Just Going Thru Some Thangs!

The Beginning

DeAnn Lain

authorHOUSE®

AuthorHouse™
1663 Liberty Drive
Bloomington, IN 47403
www.authorhouse.com
Phone: 1-800-839-8640

Published by AuthorHouse   10/11/2011

ISBN: 978-1-4634-2203-5 (sc)
ISBN: 978-1-4634-2204-2 (e)

Library of Congress Control Number: 2011913588

Any people depicted in stock imagery provided by Thinkstock are models,
and such images are being used for illustrative purposes only.
Certain stock imagery © Thinkstock.

This book is printed on acid-free paper.

Dedication:

This book is dedicated to Rodney. Thank you for believing in me when no one else did!

Thank you baby!

Introduction

This is a labor of love and one which took me through many experiences. I am grateful for having gone through every aspect of the journey; for indeed each was meant to bring me to the place I am now in my life.

For me this book is a dream come true, which also marks the beginning of a new journey in my life. I have been blessed with a beautiful gift, and I am willingly sharing it with the world.

The hope is for you my wonderful readers to read and enjoy the story. See yourselves in the lives of the characters, but most important find the courage to pursue your dreams and aspirations.

We were all created with talents and gifts and I encourage you to focus on your destiny. Be persistent even in the face of great difficulty, and uncertainty that the only person powerful and qualified enough to fulfill your dreams, is you! Get out of your own way.

Happy reading….. DeAnn Lain

Table of Contents

Just Going Thru Some Thangs!
By DeAnn Lain

Happy and sad thangs

Sunny and rainy thangs

Windy and calm thangs

Sexy and ugly thangs

That's how life is; a whirl wind of

Just Going Thru Some Thangs!

Up and down thangs

Crazy and sane thangs

Smart and dumb thangs

Right and wrong thangs

That's how life is; a whirl wind of

Just Going Thru Some Thangs!

Love and hateful thangs

Mean and nice thangs

Back and forth thangs

Cool and hot thangs

That's how life is; a whirl wind of

Just Going Thru Some thangs!

Desire and lustful thangs

Positive and negative thangs

Life and death thangs

Heaven and Hellish thangs

That's how life is; a whirl wind of

Just Going Thru Some thangs!

Chapter One
Thangs Change

It was 9:00am when Brenda James stepped off the plane in Augusta, a little town one hundred and twenty-miles east of Atlanta, Georgia. It took a lot for her to step on that 6:00 a.m. flight out of LaGuardia Airport in New York. Following her dreams to be an architect, her three years of hard work at Peaton was finally paying off. Graduation was just around the corner, and all of her dreams were beginning to come true—all but one.

Looking at her strut off the plane walking towards the baggage claim area; she appeared to have it all. Emerging as a confident carefree woman, Brenda looked like a rested visitor from a vacation in the Caribbean. In her cool shorts and sandals, she seemed not to have a care in the world. On the contrary, Brenda felt like an eagle wounded while in flight. For every footstep she took she couldn't help, but to remember the last two months of her summer as it ran through her weary mind. After enjoying her summer at home with Greg, her boyfriend, and all of her parents' praise of finally becoming the first in the entire family to graduate from college, Brenda was sucking up all of the rewards of being the first, even the promise Greg made to marry her when she went off to college three years earlier. Knowing that the days were drawing closer for her to leave for Peaton, Brenda kept wondering when he was going to pop the question. Greg had not given her any hints as to whether or not he was going to ask her to marry him. Finally, the weekend just before leaving, Greg had left a message on Brenda's answering machine, telling her to meet him down at their old high school track. Returning home after getting a manicure and pedicure before leaving for school with her best friend Andrea; Brenda rushed off to check her messages, and there it was his message to meet him so they could be alone. This was the news she had been anticipating all summer long. Spinning around like a top on a smooth surface, Brenda twirled out to the staircase shouting out to her mother about the good news.

"Mommy!"

"Yes Brenda!" Her mother said, "I'm in the kitchen."

"Greg just called!" Brenda shouted as she rushed down the stairs to the kitchen. "And he's ready to pop the question!"

"What question?" Janice replied.

"The Brenda will-you-marry-me question."

"Oh boy!"

"Why did you say that?" Brenda asked.

Janice turned away from the dishwater in the sink to dry her hands. Throwing her dishtowel on the sink, she leaned against the counter looking at Brenda standing in the doorway. "Brenda, you and Greg have been dating since high school. I think you should throw your fishing line out and see what else you can pull in."

"Oh, come on. Just give him a chance to really grow on you. He's a hard worker, and he loves me just as much as you do." Brenda stood in the doorway with a long face.

"Brenda, I hope you're right. You know I am not going to get pushy with my opinions about your personal affairs. Whatever makes you happy, I'm behind you with my mouth shut. You're my favorite girl."

"I know I'm your favorite girl Mommy, because I am who I am because of you."

"And who's that?"

"Brenda James the strong powerful woman who will one day change this world for the better."

"That's my Brenda." Janice smiled watching her daughter turn to walk away. Janice called out to Brenda. "Hey wait!"

"Yes Mommy."

"You know I only want the best for you."

"I know." Brenda smiled.

"Brenda, before you walk through that door, you will encounter a whole new world of experiences. You won't just belong to me anymore. You have my blessings. Go! How often does a girl get a marriage proposal from a guy she's head over heels in love with! Remember I'm behind you." Janice winked at her; gave her a thumbs-up with a nod and a warm smile.

"I will always love you for that Mommy. Thank you."

Brenda clapped her hands and rushed through the back door on her way to meet Greg. Janice watched her daughter dance out of the kitchen. However, she hoped that Greg would somehow drop off the face of the earth. Something about him just didn't rub her right. With his fancy cars, designer clothes, and no employment record to refer to Janice could not figure out why her daughter would want a punk like him.

Brenda got to the track a little early to meet him. She was very nervous and unsure if she should smile or look serious when he got there. Letting her mind relax, she found herself standing on the starting mark on the track as she began thinking about what kind of ring he could have gotten her. Imagining a beautiful long trail on her dress, with thoughts of Greg seeing her walking toward him, she even thought about her best friend Andrea being her Matron of Honor. The feelings she so innocently felt brought about a little sniffle of happiness from within her. Regardless of anything, it really didn't matter just as long as she and Greg were together.

Greg waited until the very last second on the clock to make his presence known to her. He was slow in his pace as he walked through the gate where she stood waiting for him. Approaching her from behind he knew that the forever they planned together, could probably be erased in just moments. A bright, sexy, intelligent woman like her was hard to find, but that didn't stop him from throwing it all away for a summer fling that got out of hand with her best friend's sister. He knew she was the best thing to ever happen to him.

As they greeted each other, Greg hugged her small frame with his large long muscular arms. Wrapping her up like a king-size blanket around a small child as he picked her up; he squeezed her with a soft sigh of relief.

"Hi, baby." He said passionately.

"What's all this sudden lovin for? You act like this is the last time you're going to see me."

"I hope not." He grumbled.

"What's up with all this can-we-be-alone stuff?" All the while, she kept the thought of him asking her to marry him in the back of her head. She knew this was it.

"Brenda, let's sit down for a minute."

"Are you sure?" She asked, "I was just thinking—"

"What Brenda?"

"Oh! Nothing Greg."

"Come sit with me my Sweet Brenda, just sit with me." Greg said as he grabbed her hand leading her off to the bleachers away from the track.

"Greg before you start – "She paused as if she was so sure of where he was leading her. "I just wanted to say that you have been the best thing to have ever happened to me, and I'm so proud to be with someone like you. Despite what anyone says, I love you."

Greg looked at Brenda silently for a few moments with a long pause. "You know I was just thinking that right before I walked through the gate. You are so loyal to me."

Brenda's face suddenly displayed a squinted profound display of confusion. She suddenly fell into a cloud of bewilderment. "Greg, what's wrong with you? This is not the way I envisioned you asking me to marry you. This is more like a sermon."

"I guess there is no other way to do this. Brenda I hope that you know I wouldn't do anything to ever hurt you on purpose." Greg had his hand on his head.

"Greg you're making me feel a little uncomfortable. What's up?"

"Lisa is pregnant?"

"And! This is her third child in what four years? At least she's slowing down a little." Brenda chuckled.

"Listen, Brenda."

"What?"

"I just need you to understand."

"Understand what Greg? I do understand that I love you, and I understand you want to marry me."

"No you don't!"

Brenda grabbed his chin pulling his face toward her. As always, Brenda had her concerned yet openhearted smile gracefully placed on her face. Greg closed his eyes and leaned over kissing her in a loving, yet hopeful gesture that this kiss will somehow ease the truth that was about to come out.

"Greg what do you want to say to me? Wait! Let me help you with the words."

She sighed for a moment as she took deep breath. "Let me help you." Placing her soft forefinger over his lips, she scooted closer to him. Right at that moment, Brenda could feel his body heat meet her cool skin from the night breeze.

"Shh! Let me know if I get anything wrong, okay?" To imitate a man's voice Brenda deepened her voice, and began to propose to herself. She only assumed that Greg was too scared to do it himself. "Brenda will you marry me? I accept! All right! Greg I said yes!" Brenda had the biggest smile on her face.

"Brenda come on stop it!"

"Greg what's wrong with you? You act as if you don't want to marry me. You said that when I graduated we were going to get married."

"I know what I said Brenda."

"And I have been planning and waiting for this day for three years. Marrying you and graduating from college have been the only two things to keep me whole and so alive. I live to love you, and I want to be the best I can because I love you. You are my future, and most definitely my forever."

"It's mine!" Greg blurted out.

"What's yours Greg?" Brenda sat shaking her head.

"The baby!"

"What are you talking about? What baby?"

"I got Lisa pregnant."

The horse's mouth began spilling all of the dirty laundry. Brenda's eyes were filling with tears of pain and disbelief about what Greg just told her. Pushing aside all of what he had just done, and instead Greg had the nerve to bend down on one knee begging for Brenda's forgiveness, and in the same breath proposed marriage in the wake of her shattered dreams. Brenda looked at him with a face that had heartbroken written all over it, with a touch of do-you-think-I'm-stupid thrown in. Oh the rage inside her yearned to slap him into oblivion.

"Do you think I would marry you after this?" Brenda stood up putting her hands over her mouth, and closing her eyes to hold back the tears.

"I was hoping we could work through this." Greg stood alongside her.

"How could you do this to me Greg?"

"Brenda–I swear it wasn't supposed to happen this way, but it did. What can I say? It just happened."

"Shit! Like this doesn't just happen! Is she keeping the baby?"

"We both decided to keep the baby." Greg said softly.

"What!" Brenda yelled at the top of her lungs. "We! When did you and I become you, me and her?"

"That doesn't matter. What's done is done Brenda."

"I want to know when did you start sleeping with her Greg?" She asked wiping the tears from her cheek.

"Around June! I don't remember, and besides that's not important."

"Oh yes it is." Brenda fell to her knees onto the gravel in front of the bleachers. She shook her head with a dry voice. "You low down dirty bastard! It was right after you made me abort our baby. You're the fucking devil. How cruel can you be? You begged me to discard my baby like a piece of trash. Then you pushed me aside for someone else, and she is having your baby; the one you both decided to keep. How fucked up is that? I was stupid to let you talk me into killing my child."

He got on his knees next to Brenda rubbing her back to console her from his unforgiving pain to her heart. "I couldn't keep on killing my seeds like that."

Brenda looked at him stoic through her tear glazed eyes. "Hmmm…. so our seed didn't mean anything to you? I guess I wasn't that important after all. Mother was right. She sensed that you were a good-for-nothing-son-of a–bitch, and I should've taken my cue from her. I didn't and now here I am".

"That's not true." He said resting his hand gently on her shoulders hoping not to make the situation worse than it already was. "You are so perfect for me. I just got caught up in the moment."

Brenda abruptly pulled her body away from his grasp taking a long unbelieving look at him. "Does Andrea know?"

"Brenda what does she have to do with this?"

"Everything! Does she know?" Brenda waited for his answer; which felt like an eternity. She hoped that her best friend might not have been aware of the events in question. Greg glanced down at the gravel on the ground and then replied, "Yes she knows."

Something came over her as she shot up from the ground with a hard frown on her face thinking, could this day get any worse. "How…no…no…no…there is no way she knows and did not tell me! How could she not tell me? I can't believe her!" A deathly silence came over her and she stood motionless looking at Greg; her simmering anger was rising to the fore of her being. "I should put my foot up your ass. I gave up the best years of my life waiting for you! And you drop me for my best friend's sister. That's incestuous you sick, demented, trifling bastard."

Brenda threw her finger in his face yelling louder than she ever had before. "I tell you what. I hope you catch something and die you damn cheat! You are nothing but a waste of space. Why are you even breathing?"

As Brenda turned to leave Greg reached out for her as she tried to walk away and instinctively she turned slapping him with every ounce of rage felt, and yet to be felt proceeding to call him every name in the book except a child of God. The sobbing echoes coming from within her sounded like a woman in travail. She was broken and shaken to the core after all that had just been revealed. Unable to take the sight of him any longer she ran like a bat out of hell out of the park. Storming through the door of the home she shared with her parents; darting swiftly to her room was the respite she craved as that space became her solace for the next few days. Everything around her seemed bland and unreal. Her world was moving in slow motion. Nothing felt familiar to Brenda—not even the pillow, which her grandmother made for her when she was three, offered any comfort. Her life was now an overturned jigsaw puzzle waiting for her to find the courage to put the pieces back together.

Where to start was the question weighing heavily on her mind. After all her packed bags sitting patiently in her room was a clear reminder to her that the other aspects of her life needed her immediate attention. With a plane to catch she had, but so much time to pull herself together to get to the destination that awaited her. Brenda was caught between a rock and a hard place. On the one hand it would break her parent's heart if she did not get the quality education they were so actively paying for, and on the other leaving so soon after the Greg debacle could run interference with her studies. After a few hours of wrestling with the idea of what to do, one truth rang clear and staying home was definitely not it. She knew that leaving would be the best thing to remedy the situation giving her sometime to get over him.

During her time of reflection and contemplation the thought of calling dearest Andrea was not lost on her. They were best friends, or so she thought, sharing everything—from dealing with the loss of their virginity to having an abortion—every emotion that could accompany those experiences they shared in tears and laughter, came rushing like a mighty wind to the surface of her mind. Brenda needed to hear a reason as to why someone as close as Andrea would betray her. The one person who knew her inside and out never once let her know that a brick was heading straight to her head. Brenda kept thinking aloud. "She never once let me know that a fucking brick was heading right at me. She didn't even tell me to scurry for cover." Brenda picked up the phone and dialed her number. It rang several times before Andrea's mother picked up.

"Hello Mrs. Gils. How are you doing?" Brenda politely asked Andrea's mother.

"Just fine Brenda. When are you leaving for school?"

"Actually, I leave in about an hour. I was hoping to speak to Andrea. Is she home?"

"Yes hold on. You have a good trip back to school okay sweetheart?"

"Thank you, Mrs. Gils."

Brenda waited for Andrea to pick up. Brenda whispered to herself, "This is a damn conspiracy. Her mother has to know what's going on. Shit! Lisa lives in the same house. Those two-faced motherfuckers are so cold."

"Hello." Andrea replied.

"Hi Andrea."

With a hint of hesitation Andrea spoke, "Brenda–" She paused for a tense moment. "I know. Greg told me. Are you okay?"

"Actually, I feel like playing kick ball or, better yet kicking my best friend's butt. What does that matter to you? Why didn't you tell me Andrea?" Brenda bitterly asked.

"What was I supposed to do? My sister and my best friend are caught up in a messy twist. I needed to stay neutral."

"Well, you stayed neutral all right. I thought friends never let friends drive drunk."

"Brenda I didn't let you drive drunk. You have to understand that Lisa is my sister, and I had to let this play out. I didn't want lose either one of you over this mess."

"Well– somebody had to be the loser." Brenda slammed down the phone and headed for her bags and the airport.

The time came when Brenda had to board the plane to Augusta. Her mother waited with her at the gate. Deep inside Brenda still wanted to cry, but she couldn't because she might not be able to stop the tears. Wanting her departure to be smooth and clean; she fought back the tears. The announcement came for the passengers to board. Brenda hugged her mother goodbye holding her little extra tight Janice felt something was wrong with her daughter. So to give her a little extra boost for her flight; she reminded her to enjoy herself.

"I don't mean to bring up the other night, but I didn't hear anything about an engagement ring. Your father and I heard you crying in your room."

Brenda looked at her mother. "Nothing to tell mommy, we both agreed that we should have some breathing room."

"I know I wasn't a big fan of you being with Greg, and I am not going to pick at you about any of the details. However, I want you to have fun and even explore other relationships. Never limit yourself until you've enjoyed your youth and your freedom. You'll understand one day. In a nut shell, there are many fish in the sea."

A soft smile graced her pained face. "I'll do my best."

"By the way you have made me so proud. I never thought this day would come so quickly. My baby girl is finally getting ready to graduate."

"Come on Mommy don't make me cry."

"I just wanted you to know I love you, but most of all I am going to really miss you. Brenda are you going to be okay?"

"Yes. I'll miss you too Mommy."

"Call me when you get there."

"I love you. I'll call you as soon as I get there." Brenda waved as she walked away.

Stepping on the plane she took a deep breath held it, and gently blew it out thinking to herself, "Self, I have two hours to pull myself together before I land in Augusta. If I don't I am going to screw up my whole life over yesterday's mess, and beside that my mother would lose her freaking mind if she knew I messed up my college career and her money over a man. I guess thangs change and I better change too!"

Chapter Two
The People We Know

Entering her dorm lobby there she was Lee her roomy for the last three years at Peaton College. Lee Jordan was from a small town just outside of Augusta. Lee Jordan was country as a sugar sandwich, but smart as a whip with a sense of humor, who was cool as ice and bold like hot spice. Lee's attitude was one of arrogance tinged with a splash of risk taking that sprinkled with fearlessness; which too many who misunderstood her, was offensive. She had a knack for doing whatever she had to get her way at all costs without regard for the feelings of others. This was not so with Brenda and Rachel, because strangely enough she had a soft spot for them both. Lee is the last to admit that Brenda and Rachel were her conscience in person. Lee could never hold a strong argument against them whenever it came to her being ruthless to someone.

Walking up the hall toward her room Brenda saw Lee flipping on some girl. Her unmistakable loud voice and arrogant attitude was on full display on the first day back to school. She is just as loud now as she was three years ago. Brenda walked up to where the ensuing drama was unfolding starring I will Snap-Crack-Pop-You LEE.

"Excuse me Alisha is it?"

"It's Asia." The young woman replied.

"Whatever! I didn't pay my money to be held up in the hallway the first day back at school. I'm sure you can understand I have a life, and you're not a part of it. Let's get things moving!"

"Listen, Lee you're just going to have to wait. I'm only one person you know. So, that means I have only two arms not ten."

"So let me help you darling." Lee replied.

Lee began moving Asia's bags ever so carefully against the wall clearing enough of a pathway so people could pass through.

Asia became incensed at the sight of her handling her luggage. "I don't want you touching my things! Step off! You don't know me like that stranger!" Asia yelled.

"Listen! I'm only trying to help you get out of my way." Lee hissed. "Ain't I nice?"

"Please I told you I'd move them as soon as I can. Don't rush me." Asia pleaded with Lee hoping she wouldn't kick her butt in the hall on the first day back to school.

"All right I'll put your precious garbage down. I can see the fear in your eyes. So, I'll give you some room to maneuver yourself and your stuff girlfriend." She snarled and being the ever present menace chided her to hurry up. "However I'll snatch you bald if you don't put a rush on it catch my drift!"

Lee was small and petite like Brenda, but she had a way with words to make you understand she was not to be toyed with. In no time the hall was clear, and was free for all to pass. Lee had a reputation of not taking anything from anyone, especially a female. She was known to put her fists where her mouth was at the drop of a dime.

Entering their dorm room behind Lee, Brenda's long face yelled out the boyfriend-dumped-me, and I didn't even see it coming. She dropped her luggage in the middle of the room. Thank goodness Lee didn't have much other than a stereo system, a very large trunk of clothes, and her keys to her convertible Mercedes she bought with her trust-fund money her father left for her. Lee was definitely a light traveler, because she always seemed to stay on the go. Brenda needed the room for her many boxes and bags, because she was a very heavy packer. She made sure she left home with everything she might need in case of an emergency.

"Hello girlfriend! Summer sure kicked your ass."

"Is the hole that big?" Brenda asked. "I broke it off with Greg."

"What happened?"

"That idiot was fucking around behind my back so much he knocked her up in the process."

"I'm sorry to hear that. Nevertheless, that's how a motherfucker is. They can't be trusted. Good thing you found out before you married him."

"You're right. I can't believe he cut me off for Lisa."

"Isn't she your best friend Andrea's sister with two different baby daddies?"

Brenda stomped her foot exasperated. "Hum! Now it's three different baby daddies on welfare, and Section 8. Hell! She's got full benefits."

"What! Leave a good sister for a trifling stunt like her. She got your man and us paying her rent with our tax dollars. Now that's some shit to remember."

"Damn it! Why me!"

"I Know why?" Lee replied.

"You do?"

"Yes I do listen up. See Greg is a piece of skunk shit. Guys like him like the smell of a nasty ass. Your ass is too clean for him. He knew you were too good for him. Greg had to get a blind fool who couldn't see beyond his zipper."

"It's like that! Huh?"

"It's always been like that sister friend. It's just that you've been committed, and focused on one man for so long you missed the things going on around you. That's not your fault. You wanted to be good. Now it's time to be very, very bad. Downright nasty if you ask me."

"Oh please! I can't stomach anything with a penis right now."

"You just need some time to heal your wounds."

"Whatever. How was your summer Lee?"

"Let me see. My mother, and I were at each other's throats as always and Rubin was off the hook. I think he wants more from me."

"Is he crazy Lee?"

"He better not be because he's going to get his feelings hurt. It was supposed to be strictly sex. No strings attached."

"What are you going to do girl?"

"The only logical thing to do is break it off."

"I told you don't mess around with these professors."

"I know Brenda. You know what? Maybe I'll give him a mercy-fuck goodbye. He may be frumpy, but he sure can work me over."

"A mercy what! Are you silly?"

"No. Whenever I give him some he does whatever I say."

"Because he knows he can get some more crazy. Lee when he finds out the foxhole is closed for business he's going to have a fucking conniption!"

"I hope not!"

"Believe me Lee a dog knows begging is the best way to get a meal."

"What!" Lee replied.

"Let me tell you something woman. Every time he sets his eyes on you he's going to get all up in your business. Even I know that a man is not going to go away as long as you keep giving it up."

"Forget it. I'll deal with this crap later. Do you know what time registration is Brenda?"

"Three o'clock I think."

"I wonder where Rachel is? Have you seen her yet?"

"I haven't seen her yet. Come on, Lee, let's go down to the lobby and wait for her."

Rachel the glamour girl was beautiful; she could cook, and dress her tail off all in the same breath. Everything about her was business. She was always rational about life. That was her strongest attribute, always managing to keep a level head no matter what. Lee and Brenda found Rachel out in the parking lot unloading the cab she took from the airport. Her clothes were ruffled, and her hair was out of place. Rachel was frustrated and just simply pissed off at the world, because her day just didn't run as it should have. Her plane was late getting in, and most of her luggage was on another flight that wouldn't be in until later that evening. On top of everything else registration was in an hour. The overwhelming happiness to see Brenda and Lee after a long summer was a delight. All three of them gathered for a group hug welcoming each other back.

"I just got off the plane, and this darn cab was so slow in getting here." Rachel ran her hand through her hair shaking it. "I must look a mess. My goodness what I wouldn't give for a cool drink to quench my thirst and five-minutes to pull myself back together."

"Come on sexy. Lee and I will help you unload and relax!"

"Not until I can get to a mirror girl."

Somehow they complemented one another very well. Brenda was laid back and thoughtful; Lee was loud, unruly, and smart as a whip; while Rachel was classy and very polished having the desire to have the world eat out her hands. Their combination was odd, but for them, they needed one another to fill one another's shortcomings.

Meeting up outside the student-union building the ladies fell in line with the rest of the student body to register for classes. While they were standing in the registration line together talking about the new faces, and the old ones occupied their minds for the moment.

"See Rebecca over there" Brenda pointed to the back of the line.

"Yeah! Why?"

"Look at her stomach. Tell me she didn't get a little heavy in the midsection. Lee, I told you she was pregnant."

"She doesn't look pregnant to me, Brenda."

"It doesn't matter now." Brenda added. "Just as long as she doesn't show before the semester is over."

"That's right. If Dean Bridges finds out she got to go." Rachel added. "If she is and he finds out, he is going to toss her off campus."

"I know because we are attending a religious institution that prides itself on having a strict policy against unwed mothers living on campus. It sends the wrong message to those who aspire to be the best." Brenda preached.

"They are full of shit!" Lee lipped off. "Remember Dean Bridge's wife kicking Professor Jones's ass in his office when she caught them having some sexual colleague talk after office hours?"

"Oh yeah! I remember." Rachel laughed while leaning against Brenda. "Check it out! There goes Mr. Fieldsman."

"He's still alive?" Brenda muttered. "I thought he might have died over the summer. Shoot! He is so ridiculously tight when it comes to money."

"Remember our first semester when he made some guy get off the line because he was short of ten-dollars?"

"That ain't anything Brenda. Remember Billy when he was short of thirty-cents?"

"Okay!" Rachel stated. "You two should stop because you see a black face on the other side of the table you expect a little slack. Ladies business is business. If it's ten-cents, then it's ten-cents and not five-cents. The school needs their money to run things. How can we study if everybody is short a few pennies? People have to be paid. Those pennies add up."

As they were gossiping like three old ladies with nothing better to do Blake Johnson popped out of nowhere standing off to the side in a crowd of people. Lee just happened to look up, and there he was.

"Rachel, guess who just stepped into my view?"

"Who?" Brenda and Rachel said in unison.

"The cream maker!"

"Where?" Rachel asked nervously scanning the crowd.

"Straight ahead." Lee indicated.

"Oh, baby, baby, baby!" Rachel turned looking at Brenda.

"Brenda tell me he doesn't give you something to think about."

"Yeah! A broken heart." Brenda replied with a less-than enthusiastic attitude.

"Girl player hating does not look good on you. That is one fine specimen of a man. He is so delicate I would eat him with a gold spoon."

"Rachel is that you talking?" Brenda was shocked at her shaking her head in response to the sexual tones in her voice.

"You know what Blake does to a sister."

"No! What?" Lee snickered looking Rachel up and down.

"Rachel don't you answer that. You know Lee thrives off the dirty thoughts about men." Brenda replied with a holier-than-thou-look on her face.

"Oh Brenda please!" Lee waved her hand at Brenda to let her know to get down off the cloud she was floating on. "Go ahead Rachel; tell me your inner-most thoughts. Forget Brenda."

"Well Lee if I must."

"Yes! You must dear friend."

"You see that body on him? I'll tell ya what! I would take my lips and kiss each corner, curve, and ripple on that masterpiece. You see that mouth? I would love to watch it eat some of my sweet blueberry deep dish pie."

"That's what I'm talking about." Lee tried to give Brenda a high-five.

"I ain't slapping you five! You and Rachel are nasty."

"Brenda I'm just being real." Rachel explained. "Look at that man. I'm young he's young, and I need the touch of some backbreaking therapy. I haven't been with anybody in over a year. I'll be dammed if I graduate without getting my hands on him at least once. Brenda you better let the freak come out of you."

"That's right girl." Lee replied. "You think of sex as a lady like a thing to give a man. I promise you when you finally have yourself a crybaby orgasm; you'll never look at sex the same way again. I promise you that you won't give anything away. You're going to be a beast if you don't get your rocks off. That crybaby orgasm will make you shout, shake, cry, and crave for more. Oh! And if you are with someone who doesn't get you off you will dismiss his ass right where he lay. I like to think of my sexual lifestyle as single, saved, and satisfied."

"Lee this is not the place for this. Anyway mind your own business. I have to go to the bathroom to give myself a crybaby orgasm. Ha-ha! At this point in my life taking a piss is the best thing ever."

Brenda walked off leaving Rachel and Lee on the registration line preoccupied with Blake's good looks and hard body. Blake felt probed by the wondering eyes behind him. Being naturally smooth and charming he strolled over to the probing eyes that kept a careful watch on his every move.

"Oh hell!" Lee tapped Rachel on her lower thigh. "Here he comes."

"I see." Rachel whispered through her teeth.

"Rachel it's now or never."

"I can't."

"You should make yourself known when he walks by."

"I'm going to clam up. Every time I see him, I get brain damage for some reason."

"Well how are you going to get close enough to him to get your groove on?"

"Dummy up. Here he comes." Rachel whispered.

Before she knew it her heart was in her throat. Blake kept a steady pace straight for her. Those bedroom eyes of his locked in on her soft satin brown ones. With a movie-scripted sexy grin his lips quietly spoke from a distance. "Hi." This let her know the feeling of attraction was mutual. Rachel looked around to see who he might be talking to. To be sure she pointed at herself. Blake nodded as he pointed his finger at her to let her know she was the one.

Blake always had his eyes on Rachel. Bad timing always kept him from approaching her. If she wasn't with Lee or Brenda, then she was handling her class work making sure she kept her grades up. It seemed he could never catch her alone when she was just on some downtime from the world around her. He knew this would be a good time to just stop, and let her know it was good to see her. With classes starting in a day or two she should have some free time to share what he felt was right. Rachel was the kind of girl that turned him on. Beautiful, good dresser, and no extra baggage, she seemed to have no worries in the world. She wasn't like the rest of the women he usually dated; Rachel was on top of her game with a no-nonsense attitude about life. Seconds before reaching his target, Rachel was overcome with fear and she began trembling as she clutched her paperwork tightly against her chest. Lee turned away gazing into space in the hopes of seeing a miraculous appearance of a star in the daylight to avoid appearing to be aware of what was going right next to her.

"Hello Rachel." Blake replied admirably.

"Hello Blake."

Glancing over to be polite, Bake acknowledged Lee's presence. "Hello Lee."

"What's up Blake?" She replied.

"Nothing much." Blake turned all of his attention back to Rachel. "It's good to see you Rachel."

"Same here."

"How are things going?"

"Great!"

"I know we just got back to school, and I was wondering if we could get together for dinner or something."

"Sure Blake. When?"

"Is tomorrow too soon?"

"That sounds good to me." She replied with a giddy chuckle.

"Here is my number. Call me tonight. I'll be sitting by the phone waiting just for your soft voice on the other end okay?"

"Okay." The strong level headed woman became a kid in a candy store.

After a long day the ladies went to hang out in Rachel's room for the rest of the night. Lucky for Rachel her roommate wouldn't be returning to school that semester, so she ended up having her own room. For her this was a good thing, because it left more room for her clothes in the closet and no time limit on the bathroom. Lee walked through the door of Rachel's room in a posed akimbo stance scanning it up and down like a mother in search of incriminating evidence.

"Rachel you sure got it good."

"Damn skippy! This is my lucky day. I find out my roommate won't be joining me, and Blake is taking me out for a date tomorrow night. I sure love when things go my way."

Mumbling under her breath Brenda replied. "At least one of us is happy with the way things are going." Brenda looked up at Lee.

"Brenda I'm happy too." Lee shouted out. "Shoot!"

"Are you sure about that Lee?"

"Yes! I am Brenda, because Rubin and I having gone our separate ways it doesn't make me feel sad."

"Correction Lee!" Brenda rolled her eyes at Lee. "Girl you went your separate way, and he has no clue it's over between you."

"Lee don't tell me you haven't broken the news to him yet?" Rachel added.

Brenda whipped her head around to look at Rachel. "No, she hasn't!"

"I will!" Feeling defenseless Lee backed down. "I will tell him when the time is right."

"Will that be before or after the mercy fuck?" Brenda inquired rhetorically.

"I haven't decided." Lee shrugged her shoulders at Brenda.

Rachel warned Lee about her action with a tone of concern. "You be careful. I always found him a little strange anyway."

"He's not strange. He's unassumingly freaky."

"I can't see him being as good in bed as you say, because looking at him with those glasses and old jackets, everything about him is outdated."

"Ladies let me enlighten your darkness. Don't be fooled by his dud look, honey child hush! He is a stud. Just think of him as Clark Kent, because when he jumps into that telephone booth and he whips on that cape everything about him changes from his tongue to his toes. Besides, kryptonite can't stop his superhero down stroke."

"I still can't see what you're talking about." Brenda asked her in an inquisitive voice. "How did the two of you hook up anyway? Because the story you gave before never sat well with me. Lee you had to go after him, because he had something you wanted."

"When you hear this you just might get sprung Brenda girl, so be warned."

"Lee whatever get on with it and spill the beans."

"Hush! Both of you; come on Lee get to talking." Rachel snapped.

"I'll keep it clean. Okay Brenda! It was last semester in his office. Remember, I had a meeting with him about my mid-term paper. I didn't think my grade was fair. So, after we sat talking for about an hour or so, the conversation rolled in another direction. He started talking dirty to me, and I needed to ace his class for the scholarship. I let opportunity lead me, and the rest is history."

Rachel asked her with a bemused looked on her face. "So why break it off?"

"He got some pussy, and I got me an A. Rubin served his purpose, and now this fool wants more. Please! Me trying to settle down with a man who gets weak over some cat fish is a joke. If I can sway him then anybody can with the right moves."

"You are so cold." Brenda pretended to shiver.

"I'm not cold. I'm keeping it real."

"I'm glad I have a conscience."

"Maybe your conscience should tell you to get some a Mandingo Brenda."

"HA-HA! Sticks and stones may break my bones, but words will never hurt me."

"You said it wrong Brenda. Not all sticks will hurt you."

Rachel pointed at Lee. "That was good Lee. Enough!" Rachel wanted to change the conversation. "You know I can honestly say I'll miss being in Augusta."

"Not me!"

"What! Not you Brenda!"

"For one the five or six buses they have running in this town stops at nine o'clock at night. There are only three television stations and two major radio stations unless you have cable or satellite. The clubs around here are like something out of the fifties when it comes to music. Oh my goodness! Let's not forget this! The music is so behind by the time they get a song here New York already heard it; mixed it, and dumped it."

Defending her hometown Lee said with an unhappy pouty frown as she replied in strong voice hinted with shame. "Brenda it's not that bad."

"Not to you, because you've lived here all your life and you haven't experienced twenty-four–hour seven-days-a-week accessibility to whatever you want. Everything shuts down by midnight here. Am I right, Rachel?"

"You certainly have a point." Rachel agreed gingerly. "Living here is no fun, but it is certainly quiet. That's why I came here to get some studying done."

"See Lee. Nothing personal girl it just that Augusta is stuck in time." Brenda smiled at her.

"Maybe I should go to New York or California to see what the East and West Coast has to offer a little country girl like me." Lee wondered aloud.

"You may live in the country, but there is nothing country about you!" Rachel said laughing along with Brenda clapping their hands.

"We love you just the way you are, because the people we know here in Augusta are nothing like you Ms. Lee Jordan!" The ladies continued to laugh aloud at Lee's expense.

Chapter Three
I'm Not in the Mood!

The first day of classes for Lee opened up an assortment of problems that would need a bigger and tighter lid to keep closed. Walking up to the door of the poetry class she needed to finish out the last of her credit hours to keep her scholarship there he was—Professor Thomas her secret lover—standing in front of the class. Wondering what was going on she stood outside of the door and opened the fall catalog. As she turned to the page where the poetry class was posted there he was—Professor R. Thomas. Closing her eyes and sucking her teeth Lee kicked the wall in frustration. Knowing she had to go in Lee knew she had to hold off on breaking off her affair with him; for fear he might hold her final grade over her head. Opening the door to walk in she smiled leaning her head to the side as she walked to the seat Rachel saved her in the back of the room. Professor Thomas kept silent as she walked in. Once she sat down he looked over at her with a doggish grin about his face.

"Ms. Jordan you're late."

"Sorry Professor."

"Well– if you intend to be late at least you should get my title right. It's Professor Thomas to you. Don't let it happen again Ms. Jordan." Stepping away from his desk Professor Thomas asked to see her after class.

Lee turned looking away from him knowing that look he gave her. She sensed it as she thought to herself, "I know what he wants and he wants it right after class." She could see his hand was fastened in his left pocket. She knew he was as a rock hard and ready to release. Lee looked over at Rachel and softly whispered, "Rachel thanks for saving me a seat."

Rachel whispered. "You're welcome."

"I thought the other Professor Thomas would be teaching this class."

"So did I Lee. We should have looked at the listing a little more carefully. I have got to wear my glasses more."

"Same here and I bet all the rest of the classes are full. In fact, I know they are. It took me an hour to find this class to give me the hours for my scholarship.

"Lee what are you going to do about your horny professor up there?"

"Hell I don't know. I've got a lot to think about."

"Excuse me ladies!" Professor Rubin Thomas said in an authoritative manner; as he directed his comment to the conversation between Lee and Rachel over in the corner where the two were sitting, "I hope I'm not interrupting anything important ladies."

"Sorry Professor." Lee apologized.

"Again Ms. Jordan you got it wrong." With a tightening grip of his hand in his pocket he looked at her with unspoken words of filthy lust in his eyes.

Gritting her teeth Lee corrected herself with a raspy overtone of leave me alone asshole. "Sorry Professor Thomas."

"Ms. Jordan not only did you come late, but you're also being very rude. I hope this doesn't carry on all semester."

Lee rolled her eyes. "No it won't Professor Thomas."

"Thank you Ms. Jordan. Don't forget to see me at the end of class."

Closing the door behind the last student Professor Rubin Thomas walked over to his desk to take a seat. Lee was still gathering up the last of her things to place in her bag. She walked toward the desk as she watched Rubin take off his glasses, while he proceeded to loosen his tie. With his elbow firmly planted in place with his chin resting in his hand he summoned her over to him.

"Come to me Lee."

"Rubin come on. I don't feel comfortable here."

"I just want to talk to you. It's been a few weeks since I've seen you. Sorry for being so hard on you in class baby. I just got a little uptight when I saw your tight little ass walk by. Forgive me?"

"Yes I forgive you Rubin." Lee distanced herself from him and his desk. "Has it been that long?"

"Yes it has! I've missed you very much."

"Little old me?" Lee hesitatingly replied.

"Yes, sit right here."

As Rubin was slapping his thigh to let her know where to place her bottom a picture of a dirty old man suddenly came into focus. Shivering quivers of disgust made her skin crawl, and the pressure was on. Lee had to give in to keep him happy and her final grade safe. Easing down on his lap she kept her eyes closed from having to see him paw at her body, while he fed his sexual hunger for her.

Weeks passed and Lee kept a closed mouth to Rubin about her intentions to break off their hidden affair. Wishing for the days to pass quicker so that the final grades could be logged Lee couldn't wait to drop him like a nasty rag. Meanwhile, Brenda kept to her business of putting her head in the books in order to keep her mind off Greg and her broken heart. As for Rachel these last few months had been great. Spending time with Blake was just what the doctor ordered for her. Rachel kept a smile on her face every day; nothing could get her down. Something about their relationship was too good to be true, but Rachel didn't seem to notice there was a problem. Brenda noticed that everything they did was on his terms from the movies they saw to when, and how long they spent time together. While spending sometime in the library one day Rachel and Brenda took a break away from the books. To break the dry, drab study mood Brenda thought she would bring up a much more interesting conversation.

"Rachel what's up for tonight?"

"Blake and I are going to the rap concert at the stadium downtown."

"I thought you didn't care much for rap music."

"After spending so much time with him it kind of grows on you."

"It seems everything he likes grows on you Rachel."

With a hint of attitude in her voice, Rachel responded, "Really."

"I think you're putting too much into this relationship. I could never figure out why he never had a steady girlfriend. Since everybody seems to think he is Mr. Wonderful. I could be wrong."

"I know you're wrong. Maybe people feel intimidated by very beautiful people like him. That's the only reason I can see. He's a lot of fun, and he is so romantic."

"That's not what I heard. If you must know I heard some things about him that bother me."

"Just stop Brenda. I don't want to hear it. I hate when people try to poison your mind with hearsay. Don't you dare! You were just in a similar situation not too long ago."

"If someone had come to me Rachel, I would have wanted to hear the truth or the half-truths. At least if whatever is going to happen happens, I don't want feel like I was the last one to know."

"I don't want to know. I really like this guy. I want to take my time and see if he could be the one for me. At first it was lust, but things have taken a different direction. I think this could be love. I think we have something special, and I want to take my time with this."

"Rachel, I'm your friend no matter what. If you need to find out the truth let it be in your time. You be careful, because sometimes when it seems too good to be true it is."

"I hope that doesn't apply to sex because we haven't slept together yet."

"Good! Don't! I got a feeling he's going to break your heart in the worst way."

"I hope you're wrong. Then again Brenda nothing is written in stone. If I get my heart broken then it was meant to be. I'll just have to deal with it."

Wishing her well, Brenda squeezed her hand. "Have fun. I am always going to be concerned even if you don't want me too."

"I know Brenda. I shall have to try and enjoy my Prince Charming."

Returning to his apartment after the concert Rachel rested her tired legs on his couch. Blake went into the kitchen to get two glasses of wine. Handing her a glass of red wine he made a toast to the two finally going out together and their two–month anniversary.

"To us Rachel two–months of togetherness you make me feel whole." Blake smiled.

"Same here."

"I am so glad we finally got together. I knew we would be great together."

"Really Blake? I'm glad you feel that way because I've been feeling the same."

"These last few months will make it official then if you feel the same."

"What?" Rachel paused as she sipped her wine.

"Tonight is the night we should take our mutual feeling to another level."

"Okay. So what level did you have in mind?"

"Come here and let me show you."

Feeling his lips kiss her neck she pushed him away. His aggressive touch felt cold and vicious to the skin; she felt something wrong. As he slid closer to resume his quest to get her in the mood Rachel twisted, and turned her head in hopes he would get the message of, "No way! Not tonight! I am not in the mood!" Rachel took both of her palms and yielded him in his seat. Blake looked at her with a puzzled look on his face.

"What's up with you? Every time I kiss you, you pull away."

"I'm not ready for this level yet Blake."

"Stop playing so hard to get. It's been two-months."

"Yeah! That's all!"

"Stop thinking and go with the feeling. You know you want me too. So why don't you?"

"It's just not right yet. We have so much to learn about each other Blake."

"We'll learn more when we take our clothes off. Once you study my sweet black ass what else do you need to know?"

"I'm not interested. Please respect my decision."

"What!" Blake shouted. "Well then respect my decision that I want to fuck you! I've been patient for two-months. What are we going to do?"

"Nothing!"

"Nothing! I'm tired of looking at you. You're fine and all, but I'm ready to put your pretty ass to work on my big dick!"

"No, I don't want to fuck you! I'm not ready yet and you'll just have to wait until I am. It's as simple as that Blake!"

"You think so? The bitches I date give it up when I demand that they do. I've been nice enough to let you wait this long. So stop playing around! My dick is hard! If you don't want to fuck, then you want to suck my dick? You got choices."

"You know what? It's time for me to leave." Rachel attempted to stand up to leave.

"Get your ass back here! You leave when I say!"

Yanking Rachel's arm like a rag doll he threw her down on the couch. As he stood over her unbuckling his belt Rachel realized he was serious about having sex with her. She scrambled to get off the couch knocking over the wine glasses on the table. As she made a dash for the door, he grabbed her leg pulling her back. Rachel screamed at the top of her lungs for him to stop. Within in a matter of seconds he became a monster with a nasty grunt. Not wanting anyone to hear the struggle going on he reached back, and with a closed fist he punched her in the mouth and about the face. He wanted to shut her up as well as to cripple her so he could have his way.

As she held her face in pain she could feel the blood rush out of her mouth all over her face and down her neck. Feeling lifeless he pulled her sluggish body back away from the doorway. Pulling her skirt off along with her panties Blake positioned her legs apart just enough to climb between them. Rachel lay there in shock and pain as she watched him undress himself. "I'm going to give you something to scream about. When I'm finished, you will ask for more. Trust me; every stroke will be good to ya!"

"Don't do this to me, Blake. Please!"

"Is that a please-I-want-it or please-hurry-up?"

"No. No. Stop!" Rachel pleaded as she coughed up blood from her wounded mouth.

"Let me show you what you've been missing! When I'm finished you'll thank me!"

Rachel had to think fast. Just as he was kneeling down to get on top of her; Rachel surprised him with a knee to his groin. He fell like a deck of cards. Feeling the piercing pain paralyze his body, Blake gave in to its command. Falling, gasping, and panting, he prayed for the Fairy Godmother of Relief to appear on his behalf. Rachel pulled herself together wiping the blood from her mouth. Standing up with the rage of a tormented bull she let loose. Kicking him about the back by stomping up and down all over him, she was worse than a trooper at war with the enemy.

"Oh shit!" He gasped in excruciating agony.

"What's wrong Blake? Something got you down? You hit the wrong woman! Oh you came upon your worst motherfuckin nightmare! Let this be the first and last time you put your hands on a lady."

With the fire of a hell-raiser Rachel turned him over on his back to look him straight in the face, because she wanted to make sure he never forgot her. With the heels of her knee high brown leather boots she stepped into his face sending his front teeth into the back of his throat.

"Every time you smile think of me. If you ever come near me again I swear on your mother's grave I'll kill you and that is not an idle threat it is a promise sealed with your blood. I'm not in the mood for this shit!"

Chapter Four
What You See
Ain't What You Get

Running through the door out of breath, Brenda panted and huffed as she looked at Lee. "Have you seen Blake today?"

"No! Why? What the hell got into you all out of breath and shit?"

"It looks like he's been in a car wreck or something close to it."

Concerned Lee turned around and stopped what she was doing. "What! I wonder if Rachel knows what's going on."

"She should now something. I haven't seen her or talked to her at all today. I know they went to some rap concert last night."

"Let me ring her room." Lee waited for an answer. After several rings Lee hung up the phone. She looked at Brenda as she nodded her head to say, "Are you thinking what I am thinking."

"Come on let's go!" Brenda replied.

They hurried up the stairs to her room. Standing outside her door they could hear music playing as they waited. They knew Rachel never played loud music. She always kept things as quiet believing that it kept the mind at peace. Her mother instilled many Southern sayings in her, and in many ways she literally lived by them. They knew something was wrong. Lee and Brenda knocked repeatedly hoping she would hear them. They took the extra key Rachel had given them to open the door. Shouting out Lee announced their presence.

"We're coming in!" Lee shouted.

"No!" Rachel shouted back.

"Get off the door! Let us in!" Brenda waited for a response.

She continued to yell through the door to Rachel. "We need to tell you something important."

"Can I see you guys later?" Rachel replied.

"Do you have company or something?" Lee asked.

"No! I just need to be alone."

"It's me, Lee. Come on girl we just need two-minutes of your time. Get off the door and let us in. Better yet, we are going to stand out here until you do."

Rachel knew that they were going to sit by the door and knock every other second to drive her crazy into submission. She let the door open from the inside. Being ashamed of her swollen face she turned to hide under the covers of her bed as quickly as she could before the door opened up.

"Okay Rachel what's wrong with you? Got your period or something? Get out of that bed! We need to talk to you." Lee said jokingly.

Peeking just over the covers Rachel said, "Go ahead."

"Will you take the covers off your head?" Brenda replied. "This is silly. Us talking to you with a blanket over your head we look crazy."

"I can hear you just fine." Rachel softly garbled from underneath the covers.

"You sure are acting squirrelly."

"Lee, I just don't feel good right now. So please leave me alone for now. I'll hook up with you guys later okay?"

"Okay! However, this won't take long. I saw Blake today, and he looks like somebody beat the crap out of him. Do you know anything about this?" Brenda asked.

Lee was fed up. She began pulling at the blanket. "Hell Rachel you're driving me nuts with this hide-and-seek game you're playing."

"Stop Lee! I don't feel good!"

Lee grabbed the blanket with all her might. It went flying into the air revealing the secret Rachel was trying to hide. A waterfall of tears came cascading down her swollen cheeks. The embarrassment of it all was too overwhelming for her, as she turned away hoping at this moment the earth would open up and swallow her alive. Lee was infuriated at the sight of her friends face.

"What the hell happened to you?"

Brenda came to rest on her bedside; as she began cradling her like a new born baby. The horror of seeing her beautiful battered face frightened her out of her wits. She looked like she was hit with a two-by-four. Brenda held her face in her hands gently like a mother to her child.

"Rachel tell me what happened to you! We have to know."

"I can't Brenda!"

"Yes you can. We're your friends. We won't let anything happen to you. You know we love you. We just want to make sure that you are safe."

"I was a fool Brenda. I didn't see it coming."

"See what coming?"

"Blake."

"Blake!" Lee yelled.

"He did this to me."

"Did what?"

"Hit me! Brenda he hit me so hard."

"Then what happened to him?"

"I hit him back."

Lee and Brenda looked at each other confused about how the hitting arrangement went. They all sat together for a few hours so Rachel could cry out all of her pain. They finally got her to tell them of the attempted rape, and assault Blake had committed against her. Brenda knew of the possibility of his attack on her. Looking at her friend in her state she did not want to be the one to tell her, "I told you so." Brenda decided to keep it to herself making sure that Rachel wouldn't feel any worse than she did right at that moment. Nevertheless, Brenda couldn't help but think about when she tried to warn her friend earlier about Blake's past relationship with his last girlfriend that ended with a broken arm, and a fractured cheekbone.

"Rachel do you want to report this to the police? He should not be allowed to get away with hurting you?" Brenda pleaded with her.

"No!"

"Why not Rachel?" Brenda pleaded with her again.

"Brenda it's over and I just want to forget this. I know I can't handle all the garbage I'm going to have to go through to prosecute him for what he did to me."

"Well you just can't let him get away with this. You have got to try and do something about what he did to you!"

"I have too!" Rachel's tears streamed down her bruised, swollen face as she tried to avoid what she knew was the right thing to do. "Who's going to believe me that after two-months of dating him, he tried to rape me?" She looked at Brenda and Lee shouting out, "Nobody!"

Lee jumped in irate with her teeth grinding against one another. "We should hunt him down like an animal and gut his raggedy ass!"

"Are you sure?"

"I just want to leave it alone okay?"

"Okay! Cool down." Brenda rubbed her back to console her. "If that's what you want."

"Well, I figure if you don't want the police to get involved then we will." Lee nodded in Brenda's direction. "Right, Brenda?"

"What are you getting at Lee?" Looking nervous Brenda stared at Lee knowing that her little mind was up to no good.

"Just give me a few minutes and I'll let you know." Lee replied.

Being the rebel and the do righter for the sake of her sister friend in need Lee was brainstorming a way to set the record straight with Blake. Coming up with a foolproof way to get even Lee and Brenda took a late night drive out to Blake's apartment complex. Dressed in black they made their way to his Cadillac Escalade. There it was in all its glory under the moonlit sky her shell sparkled from afar.

"I can't believe I'm doing this." Brenda whispered. "Why can't we just turn off his utilities?"

"We are in the morning Brenda don't get scared now. We're here."

"I'm not scared, Lee. It's just that this thing cost a lot of money."

"You're right. Thousands of dollars give or take a few pennies. Besides, our friend's face is priceless."

Lee walked over to the truck. "Well, well. Here it is the one the only key to pain."

"What are you talking about Lee?"

"After we're finished with this Blake will have a dent in his heart as big as the Grand Canyon. Look at this shit."

"Blaz-zen Blake." Brenda replied. "That's nice."

"Nope that's not nice. Even his fuckin license plate shouts out, 'It's all about me.'"

"Lee remember blazing is the main idea here. Are you finished?"

"Yep! When that jackass cranks this baby I hope it says no, because when we are finished I'm pretty sure it won't give in."

"Wait Lee!"

"What?"

"Don't you want to bow your head to say a little something before it joins the others in car heaven?"

"Why not?"

Bowing their heads in prayer Brenda said, "Father forgive us for we are about to sin. Sorry for this act of revenge against you, but we had no choice. Anyway, Lee made me do it."

"Great! One more thing. Please give him hell before you go out." Lee added. With her attitude-laced pitch she continued to say, "We would really appreciate that. Thank you."

After pouring two-gallons of a premixed concoction of nail polish remover, rubbing alcohol, paint thinner, ammonia, and bleach into the gas tank the ladies eased back to their parked car a few blocks away with their hearts racing praying they did not get caught. The ladies danced around like happy thieves in the night. Once in the car they jubilantly cheered feeling they had evened the score with Blake. With their mission accomplished with no outside interference they headed back to Rachel's room to watch over her in her time of need.

"He was so perfect the nice apartment—he even liked the finer things in life. He wasn't the typical college guy. I just knew he was into me with the heart of a gentleman."

"Well Rachel let's just say you got caught out there. If it is too good to be true, then it is."

"Brenda– I'm trying so hard to not believe that."

"You're right Brenda." Lee shouted. "All the good ones are married; in jail; got too many kids; living at home with Momma; on crack; got AIDS, or dead. Wait goddamn it! I forgot the gay ones who don't find a vagina attractive."

"Very true Lee. After Greg did what he did I felt like where do I begin who do I trust, and why should I trust anyone again?"

"I now know how you feel Brenda. Before Blake and I had been out I hadn't been with a man in over a year. I put my books first." Rachel confessed. "I got tired of trying to figure them out. The average man our age can't even hold a decent conversation."

"I hate when brothers talk with their hands." Brenda laughed in the mist of their conversation. "Wait don't forget this, you know what I'm trying to say. The entire time you're talking to him, they only use those five words, and he expects me to figure out what he's talking about. Yet, he never uses who, what, when, where, why, or how. I hate a man who is limited."

"You two need to make a switch." Lee advised the ladies to use her old remedy of older is better when it comes to satisfying a woman's thirst for passion, and conversation. "That's why I only deal with older men. They get straight to the point, no boyish games to play. Most of the guys on campus don't even know how to pee straight. The only thing they know is how to stick it in and hump let alone know how to treat a sister with love and respect."

"I wonder how Blake hid that monster in side of him from me?" Rachel inquired.

Lee patted Rachel's hand. "Listen Rachel, you couldn't have known he was that way until he did what he did. An animal like him always has a perfect shell. He was too flawless."

However for Blake, he was going to have one heck of a morning. Jumping into his one-month old Cadillac Escalade his parents bought him as a pre-graduation present he headed out to his dental appointment to have his two-front teeth, which Rachel knocked out replaced. Driving along the highway in the bumper-to-bumper traffic Blake was watching his clock hoping not to be late. As he leaned over to adjust his music for sound, suddenly a violent thrusting backwards and forward took over his vehicle. Keeping his foot on the brake made it ride like an unbroken horse on its way out of a rodeo gate.

He had a frantic look on his face as to what was happening to his ride. Adding, the crawling traffic was making matters worse as he tried to pull into a nearby gas station. Blake threw it into park, jumping out to pop the hood. *Poof!* Out of nowhere a cloud of smoke appeared. The engine let out an intense flash of fire. Blake yelled out for help, and within minutes his Escalade was engulfed in flames. All he could do was stand back away from the intense flames, and listen to fire trucks off in the distance stuck in traffic.

A few weeks had passed and things with Rachel were beginning to fall back in place. Regaining her confidence Rachel's beautiful face was healed of all traces of the attack. Still, she was very angry about how she could have been treated so badly by someone she was falling for. She needed to put aside yesterday and concentrate on her future. Therein lay her first mistake. Rather than fall she should have stood fast to reveal what you see ain't what you get sometimes.

Chapter Five
He's Got to Go!

The time had come for Lee to get stern with Rubin. Every Tuesday and Thursday he expected her to please him. Lee had become fed up with him. Feeling trapped Lee was unsure if he would fail her if she broke off the affair and left him. She seemed to have a disgusted miserable look on her face every time she had to show up for his class. Needing to find a clean safe way out of this relationship Brenda and Rachel came up with the perfect solution to help Lee get out of her situation. The fact that Rubin was married and a father of four was the focus of the plan the ladies came up with to help get rid of him.

"Okay Lee. We know you've been plotting. Rachel and I have been thinking long and hard about your little problem too."

"This is no little problem I have to keep given it up until the end of the semester. He's starting to make me feel like a whore."

"Well I think we should bring this to an end."

"Are you sure you guys can help me?"

Speaking simultaneously Brenda and Rachel spoke in a chorus. "Positive!"

"Come sit." Rachel said, "And listen my friend."

Armed with a tape recorder in her bag and her pre-rehearsed story line Lee was ready to ambush the enemy. Waiting for the class to end Lee looked over at Rachel, and smiled to queue her for her performance of a lifetime. After Rubin finished the class he closed the door after the last student walked out—just like always. While Rubin locked the door Lee clicked the tape recorder on, and hoped that it would pick up every word they said. Rubin sat like always, and Lee followed his lead like all the times before.

"I love tasting you."

"I'm glad you like the way I taste Rubin."

"Take your shirt off. Hurry!"

"What's the big rush Rubin?"

"I have a faculty meeting in twenty-minutes."

"Then this should wait because I need to talk to you."

"About what? We can talk while we're doing it. I don't mind."

"I don't think so Rubin."

"Come on Lee, Mr. Happy is on hard. Why mess this up with conversation?"

"I'm pregnant Rubin."

Rubin's lips quickly stopped planting little wet kisses up and down her face. He picked his glasses up off the desk placing them on his frozen shocked face. As he cleared his throat as if he were about to let a long speech out, Lee knew she had the fly in her web.

"Rubin is anything wrong? I hope this doesn't change anything."

"Yes it changes everything!"

"But I thought you wanted to get serious by spending more time together like a couple?"

"But a baby wasn't a part of the plan."

"Why not? I thought you loved me Rubin."

"Lee— I care a lot about you, but I don't love you. Not the way you should be loved. I have a wife and a family already. I'm not going to lie to you. I love my wife, and I'm not willing to give up all that now."

"Why did you tell me all those things about how much you desired me and that I was the only woman to make you feel alive?"

"I'm hoping you understand what I am about to tell you. All those things I said was at a time of passion you know the heat-of-the-moment kind of things. It seems when you go with the moment it makes things more pleasurable."

Lee began sobbing. She put on an act that would have fooled the best truth seeker. Rubin hugged her to console her tears of make believe. He had beads of sweat rolling down his face that was soaked up by the bend of his collar. He thought about the scandal that could come out of this if anyone found out she was having this baby; his baby scared him out of his mind. His wife finding out could lead to a divorce. Already having four kids he was sure a fifth would cripple him financially. Even worse his name could be dragged through the mud knowing this could ban him from teaching at any well-noted college institution in the South. He had too much to lose if this got out. Rubin couldn't take the chance of not stepping up to the plate to take care of the matter. The only solution was to get an abortion, because nothing good could come out of this. "Lee how far along are you?"

"I don't know yet."

Wiping his sweaty forehead he asked, "Are you sure you're pregnant?"

"That's what the pregnancy test I bought is saying."

"Let me write you a check for eight-hundred-dollars. This should cover everything including buying yourself a little something to make you happy once this little incident is over."

"You want me to get rid of it?"

"Please!"

"I don't think I could do this. This is a human being inside of me."

"Don't— don't think of it like that Lee. Just think of it as a small problem you take care of right away, because if you don't it will cause a lot of long-term problems for the both of us."

"Oh Rubin this is our baby we made together. It will be like killing a part of you. I couldn't bring myself to hurt you like this."

"Listen to me. You have your whole life ahead of you. Don't tie yourself down with a baby, and with graduation around the corner. Please let this go. I will understand."

"If you think this would be best."

"Yes I do! If you need to take a few days off from class, I'll overlook it. It won't affect your grade at all. You know I'm going to give you an A plus. I know how important your academic scholarship is too you."

"Thank you."

"Go cash this check and take care of it as soon as possible all right sweetie?"

"All right, Rubin."

"Okay I have really got to go now!" Rubin rushed off to his meeting leaving Lee sitting at his desk with an eight-hundred-dollar check in her hand. Lee clicked off the recorder and started giggling. Rachel came around the corner after she saw Rubin exit down the stairs.

"Lee what happened?"

"That fool gave me an eight-hundred-dollar check Rachel."

"Get out!"

"Yeah he did and you know what? I expected him to just blow me off. He certainly surprised the hell out of me."

"So he really thinks you're pregnant?"

"Oh yes! He almost shitted in his pants when I told him. You know he was only concerned about his career and his picture-perfect family. It was written all over his face. See why I love them and leave them? I'm so glad we did this. Rubin won't touch me with a ten-foot pole now. All he's thinking right now is, "I hope she gets rid of it quickly.""

"Well it's a good thing you got a tape of the conversation. If he tries to harass you for sex or anything like that just tell him that you are going to take the tape to the president of the school. That should keep him in line."

"I don't think I'll have to go that far. Everything about the way he hauled ass out of here tells me he's washed his hands of me. I'm glad it's over. He's got to go and his ass is gone!"

Chapter Six
A Girls' Night Out!

With midterms over the ladies decided to let their hair down at the officer's club at the nearby army base. Wanting to get away from the everyday college stuff Lee decided to treat Brenda and Rachel to a night out with the eight-hundred-dollars Rubin had given her. They were in need of some serious adult entertainment. Brenda came to Rachel's room after her last class to get ready for their night out. Opening the door Brenda shouted out, "Lee what are you wearing tonight?"

"Well silly turn around and find out."

There she was getting ready to show off her sexy self on the catwalk in a spaghetti-strap knee-length silk black dress, and a pair of three-inch sling back red leather shoes. Her hair was pulled back in a bun and accented with sliver butterflies. Lee looked the part of a heart-breaker for a weak soul. Brenda was pleasantly surprised to see Lee looking so together.

"Well, well, Lee you look fabulous darling. I didn't know you had it in you girl."

"I don't. Rachel decided to hook up my attire for the evening."

"All right Brenda." Rachel called from the other side of room with her magic wand. "Your turn Cinderella!"

Lee ran down the evening itinerary for the ladies. "Just remember free drinks and lots of phone numbers. You want to come home with something to pick from just remember you're going trick-or-treating. Make sure you have a bag to put all your treats in."

"Lee you're too much." Brenda replied.

"That's right girl. We have much to do tonight like mingle with the singles and lead the blind into our webs."

"I'm not trying to be a pigeon, a chicken, or any kind of bird Lee."

"And I don't expect you to Brenda: Do you know why I have men falling at my feet whenever I take a step?"

"I have often wondered that."

"Listen you have to give them something to imagine like a nice figure or a shy smile. Hell, even a good conversation to tease them a little. Just remember this, I have never seen a man fall out over a woman's brain. Men are special they come in categories like books, but you have to skim the first few pages to get a feel of what you're about to read. You got the good men who are looking for us smart, together, and independent women. Now the bad, well they are looking for the chicken heads of America. Now we all know women like that who will give up their children, home, friends, family, and everything that once made them whole as a person just to say I got me a man. Last—but of course not least—the confused. They're good and bad. They are looking for someone with a death wish. They will beat your ass today and bring you flowers tomorrow. You don't fuck around with bums like that."

"Listen I am not trying to go shopping for a man. I'm trying to concentrate on school, and besides I just want to dance and have some fun."

"After what you told us about what Greg did to you? Brenda come on! Don't you think it's time to forget his ass?"

"Lee you're right, but right now I'm just not ready for a new relationship."

"You didn't hear me say anything about a relationship. Just get somebody who can make you feel good for the moment. There is nothing wrong with you having a friend who can help you with your inner frustrations."

"That hasn't even crossed my mind."

"Rachel and I both know you have to relate, relax, and release. You are so backed up with Greg on your mind that you're letting the past dictate your future. Rachel has come a long way since Blake, and she's going out tonight to just have some good fun. Besides, she's ready for whatever may come."

From across the room Rachel added, "Brenda, I have to move forward. You just have to let go. I refuse to let Blake brainwash me into thinking every man is a cruel animal or a piece of nothing. He was a mistake that had to happen. I learned a lot from that experience, especially the importance of maintaining a positive outlook on my future. If I don't then I'll be stuck in the past forever."

"I can't help what I still feel for Greg, Rachel. Inside I feel chained, and the only thing to break me free is time. I can't just forget six years overnight and jump into something else. I have to fix what's going on in my life right now. Another relationship right now is a no-no."

"Brenda!"

"Yes Ms. Lee."

"Don't let this last year in school be a loss. I really don't think Greg has been sitting around the last two or three months thinking of your sad ass. He's getting his groove on at your expense and here you are losing sleep. Give yourself permission to attract better, but you first have to let go."

When they arrived at the club it was filled with the young, the old, the married, the desperate, and the many homesick army men and women looking for love or a hit-and-run. The blue dress Brenda was wearing with the bare back was going to touch base with every category of man lingering in her pathway. The ladies stood halfway between the dance floor and the bar; they set a new standard of beauty. The ladies came off as classy and strong. All eyes scoped them out as they were standing talking about where they would sit.

"Lee, I guess we got a house full tonight. I think a little fun might be something I could get into. Whatcha think you hot mamas?" Snapping her fingers to the beat of the music Rachel was ready to party the night away.

"I think this hot mama might not be lonely for long. Let's get on the floor and shake this black dress loose a little. Besides, feet like mine need to get their groove on to this pumping music. Go find us a table Brenda. Rachel and I will find us some company."

"Just remember ladies I am not going home with anyone, and make sure your behinds find me. Don't bring back any overly happy, grinning, ugly jerks please, and by the way don't you two get lost in here. I'll find us some seats; besides I'm not that comfortable in these shoes." Brenda stated with a pleasant smile on her face.

Watching Lee and Rachel fade into the crowd of people; Brenda began to fight her way through the crowd of partygoers to find two empty stools at the end of the bar. She began to sit down. Suddenly, she heard this voice from behind her; it was deep yet soft and patient. It reminded her of a handsome tall dark actor she was fond of.

"Excuse me young lady. May I help you into your chair?"

When Brenda turned to look behind her; she found herself gazing down towards the floor. Her eyes fixated on the vertically challenged gentleman in front of her smiling and thinking to herself as she bit the bottom of her lip. "When I want some fun I get a joke." She didn't want to make fun of him or want him to feel like he wasn't good enough to be in her presence, so like always she was respectful. Brenda smiled and replied using her warm, kind voice.

"Yes thank you."

"May I buy you a drink?"

"Yes."

"By the way my name is Theodore Shell."

"Hello Theodore."

"No– call me Teddy. It makes me feel taller."

"Well okay Teddy. I'm glad you're a man without a complex."

"Thank you. You still haven't told me your name."

"Oh! I'm sorry! My name is Brenda."

"What a pretty name for a very beautiful lady."

"Thank you for the compliment Teddy."

"So, Brenda are you military or a civilian?"

"I'm a civilian. I'm a student at Peaton University."

"So you're beautiful and educated! What are you studying?"

"Actually, I'm graduating next May. I've been studying to become an architect. I got this thing for beautiful structures. When I look at a building that catches my eye I get all fluttered and excited. I hope I don't sound too weird."

"No." Teddy smiled pulling his glass away from his face. "I'm impressed. I have never met a girl with a thing for buildings. I must say it leaves me wanting to hear more about you Beautiful Brenda."

Teddy's last reply made her laugh because someone actually found her interesting and different from others. Once they were acquainted with each other she found herself lost in his conversation. She learned his mother was very ill, and he had to request an emergency leave from Hawaii where he was originally stationed to be closer to home. Home for him was Columbia, South Carolina, which was two-hours away from Augusta. He wasn't very tall, but his body was very muscular. Nothing particularly special about him when she first glanced his way, but after spending two-hours talking about family Brenda felt very comfortable with him next to her and she wanted to know more about this person. After telling a dumb joke about something she heard in a movie he laughed. Right at that moment his smile silenced her. Overlooking his obvious negative she saw a shiny soul with a glare that made her warm all over. Something inside of her wanted to hold him. The joke that approached her when she first sat down immediately became this priority in her life right at that moment. Theo looked at his watch noticing it was very late. He took this opportunity to ask Brenda if she might need a ride to her destination. Theo wanted to make sure he did whatever it took to get her phone number hoping he could get to know her better.

"Brenda do you need a ride back to campus?"

"No. I came with my friends. I pray they're not too wasted to know how to get back to campus."

"If you would like to go find your friends I'll wait here for you, and if they can't drive then you can follow me back to your campus in your car."

"Would you really do that for me?"

"Of course! Anything for a young lady who didn't drink me out of my house and home. Besides, since we have shared some of our life stories I feel like a friend, and friends should help friends, right?"

"Well okay. Stay. Don't leave. I'll be right back okay Theo?"

"I'll be right here Brenda."

As Brenda walked through the club she began thinking to herself, "What a nice guy." After making her way through the crowd of people she found Lee sitting at a table with a very distinguished older man with salt-and-pepper hair. The closer Brenda got to the table the more noticeable his wedding ring stood out.

"Hey Lee may I talk to you for a second?"

"Yeah sure, but first meet Ethan Robertson."

"Hello Ethan, my name is Brenda." Brenda reached out to shake his hand. "If you would excuse Lee and I for a moment."

"Why sure ladies. Listen Lee, I need to make a phone call. I will be right back, all right?"

"Sure Ethan. I'll be right here when you return."

Lee started looking him up and down like a dog getting ready to mount as he headed off into the crowd. Her eyes were relaxed, but her mouth was wide open. Something about Ethan must have yanked her mind wicked, because Lee never looked so hot in all the time Brenda had known her.

"Lee you're crazy."

"No I am not. He's nice and very sweet. What's wrong with that?"

"Didn't you notice the wedding ring on his hand? You're playing with fire again when you start fucking around with a committed man. Married or not don't put yourself in that mix. Hello hard-headed remember Rubin?"

"Yes and yes. I saw the ring. He's not fucking his wife, but he's taking care of home. What does that have to do with anything?"

"Lee, we didn't come here to hook up with any family men. What can he do for you anyway? It's not as if he can stay out all night or spend money as if he has it if there's a wife at home. Don't play yourself. Heartbreak is no picnic in the park."

"Brenda, I know what I'm doing. Give me some credit; you know I got a head on my shoulders at times. I just want to have a little fun. Please don't rain on a girl's parade! You have to admit there are no men on campus for us. I'm not into little boys, because they always call home to mommy."

"I understand that Lee. Still, he is too old for you. This dick slinger more than likely has no heart. If he cheats on his wife then what do you matter?"

"Listen Brenda, I am not looking for a relationship or marriage. He can go home anytime he wants too. As far as I am concerned we will probably just do some of this or some of that— no strings attached. That's what's on my mind."

"All right! Just make sure you're careful. Lee the day will come when I have to tell you I told you so."

"Anyway are you finished? Can we get back to having some fun please?"

"Okay. No more lectures." Brenda sucked her teeth. "I promise."

"Don't get bent out of shape. He let me feel his dick under the table. Girl this grandpa got a python in his pants."

"Say what? Oh goodness! I can't believe you Lee. You are crazy."

"You promised no more lectures. Besides, I am young, hot, and bothered. I think I found something to handle this wildcat I got caged up."

"What? Just make sure he gets tested for everything even fleas."

"Listen, if he's in the military, he has his mandatory tests. Besides, haven't you heard of condoms?"

"I hope you're right. I feel bad for his family. His poor wife makes me not want to get married."

"I don't want to sound cruel, but his wife has no more interest in straight sex anymore. She is as dry as toast."

"How do you know?"

"He told me so. She's forty-nine, and he's fifty-two, but his dick is twenty-five."

"You're not going to give this guy any on the first day are you?"

"No. Even if I did I haven't had my back knocked out in a long time. I got feelings and I have needs. I need some pelvic relief. I've been a good little girl. It's time to be a little bad."

"It's only been three weeks since you and Rubin got it on. Lee, you decide what you want. You're a grown ass woman. Just don't sleep with him on the first date."

"I am not. I decided to break the ice tomorrow night after he takes me out to dinner. If the conversation is good and the mood is right well, this girl is going to blow up and come home smiling."

Before Brenda could reply Ethan returned to the table with a naughty grin on his face. As he sat down next to Lee, Brenda noticed him grabbing her hand to place it in his crotch to remind her of the big python. Brenda had a half-hearted smile on her face when she made eye contact with Ethan. As the evening began to die down Lee decided to stay a little longer at the club with Ethan. Rachel was on the dance floor shaking her tail off. Brenda told Lee she got a ride back to school with someone. Lee reassured Brenda she was fine and had not had a lot to drink. Lee wanted Ethan to drive her back to the campus, but Brenda reminded Lee that Rachel didn't know how to drive. Lee promised to drive safely back to campus with Rachel. Brenda was tired and wanted to get back to her bed to get some rest after being up since 5:00 a.m. the previous morning. It was 2:00 a.m. the next morning and she was definitely hoping that Teddy might give her a lift home. He seemed harmless and very eager to impress her. When she returned to Teddy at the bar she was reintroduced to his well-flavored smile. Like a little puppy he sat waiting with a fresh glass of ginger ale placed in front of her chair at the bar. Brenda thought to herself, "He may be short but the brother got charm like a flute player to a cobra. Maybe Lee was right that I should relax, relate, and release."

Brenda asked Teddy to drive her back to campus, and with that request Teddy's smile became brighter, fuller, and more inviting. When they got into his car she had noticed that it smelled like cherries ripping on a hot summer day. When they drove off he asked her what she would like to listen to. Brenda had no real requests that tickled her fancy, so she left the music up to him. He put in a soft ballad that set the tone for a new romance that was about to begin. She began thinking, "This man knows just what I like and how I like it."

The ride home was quiet except for the music playing. Brenda began to relax by stretching her feet out in the car. Looking at the highway go by in front of her, she peacefully drifted off to sleep. When Teddy reached the parking area where Brenda asked him to drop her off he parked the car, and sat for a moment before waking her up. He took a few moments to look over at her to admire her beauty. Teddy was very attracted to her, especially the intelligent wit she possessed. While she slept he took his index finger, and softly brushed it against the side of her face to gently wake her from her sleep. When Brenda opened her eyes, there he was leaning over bushing her face with his finger cautiously, so not to frighten her as he was only inches away from kissing her on the lips—the music stopped.

"Did I fall asleep? I am so rude and so very sorry."

"That's okay. You're very beautiful when you're asleep."

"I am?"

"Yes. You are absolutely delightful to sit with and look at."

"I bet you say that to all your girlfriends."

"What girlfriend?"

"The one you're not telling me about."

"Nothing to tell."

"Well on that note I'll let you get back to the base. Thank you for bringing me back safely."

"You're welcome. You take care of those books. Always, remember they come first. Hey since you're from out of town like me here is my number. Call me if you want some conversation or if you want to hang out. Please don't be shy about calling. I could really use the company, Beautiful Brenda."

"Okay Theo. I would like that."

"May I walk you to your door Brenda?"

"No thanks, but thank you for asking. That was so sweet of you. I can make it on my own. Good night Theo."

"Good night Beautiful Brenda."

After taking his number he had written on a napkin from the club Brenda exited the car taking one last good-night look at that smile of his. She hurried to the dorm door, while Teddy sat there until she was safely inside. He clicked his high beams to let her know he was pulling off. Brenda walked to her room feeling wanted and alive—something she had not felt for months.

Lee was sitting with Ethan when Rachel returned to the table to get ready to leave. Lee and Ethan exchanged numbers kissing each other goodbye for the moment. He brushed her behind as she stood up to leave. Rachel saw the hand action shaking her head to let them know they were being bad. Just as Lee and Rachel were leaving the club there he was—Blake dancing with some girl. Rachel stopped cold in her tracks with the devil in her eyes. Lee saw her reaction and put her arm around her to snap her out of her trans-like state. Lee kept rubbing her shoulder hoping to keep her calm.

"Rachel are you okay?" Lee snapped her fingers repeatedly in front of her face. Lee was hoping to get her attention away from Blake dancing across the room. "Rachel talk to me."

"I told him he had better not ever come near me. I need to go over and remind him. Here hold my bag."

"Well if you're up to it—" Lee replied as she followed Rachel to the dance floor continuing to say as she followed her through the thick crowd of people dancing, "then I'm behind you all the way."

Rachel tore through the crowd to get over to the other side of the dance floor where he was dancing. When she motioned through the crowd she grabbed a drink off a table in her path. Rachel stepped right between him and his dance partner. Rachel took the rum drink and threw it in his face. Blake looked shocked, and bewildered at the sudden appearance of Rachel in front of him. His dance partner was pushed to the side by Lee to make sure Rachel had enough room to clear the dirty air between her and Blake.

"Excuse me honey." Lee advised his date, "Blake and my friend Rachel have something to talk about. If I were you I would take my hustle to the other side of the dance floor."

"Didn't I tell you to stay clear off me?" Rachel threw her hands in his face.

"What in the fuck are you thinking throwing a drink on me?"

"You stupid motherfucker didn't I tell you not to come near me again?"

"Yes, but I didn't think you were serious. By the way what do you want Rachel?"

"To tell you how much I hate you!"

"Well if you had let me fuck you, you wouldn't be saying that."

"You tried to rape me."

"Okay I can see you hate me, but if you only had cracked those tight thighs then you wouldn't be crying. You could have had a little pleasure you fuckin bitch. Now what do you want Rachel if you don't want me, or some dick what do you want?"

"That's how you see me— why? You tried to rape me and then you beat me when I said no."

"I did not. You're acting stupid. You don't know what you're talking about."

"You did! When a lady says no and you don't stop then its rape you animal."

"Rachel please take your uptight high-society-wannabe ass out of my face before—"

"Before you what? Hit me again. Blake if you ever lay a hand on me again I promise you I will kill you with my bare fucking hands. Only God will be able to save you when I jump on your sorry ass. Try me!"

"Get lost you dick-teasing little stunt."

"Not in a million years. Every time I see you it only gets worse, and more people will hear me scream out what you did to me. Just think of me as Blake's Black Cloud."

Rachel began to yell loud enough that people in the club stopped dancing to look over to see what was going on. Blake tried to make his way through the crowd to get away from her, but she followed him all the way out of the club to the parking lot, yelling out what he had done to her. Blake jumped into his car and drove off into the night leaving his date behind at the club. Rachel watched the taillights disappear. Lee clapped her hands to congratulate her friend for finally getting it all off her chest. Throwing her hands up to the sky Rachel let out a big laugh.

"Before he enters a room he'll check to see if I'm there."

"After that he sure will Rachel."

"Did you see his face Lee?"

"I sure did, but I'd rather look at my girl. She's back. Good for you Rachel."

"Damn! That sure felt good. I can't wait to tell Brenda. By the way Lee, does this make me a bitch?"

"Yep!"

"Good! At least I'm a fine one. This was certainly a girls night I will never forget. We got to do this again!"

Chapter Seven
Mr. Sellout

With Christmas break just around the corner Lee and Brenda headed home for the holidays with their families. Rachel decided to stay behind to take advantage of earning some extra money; adding she just wanted to have some personal time away from her family. Rachel took an open invitation from one of her professors to house sit, while he and his family vacationed for the holidays. This job would pay for her out-of-pocket expenses that her academic scholarship had not covered.

Rachel was addicted to her make-up as well as keeping in style with the latest craze of the day. She was a fashion addict who couldn't keep her cool whenever the seasons changed if she didn't update each pair of shoes, pants, dress, or hairstyle. Rachel's money flow was not what she had needed to update her wardrobe. She decided to look around for some work on the weekend. Luck had always been on her side, and it just so happened there was an ad in the Augusta Journal seeking a weekend sitter for two small children. The ad preferred a college student attending Peaton. Rachel figured this was easy money, and she didn't have to stress out over getting her nails dirty.

On the day of the interview she knew being a glamour girl was not going to get her the job. She had to pull out the jeans, and sneakers to fit the norm of the average hardworking college student. Stripping her face of all the make-up she wore, and pulling her hair back into a ponytail was the only way to make herself picture perfect for the part.

The cab dropped her off in an exclusive rich section of West Augusta. Walking up the driveway, she looked at the address that Samantha the lady on the phone had given her just to make sure she was in the right neighborhood. When she got to the front door Rachel hesitated for a moment before she rang the bell. Thinking to herself that she might be a little underdressed for the rich people behind these doors she pushed the doorbell, and she could hear the chimes sounding off in the house. After a few moments she could hear the door click, and a tall blonde woman with sea blue eyes appeared from behind the door.

"Hello. I'm looking for Samantha Daniels."

"Yes. I'm Samantha. You must be Rachel Tims."

"Yes I am."

"Come in Rachel. My husband will be down in just a moment. Would you like something to drink?"

"Thank you."

"What would you like to drink?"

"Some water with ice and lemon. Thank you."

"I'll be right back. Have a seat and make yourself comfortable."

When Samantha left the room Rachel sat down on the plush furniture that was as soft as air. Observing the large room she was amazed at the beautiful things they had. It was breathtaking to see such class and taste. She knew money was spilling out of their pockets, or at best somebody got a damn good job. Moments later Samantha returned with Rachel's drink.

"Rachel here you go."

"Thank you Samantha."

"So, I take it you attend Peaton University."

"Yes."

"Tell me a little about yourself."

"Well, I'm a senior at Peaton. I'm studying Business Management. Originally, I'm from California where my family still resides. I have four nephews and one niece. Right now I am currently house-sitting for my English professor, while he is on a holiday vacation with his family."

"Okay. It's good to see young people using opportunities like house-sitting to make ends meet."

"Thank you Samantha."

"I was very fortunate Rachel not to have to work while I attended college. I can't imagine working and worrying about bills and class work all at the same time. I must say I respect a person who can balance such a load."

"It is hard, but it makes me respect money a lot more than I used to. I've become a better person because of it."

"Really Rachel?" Samantha had a smug, snotty look on her face as if what could this little shit convey to her about money that she didn't already know. "Please tell me."

"I can only speak for myself. What I found was when parents always foot the bills; you don't know what struggles they go through to make sure you have the things you need. Not until I had to take care of my own finances did I understand what it took to make sure ends meet. I absolutely love being independent of my parents. I'm a better woman because of it."

"Well that's good for you. You must be the first to attend college in your family."

"No. I'm the youngest of four and we have all gone to college. My three brothers all have masters. I hope to complete my studies this spring. When I graduate in the spring my parents would have seen all of their children complete college."

"I see. It's not often to hear of a family like yours to have all the children be outstanding citizens who have kept a positive path in life."

"My parents have a strong belief in God and a strong outlook on the future." Rachel thought to herself, "What black people can't be educated? Not all black families have to be single parents and have a shit-load of fuck-ups. Surprise, rich bitch. I am an educated sister who just happens to have three brothers with college degrees and some."

"You know what you're honest, and if your professor would leave you his house then maybe we can give this a try. I just happen to know the President of Peaton; we mingle in the same social circles. I will speak to her about you, and if she gives me a good recommendation then you're hired. Before, I can offer you the job my husband would need to meet you okay? Let me go find him. Oh! Here he comes now."

Mr. Daniels triumphant entry into the room put Rachel in a permanent state of shock and awe. He was a fine specimen of a black man she had ever seen and his swagger only compelled the enormity of his gorgeous body. Phillip was definitely wig-flipping fine. Her eyes locked in on him like a missile on its target. Since Blake, she had taken on a very meticulous attitude about what type of man she was attracted to, but Phillip Daniels certainly was her type.

As he walked toward her extending his hand she felt a hot rush take over her body. The blood hurried straight to her head, and the room became a little fuzzy. Cracking a smile was something very hard to do right at that moment. She was trying to hold back all the drool building in her mouth.

"Hello. I'm Phillip Daniels and you must be Rachel Tims?"

"Yes. Good to meet you Mr. Daniels."

"Please call me Phillip."

"Not a problem Phillip." Rachel smiled.

When he shook her hand to greet her, she became undone as to how to keep her cool. Everything about him made her restless. For Rachel, she had an instant attraction to him, but after he kissed his wife reality stepped in. She figured that the brother was clueless, and the movie reel rolling in her head of this fine brother who got it together, suddenly cut to a black and white lens of a sellout.

"So, Rachel Tims tell me a little about yourself."

"I was telling your wife that I am from California, and I am a senior at Peaton. I'm studying business."

"Really! I don't know if my wife mentioned that business is my favorite subject. Running a business is what I do. I am the president and owner of my own computer-design company."

"I see that you're good at what you do. Your house is absolutely beautiful."

"Okay let's talk about what I expect of you on the job. I know you're young and you can get side tracked from what you need to do. I expect your undivided attention when you're with my children. No swearing or yelling in my house, and if you can't get away from some campus party or something please call ahead if you plan on being late."

They talked about school, his two sons, and what the job entailed. Laying down the law as if he were a dictator seemed to be part of his personality. Adding, as a businessman he came off cold and straight to the point. His good looks made him more appealing than he really was. She felt like this ball-breaker was making more of the job than he needed to. Therefore, Rachel laid down her expectations of the job she would be taking on. Rachel let Phillip know what her desired income would be for taking this position. Being a businessman he looked over the investment in front of him. Scanning everything from her clearly painted manicured nails to her neatly laced sneakers Phillip was taken with her polished demeanor. She was very polite, attractive, but most of all her rich brown eyes proved to be warm, alluring, and filled with lots of serenity.

After Samantha left the room Mr. Daniels proceeded to tell Rachel why their family needed to hire a sitter for the weekends. He told Rachel that Mrs. Daniels would be volunteering her time on the weekends at a mission that was located in the downtown area of Augusta that serviced the underprivileged members of our community.

"I'm glad to see a young lady like yourself willing give up your weekends to earn some extra money for school. When I was in college I found myself giving up my weekends to just get ahead. I know how important it is to a college student to have some fun on the weekends. I was there once before, but I can tell you it will pay off one day."

"I sure hope so."

"Keeping a picture of what you want in your mind I can promise you will get it Rachel."

"I'll make a note of that."

"Well, Rachel you seem to know how to handle your ambition. It's in your blood, and don't tell me it's not. The way you negotiated your pay and your limitations—I like that in a person because it tells me you're upfront. You know how to put your cards on the table. I can tell you play only what you have, and sit back to see where it takes you."

"Yes!" She thought to herself, "finally someone who can read my ambition without me telling them the plan. However, the only things that shoot him out of the water; was that he has a white wife, and that's not good. Also, his dictatorial business-minded attitude sucks and that definitely ain't good."

Time slipped by unnoticed as she acquainted herself with the children. Mrs. Daniels put the children to bed and bade farewell to Rachel. Phillip looked at his watch realizing it was too late in the evening for a young lady to be traveling home alone. Like a gentleman he offered her a ride home which she accepted. While driving Rachel to her professor's house where she was staying for the Christmas Holiday, Phillip took that opportunity to have a more open conversation to let Rachel know he was at least human.

"Rachel– I'm not the easiest person to get along with sometimes. Being a businessman has its perks, but one of the drawbacks is being ruthless and self-centered. I have to keep that mindset in order to survive in the shark-infested waters out there in the business world."

"Phillip, you have been very cordial towards me. I can't imagine you being anything other than very professional."

"I am very professional, but I have those days when I am biting off everyone's head."

"Please alert me prior to any outburst that might prove disturbing to me." Rachel quipped with a soft smile.

"I will." Phillip looked over at her noticing her warm smile.

Pulling up to her front door Phillip reminded Rachel that he would be expecting her that weekend once his wife gets the go ahead. Rachel exited the car with a beaming light of accomplishment. While walking up the small stone path to her door Phillip watched her every step. Rachel had no idea that she left a spark on this headstrong, focused businessman with her down-to-earth simple chance meeting. Phillip was hoping she would bring some relief to his hectic weekends. Moreover, the fact she is black was something he wanted. Rachel was perfect for the job. She is a smart educated black female with a strong sense of family values. Most certainly, she was not the everyday norm Phillip came across in his rich world. Rachel was a prime example of a minority on the right track to success. Rachel Tims is the real deal.

The click of the lock sent her mind into a tail spin of thoughts, which was promptly interrupted by the phone ringing in her bedroom.

"Hello!" Rachel responded hoping that the other person on the line was worth the interruption.

"Guess who?" Was the jubilant response spilling out of the other end of the phone. "Lee!"

"What's up glamour girl?"

"Nothing much. However, I just happen to have on a pair of jeans, sneakers, and my hair is in a ponytail."

"Rachel who's paying you a million dollars to perpetrate a fraud? You must be desperate to be so casual. When you go to bed you're a fashion statement. What's up?"

"Nothing! I had a role to play at an interview for a babysitter on weekends. It happens that attending Peaton was a definite plus, but flair and a sense of fashion, well it wasn't even a blip on their radar."

"In layman's term you got the job?"

"Yes!"

"How many brats are we talking here?"

"Two very nice looking biracial kids."

"Bi who? You don't say another sellout."

"Bull's-eye."

"I can't figure out why a brother would just shit all over the sisters. Hell—he couldn't even get with a Spanish girl. Motherfuckers just completely think vanilla is the only flavor on the shelf these days."

"Lee listen honey we all know the sisters got it going on. That's all I need to know."

"Well, I need to know something."

"What? Because I don't have any money."

"No! I need to come back a week early. I was just wondering if you can put me up till we move back on campus. My mother is cutting loose once again."

"Sure I can use the company."

"Rachel you're a doll."

"I know."

"What's wrong girl?" Lee could hear the uneasiness in her voice.

"Oh— nothing! Just thinking about Mr. Sellout."

"Say it ain't so. You got hot and bothered. Your panties wet huh?"

"Yes! Fine, rich, smells good and just so damn delicious. Let me change my panties, because Mr. Sellout did even see me."

Chapter Eight
You Changed the
Way I See You

Saturday morning came and Mr. Daniels called asking Rachel if she didn't mind bringing an overnight bag for the weekend. Mrs. Daniels needed to spend that Saturday evening working late at the mission. Phillip had some work to finish in his office at the house, and out of gratitude a cab was sent to pick her up. Rachel arrived on time for her first day on the job. She rang the doorbell and a friendly older black lady answered the door.

"You must be Rachel."

"Yes! And you are?"

"I'm Anna the housekeeper, cook, and slash whatever needs to be done."

"Hello Anna."

"Come on in. You sure are a pretty little thing. It's about time they added some more color to this house."

Mouth have mercy Anna was getting ready to unleash the truth. No one had prepared Rachel ahead of time for the woman whose mouth was honest and brutal.

"What do you mean?"

"The last babysitter was a little white girl from some private school on the hill."

"What happened to her?"

"She wasn't very good with the idea of having two little black boys being her boss."

"Really! I take it the only purpose she has for chocolate is to eat it." Murmuring to herself.

"When was the last time you ever heard of a rich little white girl being the help in a black man's house?"

"I guess no matter how much money you have you're still a second-class citizen."

"You sure said a mouthful."

"I hate to sound nosey, but I was wondering what is Mrs. Daniels like."

"Always trying to make sure her husband forget he's black. The babysitter before you was one of her country club friends' daughters. Mr. Daniels wanted to give the job to my niece, but Mrs. Daniels must have thought her dreads were a little too ghetto to have around the house."

"Don't tell me she has a problem with color."

"I couldn't tell you." Anna sounded somewhat unsure how to answer her question. "No. I just think that she is confused about how to live in both worlds. Samantha's forgetting that she has two sons with brown skin, and when they get older in the real world they'll be called an endangered species. Get my drift?"

"Got it! Is she nice?"

"I couldn't tell you that either. She just tells me what needs be done, and I do it. She is not one to share much of a conversation with the help."

"How long have you been working for them?"

"About five-years and you know what? Samantha has never asked how I was doing, and she even makes me work on Martin Luther the King's Day."

"That's so sad."

"It's all good. Whenever I come in on that day Phillip sends me home as soon as possible with an apology that she forgot what holiday it was. Let me get out of here, so I can get me some needed rest this weekend. I'll be seeing you soon Rachel. You sure are a pretty little thing."

"Enjoy your weekend Anna and thanks for the compliment."

The family housekeeper showed her to the den. There she found Phillip and his two boys playing on the floor. The kids were laughing and jumping all over him. The hard-headed businessman seemed more like a papa bear with his cubs. Something about seeing him right at that moment with his sons showed his instinctive paternal concern. Rachel smiled at the kids jumping all over him. He was having such a good time with his two sons. It seemed nothing could take his attention away from them. His childlike gestures sounded so sweet. At that moment Rachel could see that he was a patient father with a gentle side.

Tending to the children was easy, because her first day on the job passed by rather quickly. She played hide-and-seek, colored with crayons, and they even played cops and robbers. The boys had a fun-filled day with Rachel, and she had a fun-filled day with them also. The boys were in bed by eight o'clock. Having nothing to do she decided to take a personal tour of the house. Rachel walked through the elegant rooms admiring the marble floors, and the beautiful patterns in the designs that lay carved in the marble. Rachel couldn't resist running and sliding along the smooth surfaces. Letting her fingers do the walking she took the opportunity to feel a real Persian rug with its fine wrap and tight filling. The harmonious, rich color of the floral layout was something of true quality. The majestic ceilings, gold-trimmed bathroom tiles, along with the long spiral stairway, were only seen in the finest homes of the rich.

In and out of the many bedrooms upstairs tasting a little bit of the rich world she thought, "This is something I would have." Rachel was soaking up the many ideas she would use in her mansion one day. To conclude her private tour she needed to soothe her parched mouth. As she found her way to the kitchen there he was, Phillip sitting at the kitchen table with a drink in his hand. He looked a little frustrated after a long day of work. Rachel wasn't sure what his mood was, so she smiled heading for a glass on the counter to pour herself something to drink.

Phillip looked up from his glass. "Rachel, I thought you might be asleep or something."

"No. It's not quite my bedtime yet." She opened the refrigerator to get something to drink.

"Same here. Hey are you up for some pizza?"

"Sure."

"Great! What would you like on it? The sky is the limit."

"How about some extra cheese, mushrooms, and sausage?"

"Great choice of toppings. I love variety. Let me call it in."

While Phillip was calling in the order Rachel sat down at the table with her glass. She wondered what in the world she was going to say to this man. Rachel needed to remember to keep clear of anything that may point to him being a sellout by marrying Samantha. Deep in her heart she hated the fact that a man like Phillip with money, and power would just pass up the chance to be with a black woman. A woman like Rachel never let emotions get in the way of making money as far as she thought she was still on the job. Phillip hung up the phone after ordering the pizza and returned to his seat at the kitchen table.

"Okay the pizza is on its way. You don't mind if we talk a little? I like to get to know the people who work for me on a personal level just as you will get to know me."

"No. I don't mind. It's not often you get to sit and kick around with your boss."

"So what are your plans after graduation?"

"Well, everything is up in the air right now. I've been sending out résumés, but my phone isn't ringing off the hook yet. If nothing comes through there is always grad school."

"It's good to have a second plan."

"My daddy always taught me to keep a backup plan ready at all times."

"Your father must be very proud of you."

"I would hope so."

"How many siblings do you have?"

"I have three big brothers who have made dating a complete nightmare for the guys who took me out. I must mention all my brothers are six two and taller. Most of the guys who picked me up at my front door were seated in the living room having each of my brothers introduce themselves one by one. I tell you, my dates would mostly shake my hand bid me goodnight all in the same breath."

"You're a lucky girl to have brothers looking out for you."

"Yeah. It has its pluses."

"I bet your boyfriend never steps out of line."

"What boyfriend? I wish I could find a good man. The men I meet they don't think like me."

"How do you think?"

"Well, I'm not the kind of girl to just pass myself around like a can of beer, so that everybody can get a sip. You never know what germs people can leave behind. When a guy hears I'm not about sex, and I challenge him every step of the way he turns and runs. I'm starting to figure I'm a little too headstrong for them."

"No. You're perfect. You are obviously a beautiful woman."

"Thank you."

"I know what the problem is."

"Please tell me."

"A man doesn't expect someone as attractive as you to be wise, and secure in her sense of self with a plan about how she lives her life."

"Come to think of it you're right."

"I know I'm right. When a man finds out you have a brain, it confuses him. The ones that walk away were after one thing, but a real man will hang around until the time is right for the both of you. Always remember that."

"I will."

The doorbell rang interrupting their conversation and Phillip stood to answer it. "That's the pizza. I'll be right back."

The pizza was devoured in a matter of minutes with only the carton as evidence of their damage. The atmosphere was ripe and with sleep a little late in coming they decided to watch a movie. Both tried to find something worth watching but to no avail the reception was poor due to the weather. Phillip was frustrated with his satellite contraption, which he pays a pretty penny for on a monthly basis. Once again it was money WASTED. The feeling in the room was tense yet void of substance. Rachel thought of a way to liven things up a bit with some chit-chat.

"May I ask you a question Phillip?"

"Yes you may." Looking at her quizzically.

"How old are you?"

"I'm forty-years old." He smiled.

"You're so polished for your age."

"Like a piece of silver? Are you telling me I look old for my age?" He jokingly responded with a seriously painted face.

"No!" Rachel laughed. "Actually, you look rather young, and yes you're very mature. Your head is on straight. That's what I meant to say."

"I'm glad you noticed. By the way please put your feet up and relax. Right now, I'm not your boss the kids are asleep, and you're not on the clock."

"My parents taught me not to put my feet on the furniture."

"Okay miss prim and proper you got me there, but keep in mind when you come here to work. This is your home. I want you to feel comfortable, relaxed, and happy to be sharing my personal space."

"On one condition."

"Sure what?"

"Promise you will not take things too personal. Believe me it's never that serious."

"I think I can handle that."

"Fair enough."

After putting in a DVD they watched the movie drama until the credits rolled or at least he did. Phillip looked over at Rachel asleep on the couch. He whispered her name softly to see if she could hear him, but she was out for the night. Without waking her up he got up to get a blanket to place it over her. Captured by the full essence of her beauty he took a few moments to admire her while she slept. He was dazzled by her beauty as he stared at her; wondering what thoughts might be running around in that gorgeous head of hers and what possibility if any, might there be a thought about him.

Rachel awoke briefly just as he exited the room. She could see him standing in the doorway watching her, and then he turned the light off. She thought, "You changed the way I see you." She closed her eyes and drifted back off to sleep.

Chapter Nine
No–She Didn't!

Ethan was a dog who needed to be fed his cat chow, and Lee made it her point of duty to feed him well. He kept a low profile, while he cheated on his wife. He felt confident that he had the shade pulled over her eyes. So, like all confident well nourished bow wow's he let his guard down and began spending more time away from the house.

Lee and Ethan with every successful tryst became carefree, wanton, and reckless in their behavior. They did any and everything within their power to the push the envelope as far as they could. On some occasions their cars served as the backdrop for their risqué act. The park near downtown Augusta saw its share of violations, but it was the bathroom of his office that bore the brunt of the burden that was Lee and Ethan.

Spending extra time at work was becoming more pleasurable than he thought it to be. There on his leather couch they enjoyed wild crazy sex. Making love to his mistress in his office was the perfect cover for him, and it served his over sized ego well. Given the tenuous nature of their relationship he knew the time would come for him to face the music about his inability to perform at home and abroad. With graduation fast approaching the opportunity to go their separate ways was the perfect solution.

"Lee, I'm going to miss you very much when you leave after graduation."

"I don't have to if you don't want me to."

"You're young. What do you want with an old man like me?"

"Well an old man like you shoot! You've been driving me up the wall in case you haven't noticed."

"For now maybe. I'm not getting any younger, and my wife is becoming increasingly inquisitive about me staying out late. I can't keep up this charade much longer."

"You don't have to. Why don't you leave her?"

"Lee– I would leave with nothing. She would take everything I worked for like the house; the car, and the alimony. After being together so long I don't want to start over with a completely new family anyway. I'm too damn old for that."

"Ethan if she doesn't satisfy you then why stay in an unhappy situation?"

"Lee, you just don't throw away twenty-five years of marriage. I've been married longer than you've been alive."

"So, why are you sleeping with me?"

"Because you let me! Wait a second Lee. I'm sorry."

"You better be!" Lee replied.

"Lee— I shouldn't be sleeping with you, but you do something to me. The night in the club when I looked at you, I couldn't keep my eyes off you and I know I can't keep my hands off you."

"Ethan, you still didn't answer my question."

"What? Why don't I leave my wife? I guess Lee when you've been married as long as I have things change, and people change. There was a time we used to spend hours just talking and spending quality time together before the children were born. Now that the boys are grown we never found our way back to where it all began."

"So that's why you sleep with me. Your kids are grown."

"No. Lee did you hear a word I said?"

"I guess not."

"See Lee— you are too young for this stuff. Only someone my age could understand and feel what I do about my relationship with Victoria."

"You don't have a relationship with Victoria. You have years and children not the passion we have. When we make love it is so powerful. You look so happy when you're with me, and I know you don't feel this way when you're with her."

"Lee, you're right but there are some things that should be left alone like you never talking about your family."

Lee cuddled closer to Ethan and asked, "I take it you want to change the subject. Okay! What do you want to know?"

"What are your parents like?"

"My father was a good man. He loved me more than life itself. There was nothing he wouldn't do for me, but all of that's over now that he's dead."

"That's it?"

"What else do you want to know Ethan?"

"Where does your mother come in?"

"Oh— her! She's alive and well."

"Tell me about her."

"Okay Tina Jordan. Let me think. Oh! She spits fire like a dragon, and she can't seem to find the good in things around her. In a nutshell she's a miserable human being."

"Umm! I take it the two of you don't get along."

"That's an understatement. She is definitely not in my corner. It's been like this for as long as I can remember, and when my father died things only got worse between us."

"Have you tried to sit down with her and talk about what went wrong?"

"Tina doesn't have the time for sitting and talking with me. My brothers have a better relationship with her."

"It's sad to hear that a mother and her daughter can't share a close bond."

"Well that's just how it is sometimes." Lee wanted to change the subject, so she shifted her position to one of dominance. "I don't want to talk about this anymore it's too depressing. I think we should find something more interesting to talk about. Better yet, let's make love just one more time before it gets too late."

Deep in the throes of their illegitimate sex the phone rang. It was Victoria calling from her cell phone to alert Ethan of her presence in his neck of the woods as she pulled into the parking lot just outside his office building. Already in the area visiting her girlfriend's house Victoria decided to kill two birds with the same stone, and pop in if but for a minute to say hi to hubby dearest. When Ethan picked up the phone things on his couch were certainly coming to a crescendo.

"Hello. This is Sergeant Robinson."

"Hi honey!"

"Victoria!"

"Hey how about dinner for two? Me and you at Toni's."

"That sounds great. What time?"

"About six o'clock."

"Okay I'll finish here and meet there." Ethan looked up on Lee's smiling face with fear ripping through the brain cells in his salt and pepper head. His blood pressure was about to shoot through the roof as Victoria made it clear to him that she was in the parking lot and within minutes would be in his office.

"No! Wha! Wha! Wait Victoria I'll be down in few minutes."

Ethan without warning went from sunrise to sunset. Out of nowhere Ethan's relaxed face was filled with desperation. He lost his balance falling off the side of the couch onto the floor. Lee looked at him wondering what in the hell got into him. Stuttering and gasping into the phone Ethan couldn't gather his words to form a complete sentence.

"I'll be up in few seconds."

"That's all right Victoria! I'll come down to meet you!"

"Too late. I'm coming through the front door as we speak."

These damn cell phones. Oh well."

He had to think fast or risk being found out for his indiscretions. Slamming down the phone Ethan leaped up like a wild fool running from the devil telling Lee his wife was walking up the stairs toward his office. Lee grabbed her clothes, and began getting dressed in a rush hoping not to get caught by his wife. Ethan was pulling himself together as fast as his hands could help him. Scurrying around he scrambled to find a hiding place for Lee pointing to the only place suitable which was underneath his desk. He was in a hurry, but Lee had other ideas.

"Lee hurry she's coming up the stairs!"

"I know! Damn it! Isn't this some shit!"

"Get under my desk Lee."

Lee stepped back with a look that let Ethan know he must be warped or something. "Are you crazy? That's a tight squeeze under there. I'll go in the bathroom."

"No! Victoria might need to use it. This won't take long. I'll get her out of here as soon as she walks in." Lee stood with her arms crossed thinking about it. Ethan was losing precious time before Victoria made her way up the hall. Ethan was rubbing his head trying to get Lee to agree to hide under his desk. "Come on Lee! Please hurry up. I can't let Victoria catch us like this. Please! Please! Please! Come on Lee!"

Lee saw that Ethan was coming apart, and besides she didn't want him to rub his head bald. "Okay you had better hurry up. I am not going to sit under there no longer than five-minutes. Got it?"

"Yes Lee, I got it. Hurry up! Get under the desk."

Lee pushed the chair aside to squat down and crawl under the desk. While he scanned the room to make sure to remove any incriminating evidence not a moment later the door to his office swung open, and in walked Queen Victoria in all her splendor, pump, and pageantry. She had a smile rivaling the neon lights of Broadway, and a hello so loud it sounded if it was coming through a mega phone.

"Hi sweetheart!"

"Well hello there Victoria. What brings you by?"

"Why so formal Ethan?"

"Oh . . . nothing."

"Well, I stopped at Minnie's house to chitchat, and since I was in the area I thought I would surprise you. It's not often I come by the base to visit."

Ethan thought to himself as he looked down at the opening under his desk, "What a day to want to visit me at the office." Returning his attention to Victoria standing over by his desk Ethan ran over to grab her arm to leave. He seemed flushed and hurried in his pace to leave. Victoria noticed his uneasy state because of his loss of words and sweaty forehead; she asked him if everything was okay.

"Ethan what's wrong?"

"Oh ! Nothing! I was just finishing up some old paperwork. You know I hate leaving things until later. Well, since I'm finished here let's get something to eat. I'm starving."

"Good idea. It seems like ages since we've been out."

"You know you're right. Come on let's hurry up and get some juicy steaks."

"You sure are in a hurry."

"It's just that I'm starving, and just before you called I was getting ready to come home to get some dinner."

"It's been a long time, Ethan how about an appetizer."

"I know honey." Ethan said trying to pull her out of his office door. "This is not the place for making love baby you are my wife not a cheap whore." Victoria pulled against Ethan trying to get her out of the door in a playful sway. "I would hate to get caught in a compromising position Victoria."

"Ethan this could jump-start that motor of yours. I want to learn how I could be more adventurous with you." Victoria grabbed Ethan's tie pulling him closer to her, and whispering to him in a seductive tone. "Having sex in places that offer the element of surprise and taking chances like this can do wonders for our sex life. Let me show you how much I miss you."

"Please Victoria!" Ethan tried to pull away from her without trying to seem too obvious. "Please I just can't do it right now. I hate being put on the spot."

"I don't want to do that to you. After dinner then we will give it a go."

"Yes! But not here! Let's wait until we get home. We can take our time if we were home. Please honey!" Ethan stood erect and stressed hoping Victoria would hurry out of his office.

"As soon as we get home okay, Ethan?"

"I promise baby!" He let out a big sigh of relief. "Anything you say. Now let's go."

Hearing the door close Lee sat underneath his desk for a few minutes to make sure that they were gone. Climbing out to gather her thoughts, and to stretch her cramped legs Lee felt jilted and replaced by his wife after she had just given herself to him. She walked down the stairs and out the front door to the parking lot feeling like the sperm receptacle she had reduced herself too. Lee jumped in her car shifting it into drive, and headed out of the parking lot back to school. Lee noticed Ethan and his wife sitting at a stop sign just ahead of her. Lee felt she should get a firsthand look at Victoria being she had never seen her before in person.

Driving up from behind them she noticed them at the stop sign ahead. Lee swerved around them to sit side by side at the sign. Rolling down her window to get Victoria's attention Lee yelled, "Excuse me, I was wondering if you could give me some directions. I need to get back to Peaton University from here."

Victoria looked out of the driver's window and gave Lee a kindly smile. "Why yes! Pull over to the side and I'll tell you how to get there."

Lee responded with a smile. "Great!"

Ethan was sitting in the passenger's seat wondering what in the hell this girl was doing. Trying to make contact with her from the passenger side Ethan's eyes grew bigger than the moon. He looked over at Victoria nervously looking muddled. He leaned over looking out of his side view mirror, and asked, "What are you doing Victoria?"

"Pulling over silly. Can't you see the young lady is lost? I'll be right back."

Looking like an old tomcat cornered by two she wolves he was preparing an escape route when the time came for his demise. Ethan was beside himself thinking, "What the fuck is wrong with this girl? Why is she stopping my wife?" He looked in the rearview mirror to see what was going on. Ethan sat in the car waiting for all hell to break loose. Everything seemed to be calm for the moment. Then Victoria came to the passenger door where he was sitting. Looking at the side view mirror he began heaving harder and harder the closer Victoria got to the car. He was hoping she wasn't coming to snatch him out of the car to explain why this lady said she just finished screwing him in his office. He was lost in his sweaty anticipation when Victoria leaned over looking in the window.

"Ethan are you okay?"

"Yeah– I just feel a little flushed."

"Honey you're wet all over. I hope you're not coming down with something."

"I must be really hungry. My stomach is just a little upset."

"Sweetheart this young lady is lost. Can you get out and help her? You know how bad I am with directions."

"I'm really hungry. Let's just go. Tell her to stop at the front gate and somebody will tell her how to get where she needs to go." Ethan looked in the passenger's side view mirror to see Lee standing with one hand on her hip winking and blowing little pet kisses at him.

"Ethan!"

"Yes Victoria!"

"Let's not be rude. She must be from out of town. What if it were me? Wouldn't you want someone to help me find my way? Come on. Be nice."

Ethan stepped out of the car with a less-than-pleasing frown on his face. Slowly putting on his military hat and closing the car door he strolled over grunting under his breath, "I can't believe this girl! Crazy ass woman! I could choke the shit out of her!" He stood there looking Lee directly in her eyes. Victoria was too busy being nice to notice the tense cold stare on his face. Lee smiled at him hoping he would smile back, but she knew he was pissed when he didn't even blink an eye.

"Hello sir! I'm sorry to stop you, but I'm a little lost. I came to see my boyfriend, and suddenly he was called away. Dumb me let him leave without telling me how to get back t the hotel. Come to think about it, he didn't even kiss me goodbye. Excuse me—I'm just thinking aloud. Okay! Let me think. Oh! My hotel is next to Peaton University."

Ethan thought to himself, "She must have been to the base at least twenty or thirty times, and now she wants to know how to get back to school. This fucking girl is messing with me." Ethan pulled on his collar loosening it to speak. "Okay listen up. Take a right at the front gate and then a left at the first light you come to. It will take you straight to the highway. Make sure to read the signs. They will take you directly to your destination." In a soft whisper under his breath the angry Ethan Robinson mumbled, "And hopefully into oblivion."

"That seems easy enough. Thank you for the directions, and your name sir?"

"Ethan."

Lee turned to Victoria. "And yours madam?"

"I'm his wife Victoria. And yours?"

"Lee. Lee Jordan."

"What a pretty name. A young lady like you should be careful out here. Sometimes you can run into some of the craziest people."

"You're so right. I'm glad I ran into the both of you. You seem to be very nice and kind. Most people would have just kept driving." Lee looked over at Ethan smiling.

Victoria kept the conversation going by asking, "So where are you from Lee?"

"A small town not too far from Atlanta called Stone Mountain."

"How long will you be visiting?"

"I haven't quite decided yet. I'm trying to get a good feel of the area. I might want to settle here one day if my boyfriend wants to take things to another level."

Victoria smiled. "Lee this is the perfect place if you're starting out. It's easy to raise a family and to have a peace of mind. It is so quiet and beautiful. That's why I fell in love with Augusta."

"It's nice to see a couple such as yourself so in love Victoria."

Victoria looked over at Ethan with love in her eyes. Lee even took the liberty to look deep in his eyes to see his expression. Ethan let out a chuckle when Victoria began telling Lee some of her inner feelings. "I have loved this man since I can remember, and I would still like to think we still have that spark of passion after all these years together."

"How long have you two been married Victoria?"

"Twenty-five years, but it seems like yesterday right Ethan?"

Ethan looked dumbfounded at Victoria just as he answered her. "Oh yes. Just like yesterday."

"Stop sweetheart. Lee, he's just grumpy because he's hungry. All men get like this when they get older. They must have their dinner on time or they get grumpy right Ethan?"

"Yes Victoria! I don't want to sound rude or anything, but I've had a long day at the office, and we must make our reservations for dinner. So, you get to your hotel safely okay young lady?"

Victoria stepped in to excuse Ethan's rude behavior. "What did I tell you Lee? They get grumpy when it's dinnertime. Let us get out of here. Good luck with your boyfriend, and I hope to see you around."

Lee smiled at Ethan and then turned to Victoria with a wide smile. "Same here! Thank you for your help. Bye Victoria! Bye Ethan. You take care and enjoy your dinner." Lee watched Ethan and Victoria drive off toward the exit gate of the military base. She could see Ethan watching her as she got in her car.

Ethan's heart rate declined tremendously knowing that he was out of danger of being found out. However, Lee was wondering what in the hell he is still doing with that old crow. With no thought to the fact that she was a third wheel, which was only a cooling for a man who had her at his beck and call Lee's conscience was scratched out by some critter, and there was not much in the way of decency to expect from her. Lee let the warm December wind hit her face as a thought came across her mind. "I bet he is saying no she didn't!" Lee chuckled as she hit the highway.

Chapter Ten
Do You Need
Anything?

Phillip and Rachel hit if off their first weekend together by sharing different memories about their lives and life's many challenges. For the many weekends that would come and go they would begin to understand each other more and more. Finding a friend in Rachel was something Phillip never thought possible, especially knowing that she was only there to work for him. Nevertheless, what he found was someone who cared deeply for the being he was more than the human. Beneath the rough exterior was a laid back gentle spirit willing to share his knowledge with the world. Prior ill feelings toward being a sellout by now were abandoned. After all, he was well within his right to choose a partner he believed in his heart to be the most compatible.

Samantha the once stay-at-home mother of two was spending less and less time at home with her family. Her missionary endeavor was beginning to consume most of her time. Not leaving any personal time for her husband was putting a strain on their marriage. Phillip was noticing the lack of conversation between them since their last argument. Something about Samantha was changing, and Phillip was wondering if she was having second thoughts about their family life. With the boys becoming school age the conflict between them started to bring to light the many issues they thought they had overcome. The once happy interracial couple began to show signs of pressure. There were major differences of opinion about the education of their boys. Phillip on the one hand wanted the boys to attend public school. For him it was about them being level headed with a clear understanding about their lives as biracial children. Samantha on the other wanted the best school money could buy.

The expensive private schools Samantha picked out did not encourage much of their African-American heritage. The ratios of minorities were less than favorable to their ethnic reality. Her lack of understanding of Philip's point of view was due to her privileged upper middle class background. She was a proud card carrying member of the elite and was not about to have that revoked any time soon or under any circumstance.

Samantha's marriage to Phillip was not without resentment, and outright boycott on the part of both families. Her father called into question her sanity based solely on her choice in mate, and was not shy about his feelings for Phillip. Her mother was ashamed of her finding no reason to assume the traditional role the mother of the bride did. They both disowned her for a time, but finally accepted Phillip not because he was a nice guy with a Harvard sheepskin, but because they loved their daughter, their only daughter.

The day of their wedding brought out ninety-nine percent of her guests on the list that just so happened to be white, and out of touch. They came to see the family's first induction of color into the family. Phillip had a list of his family members who did not show in protest to his relationship. The fact that Samantha's father had a Confederate Flag hung proudly in his front yard left his family less than welcomed. So he improvised by inviting the chauffeur in to add a little flavor to the pews in the church.

Assuming his wife wouldn't take off for the Christmas Holiday Phillip didn't want to be alone, so he invited Rachel to spend the holiday with his family. Blown away by his invitation, she was elated that he thought of her as someone special enough to be extended such an invitation. Rachel arrived just as Samantha was leaving for the mission. She waved as she pulled off in her black Mercedes. After the housekeeper let her in Rachel went to look for the kids and Phillip. The kids were sleeping, and so was Phillip. Anna, the housekeeper left minutes later and wished Rachel a Merry Christmas. Heading off to the kitchen to get something to drink, Rachel suddenly realized that there was nobody cooking for Christmas the next day. The kitchen was as clean as a whistle. She thought about her mother's cooking the day before. Just the smell of her mother's homemade apple pies made it seem a little more like Christmas. Her trip down memory lane was interrupted with a kiss on the cheek from Phillip who crept up on her from behind her. It was a thank you for coming as well as a cry for help. Rachel sensing something was wrong saw it fit to inquire.

"Anything wrong?"

"We do have a little problem."

"Hope I can help."

"As you can see we don't have a Christmas Dinner. Normally, we would be visiting Samantha's family, but because she is working at the mission and I can't cook I was wondering–?"

"Sure." She replied before he had a chance to complete his sentence.

Rachel may have been a glamour girl, but her mama made sure that her little girl could throw down in the kitchen. Rachel made a list of everything they needed to make a Southern Style Christmas Dinner. Phillip took care of the shopping while Rachel got busy with the preparations. The house felt as though a Christmas spirit had finally arrived, and the air felt crisp and clean. Kids, a friend, and some good Southern Soul Food was all Phillip needed to enjoy his holiday.

Rachel and Phillip got to work in the commercial-size kitchen that had everything you could imagine to make a meal fit for a king. Rachel took charge like a captain to her battleship. Phillip was as lost as a lamb capable of being led to the slaughter. This Ivy League graduate had two left hands and ten thumbs when it came to the kitchen. Anna was the one with the responsibility of feeding the family through the week, and on weekends that was the task of the chef in a fine restaurant.

Rachel talked Phillip through the process of cutting up collard greens, slicing fresh yams, and washing and cleaning a turkey for baking. He was a little stiff at first, but as the cooking lessons jumped from dish to dish he began enjoying the fun of cooking a family dinner in his own kitchen. Rachel glanced over after putting the yams in the oven, only to notice Philip was having difficulty with the collard greens. Standing beside him she took the knife and demonstrated to him how it was done. The only thing going through his mind was how sexy she looked cutting collard greens. Allowing him to finish on his own Phillip stayed close to the counter in order not reveal his excitement after her hands on cooking lesson.

"You are amazing." He said smiling.

"Why did you say that?" Glancing at him through the corner of her eyes stay paused and replied, "Because I know how to cook?"

"Not just that, but you seem to be enjoying it."

"Explain." She continued as she opened the oven to baste the turkey.

Only God knows what was going through Phillip's mind as he absorbed every sway of her hips.

"I mean this can't be the first time you've cooked a big dinner like this."

"No it's not. I have been a constant presence in the kitchen since I was in the womb. Both of my parents are from North Carolina, and my mother always believed that a woman, rich or poor should know how to feed her family no matter what. To this day, whenever I'm home from school she makes sure I am standing side by side with her in the kitchen."

Phillip was smiling at her as she spoke about all the things her mother had taught her in the kitchen. He watched her creative hands pull together each dish into a wonderful treat for the soul to enjoy. Phillip had not had a home cooked Southern meal in years. Samantha was no cook! She was not fond of the Southern flavor or the calories it contained. Southern food was the one thing from Phillip's past he had to eliminate by being married to her.

Rachel and Phillip talked as they prepared Christmas Dinner for the next day. By the time they finished it was nine o'clock. Phillip marveled at the scrumptious meal that only loving hands and a warm heart could prepare. Just as Rachel finished cleaning up in the kitchen Samantha came home. Following the laughter that was echoing out from the kitchen she walked in and Phillip turned to greet her. He walked over to kiss her gently on the lips. He grabbed her hand and led her to the festive table of soul food sitting there. Samantha forced a half-hearted smile to appease her husband so not upset his happy medium. Samantha glanced over at everything.

"Rachel everything looks very inviting."

Rachel smiled. "Thank you Samantha."

"Good thing you know how to cook because I just didn't have the patience to learn. We always had a maid in our home to do the cooking when I was growing up." This was a lame attempt to justify her lack of culinary skills. Samantha paused for a moment. "Rachel would you excuse us for a moment? I need to discuss a personal matter with my husband."

Samantha didn't worry about Rachel being a threat to her marriage; she only thought of Rachel as being a young girl just trying to get ahead. In her mind, Rachel didn't have the qualities she thought would impress Phillip. She trusted Phillip with Rachel because in her eyes she was the best thing to ever happen to him, and he was fiercely loyal to his children.

Samantha came home to tell Phillip that she needed to stay at the mission for the night to help set up for the Annual Christmas Dinner the next day. She told him that she would be home first thing in the morning to see the children open their Christmas gifts. Moments later she left for the mission again. Samantha didn't even stop long enough to kiss the kids hello let alone goodbye. When Phillip walked back into the kitchen alone he had disappointment scrawled across his face. It was clear to Rachel, Phillip was not okay. If only she could hold him and have his pain all disappear.

"Is everything all right?" She queried. "I hope I didn't anger Samantha by cooking in her kitchen."

"Please! Samantha doesn't even know where half of the pots and pans are. Don't let that bother you."

"If you say so. Did she leave?"

"Yes. She needs to help set up for Christmas Dinner at the mission. Well– we won't let that get in the way of us enjoying the Christmas spirit."

"Okay!" And with a pleasant exchange of smiles the evening picked up right where it left off prior to Samantha's entry.

Christmas morning came and the children were up so early leaving doubts as to whether or not they slept. You could hear their little voices shouting out as they jumped down the spiral stairway. Phillip knocked on Rachel's door to see if she might be awake. Rachel had already started putting on her robe when he knocked. She opened the door and there he was standing and waiting to make sure she came down to see the kids open their gifts. He led the way down the stairs in a quick strut to make sure he didn't miss one tear of the Christmas paper hiding the surprises. The smile on the boys faces was the only approval Phillip needed to know that they were truly happy with what Santa brought them for being good all year.

Phillip disappeared into the den only to reappear with a gift he graciously handed to Rachel as he knelt beside her. "This is for you a token of my–"Phillip paused to fix his slip up. "I mean our family's gratitude for being so nice. It's nothing fancy, but I hope you like it. It's the least I–"He paused again to fix his slip up again. "We could do."

"Phillip, you didn't have to get me anything."

"I know that, but you are deserving of it."

She opened the box carefully to reveal a Cartier watch encrusted with diamonds. Her eyes grew larger than the moon and her jaw dropped to the floor as she grabbed her chest in absolute amazement. Rachel knew true quality when she saw it.

"Wow!" She said happily gasping for air.

Mission accomplished! She had the response he hoped his personal gift would illicit from her. This beautiful woman lit up brighter than a morning star.

"This is so thoughtful of you, Phillip. I mean you and your family. You just don't know how much this means to me."

"Please wear it on your first job interview. You must be on time in style."

"I will cherish this deeply. This is my centerpiece to success. I can't believe I have my very own timepiece."

Breakfast was in order as they sat to enjoy a hearty meal minus Samantha. The phone rang catching everyone off guard. Phillip answered hoping it would be a member from his side of the family calling to wish them season's greetings. Instead it was Samantha calling to tell him she was sorry for missing the kids opening their gifts. Phillip didn't get angry, but he was disappointed for the kids that their mother wasn't there. The conversation was brief, and to the point and without hesitation he returned to finish his meal.

One of the boys asked Phillip where their mother was, and he explained to him that she was helping other unfortunate people who didn't have anywhere to spend Christmas. As the day progressed Phillip, Rachel, and the kids sat to have Christmas Dinner together. Still, Samantha wasn't home.

After they ate everyone went to the den to sit and watch some holiday shows on the television. The hectic day and all that love filled cooking wiped the boys out within the hour. Phillip and Rachel had the task of putting them to bed. With her job a success she went to pack her things and leave for the night in order to let Lee in the next morning.

"Phillip, I'm getting ready to go. Do you need me for anything?"

In the back of his mind he truly wanted her to stay the night with him. Her time with him and the kids was so good. "Do I need anything? No. I just want to thank you for spending Christmas with the kids and me. I wish Samantha was around, but she is doing what she loves helping others."

"You're lucky to have a wife with such a big heart."

"I guess I am."

"Again, Phillip thank you for the gift it means a lot to me."

"Rachel–"He stopped to catch his breath for a moment. "You are a very special young lady and deserve to be treated as such."

"Thank you! Well my cab is blowing." Rachel looked into his eyes she felt it. That thing she was looking for–love. The atmosphere in the room was warm with romantic overtones. She knew she had better leave before she jump ahead of her heart, because she was still unsure if he saw her the way she saw him right at that moment. "Goodbye Phillip." The cab outside was in the right place at the right time and with a quick hug between them she was out the door.

Phillip was consumed with emotions he thought was only for Samantha as he watched the car disappeared into the darkness of the thin night air. This sudden thought of her leaving left him thinking of what he must be missing in his life. Phillip knew that he and Samantha were drifting apart slowly. They had not made love in six weeks. He wanted to enjoy his wife, but it seemed that she had not made time for a tender moment to occur. With the mission and his long hours during the week it left little to no time for love making. Still all was not lost.

When Samantha returned home that evening from her charity work that took up the whole day she found Phillip sitting in the den with a glass of brandy swirling in his glass. He was consumed by his thoughts so much so; he had not noticed his wife entering the room.

"Phillip darling I'm home."

He looked up as he greeted her in his own way. "Yes Samantha."

"Where are the kids?"

"Look at your watch."

"I am sorry for being late." Samantha walked over to the couch, and kissed him softly on the forehead. "Things just got so busy."

"Your children come first, or did you forget?"

"Of course I did not forget!" She snarled.

Phillip fell silent for a bit, and then he continued his third degree interrogation of her whereabouts. "So where were you, Samantha?"

"I was at the mission." Samantha stopped in her tracks unsure about his line of questioning.

"I called an hour ago and they said you left."

"I dropped off a few co-workers. Is that a problem Phillip?"

"Not a problem Samantha! If it's not for you then the same is true for me."

"Fine then!" She said sarcastically. "Let's drop it then."

"It's Christmas? Besides, you didn't spend it with our children!"

"I'm sorry! And the operative word there is OUR."

"Don't tell me sorry. Tell OUR children."

"Phillip, I am your wife not an employee."

"Don't you think I have a right to question my wife? My wife who is never home anymore! So what am I supposed to do? Sit back and ignore what's going on?"

"Well– I see!"

"See what Samantha!"

"You're making more out of this than there is. I am not going to explain myself because I don't have too. It's late and I am very tired. I'll sleep in the guestroom. Good night!"

Samantha stormed out of the room. Frustration gave rise to anger as Phillip threw his glass into the fireplace pained by her lack of caring about how important he values family time especially during the holidays. Seeming not to care if he might be hurt due to her actions, she never considered the fact that Phillip's parents had passed away a few years back. Adding, his extended family had distanced themselves from him. Samantha couldn't see how her extracurricular activity was impacting him negatively.

As for Rachel she curled up in her soft bed as she gazed at her Christmas present from Phillip, and smiled as she thought out loud. "Do you need anything? Damn! I can't believe I said that!" Just for a moment she admitted to herself, "Yes! I do need something–Phillip!"

Chapter Eleven
The Things They Do

The air was stiff with a deep chill to it. Lee ran to the door and rang the doorbell over and over again. Rachel hurried to the door. "Who is it?" She yelled.

"It's me. Lee! Hurry up! It's cold out here!"

Rachel yelled at Lee through the door as she opened the different locks. "You were supposed to be here this morning. What time is it?"

"About eight o'clock."

"Lee what took you so long?"

"I met Ethan on the way here." Lee found her way to the kitchen with Rachel tailing not far behind pointing the way. "Things got a little out of hand. You know what I mean."

"No – I don't know what you mean, but your smile says it all. You have been dick whipped."

Lee looked through the cabinets for some tea bags. She found some on a top shelf above the stove. "Call it whatever you want, but I'm happy. Anyway, guess who I met today?"

Rachel sat at the kitchen table where she left her hot cup of lemon tea before Lee rang the bell. "Who?"

"Victoria!" Lee replied.

"Who is she?"

"Rachel!" Lee looked at her with a look of how-could-you-not-know on her face. Rachel shrugged her shoulders, and Lee snapped her fingers to help Rachel remember.

"Lee– I don't have a clue about who you are talking about."

"Okay! I ran into Victoria Robinson."

Rachel looked above her mint green teacup midway into sipping. "How did that happen?"

Lee explained to her what went down on the army base. Rachel was listening with an open ear to catch every detail. Lee laughed about the situation she had put Ethan in, while dogging his wife to Rachel about how stupid she was to be standing face-to-face with the woman who just got her husband off. Rachel let Lee know how she felt about what she did.

"Lee, you must be off the wall to do something like that. You are crazy."

"Oh, it wasn't that serious! I just wanted to have little fun. Stir up a little excitement for the game."

"What game Lee?"

"Rachel what Ethan and I have are no promises broken, or love lost or gained. I'm just having a little fun."

"You are playing with fire, and with fire you—" Rachel stop short from finishing her thought when Lee jumped in.

"You get burned! I know Rachel, but if you know how to play with the flame then you don't have to get burned only a little warm."

"Okay Lee. Don't be a smartass. Don't say I did not tell you so. Besides, how can you be happy sleeping with a married man who could pass as your grandfather?"

"At least he's married to a black woman."

"And what is that supposed to mean?"

"Oh nothing unless you want it to mean something Rachel."

"Something like what?"

"Well just by looking at the expression on your face it says you get mighty uptight when a certain—"

"Stop! I'm not getting into this with you."

"Okay Rachel let's change the subject. By the way how was your Christmas with the trader and his family?"

"I thought we were changing the subject."

"I did. I just want to know if you enjoyed your holiday."

Rachel looked at Lee. "Yeah right you do! I had a great time and that was all?"

"Okay. I am assuming and I am only just assuming that expensive yet rich looking watch on your wrist was a gift with no strings attached.

"Lee the only thing I'm going to say is this. There are no strings attached."

"That's all you're going to tell me?"

"Yep!"

"Are you sure?"

"Okay Lee I'll tell you a little more, but just a little more."

"Make it juicy Rachel."

"We have become good friends. I've even learned a little about his family and friends. Taking all of that into consideration when I think of him, and his family I don't think about a black or white couple anymore. Phillip is an honorable man doing right by himself and his family. It's not a big deal."

"Rachel that wasn't juicy."

"What did you expect? My vagina is between my legs not on my forehead, moreover his wife has one too."

"Okay but I have to say this Rachel in the real world he is still a sellout. You can pour black paint all over their lovely little family portrait, and let me tell you. When it dries you will still see his white wife."

Rachel sucked her teeth. "What am I doing? Look at who I'm explaining myself too? Ms. Home-Wrecker herself."

Lee lifted her teaspoon out of the sugar bowl to stir it in her bitter tea. "Who me? I know screwing around with Ethan makes me a home-wrecker, but you are faking it until you make it and that watch is certainly helping your cause."

"You know Lee, I know this is hard for you to comprehend, but some people do give nice people nice things just because they deserve it."

"Whatever, but time will tell what his intentions are, and yes Rachel time will make the heart grow fonder."

Rachel stood up to put her empty tea cup in the sink. "Wrong! Its absence that makes the heart grow fonder. Get it right."

Rachel wanted to change the subject, and she thought of the one thing that would work without revealing any truth or falsehoods about Lee's observations. Like a fish she took the bait.

"So you and your mom fell out again."

"What else is new? I can't seem to do anything right. Even the way I breathe is wrong Rachel."

"Lee what's really going on?"

"From what I remember my parents had a lot of problems. They would argue and fight late at night when everybody was asleep, but I could still hear them."

"Do you know what your parents were fighting about?"

"Her infidelity."

Rachel turned in shock at Lee's admission about her mother. "Your mother cheated on your father? I can't believe it!"

"Believe it! Tina comes off as the mother of the year, but she couldn't come off as the perfect wife to my father. He saw straight through her."

"Really!"

"Yes really Rachel my dear mother did the dirty deed behind my father's back at a time when he needed her the most. When he was diagnosed with cancer he spent a lot of time in and out of the hospital. He had changed from this strong middle aged man to a fragile old soul in just months. She was so selfish she couldn't even wait for him to take his last breath."

"Damn!" Rachel was stunned at her family's dirty laundry. "That's deep Lee. Who did she fool around with?"

"My fathers' older brother. His name is Keith Jordan."

"That's a damn shame, but what does that have to do with you?"

"A hell of a lot! When he died he left my two brothers one hundred- thousand dollars each. That left 1.3 million in his estate in cash and three homes. He left my mother the house here in Augusta and the rest to me. My father left me well over eight-hundred thousand dollars, and that my darling made my dear mother Tina, furious with me."

"Why did he do that?"

"My father made it clear in his will, that he didn't want her to have anything of his if he could help it. So, all she got was a house."

"He sure left you in the middle of a mess."

"I know. It just makes me miss my dad more and more every day. Emotionally, I'm homeless. I don't feel connected to mother at all. When I'm at home nothing feels like it should since my father passed away. Somehow I'm just a visitor in my own home. What's a home without my dad?"

"With all the money he left you why don't you just move out?"

"His will made sure that Tina let me stay in the house until I graduate from school, and as soon as I do, I'm going to get my own place. Then I'll be free of her. I just want to fulfill my father's wishes."

After bringing all of Lee's things into the house Rachel decided to turn in early. Lee called Ethan hoping he wasn't angry with her, because of her display of unpredictable, careless behavior earlier that afternoon. Lee wanted to finish what they got into earlier that day. Waiting for his call Lee rumbled through her things pulling out some of her sexy gear for a quickie with Ethan. The phone rang and Lee ran like a track star across the room to grab her cell phone. She placed the phone to her ear hoping to hear his naughty voice.

"Hello!" He replied in a less than welcoming tone. "What do you want Lee?"

"Ethan that was fast. It normally takes you a few minutes to get back to me."

"I know. I'm at a twenty-four hour supermarket picking up some things for Victoria."

"After you finish Ethan can you stop by, and see me just for a little while?"

"Lee–"Ethan stalled to think about what to say. "I don't think that would be a good idea right now."

"Why?"

"Because I'm mad at you! What were you thinking today? I told you don't play games with my marriage, and above all stay clear of Victoria."

"I'm sorry baby. I just wanted to see what she looked like."

"I could have shown you the picture in my wallet. Don't mess with me Lee."

"I'm not baby. I know I've been a bad little girl. That's why I called you to make up in my own special way. Just the way you like it."

Ethan gripped the phone a little tighter knowing what he might expect from Lee's adventurous side. "The black."

"Uuh!"

"Lee the pumps."

"Well, of course Ethan."

"Lee, I was just with you this afternoon. What are you trying to do? Kill me!"

"No! I want to give you something to dream about tonight."

"You know how I hate saying no to you Lee."

"So don't!"

"Only for a few minutes Lee. I've got to get back."

"No problem. How long before you get here?"

"In about fifteen-minutes. Lee please make sure you're waiting right by the door. You know how I hate to wait."

"Okay I'll be right by the door."

Lee hung up the phone and jumped into the shower to freshen up. When she finished she put on some apple spice scented body lotion. She brushed up her hair into a pinned ball pulling down several strands of hair on each side of her ear with a soft twist to each one. Grabbing her black thong she stepped into it like a fireman jumping into his work pants. She knew wearing her silk black sheer strapless bra with her eight-inch leather hooker shoes made her feel powerful. Lee knew when Ethan saw her; he was hers for the moment.

Over the last few months he could not resist her youthful body. Spontaneity brought out the passion between them. Dashing through the store like a wild turkey on the loose; Ethan was trying to save time as he looked for the items his wife needed him to pick up. As he stood at the checkout line breathless and flushed from his shopping experience the line he was on was taking forever to move. Keeping a close watch on the time he grew increasingly anxious to get to her.

Once he paid for everything he snatched his bags leaving his change behind, as he whisked his way out to the parking lot hitting the highway in maximum overdrive. He pulled up to the house hoping she would be waiting by the door. He rang the doorbell anticipating it would open immediately. However, Lee heard the bell, and she wanted him to anticipate what would be his surprise.

Lee loved giving Ethan something different each time they encountered each other. One day she could be the Avon lady with a horny itch that needed to be scratched or a mail lady who needed to deliver a hot package that was overdue. She let him ring the bell a second time. As he was becoming frustrated with the wait at the door the lock clicked and the doorknob turned.

The large oak door slowly opened up. Lee stepped from behind the door with a devilish look about her face. She greeted Ethan closing the door behind them. He turned to look at her in her sexy attire. Ethan stood silent for a moment, while his erection grew to its full strength. Lee could clearly see his excitement formed in his pants.

Gracefully walking toward him with her eyes staring straight at him, she smiled. Ethan returned the gesture grunting as she got closer and unzipped his pants. He grabbed her, and like a dog began giving her long licks up and down her apple spice scented neck. Lee was unbuttoning his pants anxious to get them undone. Her nipples were standing at attention stopping him dead in his tracks. Lee began moaning and groaning as he tasted each of her breasts. His hand was grasping her buttocks to hold her in place, while he enjoyed every inch of her.

Ethan laid her down on the ceramic walkway kicking off his pants to get his legs out. Lee spread her thighs as he positioned himself between her. He always had a serious look on his face when making love to her. Ethan was slow in giving it to her. He wanted to make sure she felt every inch of his monstrous fit. A long stroke with a hard hit was his style. It was enough to make Lee feel his commanding impact. No matter the place or time he always had the magic touch. Lee spread herself wide to make room for his large frame. Ethan's endurance was strong and on time for every sexual event. With each landing Lee wanted more and more of his thrust up against her. Her body was wet from the dripping sweat falling from Ethan's hot skin. All of her baby fine hair on her body lay soaked, and curled from the moisture they created. Just as the moment of the climax became evident Lee began tensing up, and like all the times before she began pressing her nails into his back then squeezing her legs against his waist. All the while her toes were pointed like a ballerina in perfect form.

They lay on the floor resting from their wildish act that had just been performed in the doorway of a stranger's house. The floor underneath them was steamy and foggy from their body heat. Ethan loved the smell of Lee's apple spice lotion after hot sex. He always took the time to enjoy her scent by smelling behind her ears and behind her neck.

"I love the way you smell Lee."

"You do?"

"Yes! I do."

"Oh! Ethan you know how to give it to me!"

"You know I like to give it to you the right way."

"Yes! I know."

"I only want you to feel good Lee. I hope this will hold you for a while."

"Why? Because Daddy's little girl has been naughty today?"

"No. We have to cool it for a while. Victoria has been nagging me about spending more time at home."

Lee sat up next to Ethan looking over at him. "So what are you suggesting?"

"Lee once a week or just when I can get away without hearing her mouth."

"Well okay. Just as long as I can see you is just fine with me. When will I see you again?"

"I don't know Lee."

"What do you mean you don't know?"

"I don't know! Victoria is nagging me about where I've been and who I've been with. I thought spending more time in the office would give me the extra time to spend with you. But, today was too close for comfort for me; my fuckin heart can't take this shit much longer. I don't want anything to jump off. We have to cool it a little bit. I hope you understand."

"No! I don't. I need you Ethan."

"Lee don't you think I need you too! Listen baby after a few weeks we will be back at it the way you like it. Let me get back before she misses me. Come on. Give me a smile. Call me at work in a few days okay?"

"Okay Ethan. I want you to know that I –"

"I what Lee?"

"I am going to miss you."

Ethan left just moments after he arrived. For the time being she was happy just to get off before she turned in. It made her sleep better. Lee climbed into bed very slowly resting her drained body on the warm flannel sheets. She was out like a light.

Retuning home from seeing Lee, his wife lay in their bed with a long white silk gown. Her long black hair was tossed over her shoulders. The sheets were turned back, and the lights were dim. Victoria thought adding a little romance would help bring about a night of love making with her husband. Ethan walked in the bedroom after taking a shower to ensure he cleaned himself of all traces of another woman's musk. He noticed the music playing, and the smell of three scented apple spice candles burning in the bedroom. Victoria noticed the lack of sex in their bedroom and the many nights of keeping his back turned. She reached out to touch him in hopes he would respond. Ignoring her needs, and wants to make love with her husband of twenty-five years he just lay motionless. Victoria wanted to make sure having a night of passion with her husband was going to happen on this night. When Ethan lay in the bed she turned to look at him.

"What took you so long honey?"

Ethan cleared his throat. "Construction on the highway. I thought you might be asleep by now."

"No! I was just waiting for you to come back. Did you get everything I needed from the store?"

"Yeah, and a few extra things I saw on sale."

"I miss you." Victoria tossed her hair to the side and moved her warm body closer to his turned back. "It's been such a long time since you've touched me. I thought we could talk a little, then touch a little, and then kiss a lot."

Ethan closed his eyes knowing he didn't have the energy to perform. "I am just so tired right now."

"Don't worry Ethan. I'll do all the work!" Victoria pulled back the sheets from around Ethan's wrapped body exposing his bare chest. "You just lay back and enjoy the service."

Victoria began kissing, and rubbing his chest to get him aroused as she kissed his hairy chest from shoulder to shoulder. Ethan lay there thinking about Lee hoping he could rise to the occasion. After fifteen-minutes of foreplay Ethan realized he could not get a hard-on to make love to his wife. Victoria knew it had been a while since they had relations with each other. After playing with his lifeless penis for a few minutes she became a little concerned about his lack of excitement from his manhood.

"Ethan is there something wrong?"

"No! Why?" Ethan looked away from her after he answered.

"Then why aren't you responding?" Victoria noticed his response seemed cold and empty.

Ethan kept his eyes focused on the flickering candles across the room. "I'm tired, Victoria. That's all."

"Is it me?"

"Of course not Victoria. What makes you think that?"

"Well, you're not responding the way I hoped you would. I mean if it's not me then what?"

Ethan started thinking of something to say to not make her think he wasn't interested in her sexual advances. Knowing he just finished making love to Lee left him with no fuel in the tank to drive, although his wife thought it should be otherwise. He needed to throw her off his shady trail to not leave any food for thought; he let the lies roll right off his tongue.

Ethan turned to Victoria with a depressed look on his mug. "I've been having a little trouble these last few months."

Victoria had a fretful stare on her face. "What kind of trouble sweetheart?"

"Well you know when you get my age things just don't happen when you want them too."

Victoria patted his hand. "Why didn't you come to me?"

"I'm a little embarrassed about this."

Victoria let out a big gasp of air and hugged Ethan. "You don't have to be embarrassed with me. Is that why you've been acting the way you have these last few months?"

Ethan nodded his head looking over and strangely enough he was bewildered at Victoria's reaction. "What can I say?"

"Oh Ethan! I am so sorry for being a pain in the ass. I should have known something was wrong. I thought you were having an affair. Not to say this is not something to take lightly. Look at me forcing myself on you. I'm so sorry!"

"That's okay. I should have said something to you."

"I'll tell you what. Let's deal with this later and just hold each other. I love you Ethan, and there is nothing I wouldn't go through with you."

"I love you too. Good night honey." Ethan kissed his wife as he lay back with her in his arms.

"We'll follow up with the doctor just to make sure you can resume our passion." She said before drifting off to sleep.

The next morning Lee awoke with thoughts of the things they do when they have been together. Her dirty mind loves to replay her trysts with Ethan. This is like her cup of coffee that gets her going in the morning.

Chapter Twelve
A New Beginning

"Brenda it's about time you called him. So where is he taking you tonight?"

"Dinner and a movie."

"I bet this guy falls for you!."

"I hope not."

"Why not?"

"I'm just not ready for another headache, heartbreak, or the crap that goes along with getting your feelings hurt."

"See that's your problem. You are still letting Greg hold you back from enjoying the other fruits on the tree."

"Please Rachel! I am not."

"Oh yes you are Brenda! He's not the only man that's going to break your heart; in the real world you get your feelings hurt every day. Should you just kill yourself?"

"No! I'm not that far gone. I just need some time to gather my thoughts and feelings."

"You've had a whole semester to do that. Now it's time to get back in the game. Wait now! Not the game of love Brenda, but to just have some fun with the opposite sex. What's wrong with you being happy unless Greg has driven you to fear?"

"I am not fearful."

"I'm glad to hear that, because no matter what happens no one has the right to control you."

With a promiscuous yet zestful tone Rachel looked sideways at Brenda. "Make sure to take some condoms with you."

"I am not that desperate."

"Things change. Take a chance."

"With my life! No way! Greg has been the only man I have ever been with, and I just knew he was the man I was going to marry. Things were going as planned. Marrying my high-school sweetheart and the man I gave my virginity too. Sleeping with someone new I wouldn't know what to do in a position like that if it came up now."

"Brenda, you're living in fairytale state of mind. Besides, you never know what will happen. I didn't think Blake would do what he did to me, but he did. That is not going to stop me from wanting to enjoy sex or men. You should get with the life cycle since you haven't been with anyone other than Greg. Now you have to remember he's a sour grape, and I bet you Theo is crisp and is as sweet as an apple. He may be short, but then again big things come in small packages, and packages like that are always full of wonderful surprises."

"That may be so. Still, I have a lot of reservations about the male gender these days."

"Why are you going out with him tonight?"

"To get away from this campus and have a little fun."

"If those are the only reasons please tell Theo you do not intend to go any further than just a friendship. By the way please don't give that man a sob story about how you got your heart broken, and you don't trust men. You're only telling him you're still a little girl who can't handle grown-up things."

"I promise Rachel. I'll let him know where I stand."

"You don't need to be standing. You need to be on you back getting your rocks off!"

"You're so hilarious. Ha-ha-ha! I have to go. See you later Rachel."

After the movie Theo and Brenda went to an all night diner where they sat, and talked getting to know each other over some buttermilk pancakes and orange juice. They laughed and even joked over everyday matters. Brenda was having a great time with a man she found charismatic and warm. By the time they left the diner midnight had come and gone. The streets of Augusta were empty and damp from the early morning dew that fell while they sat in the diner.

Once the doors unlocked Theo cranked the engine to warm the car. The sudden flow of conversation they shared in the diner became still. Brenda sat with her arms crossed trying to squeeze away the chill in her body. Theo was adjusting the radio to find something to capture the mood. Looking over at her, Theo saw she was a little cold from the car sitting in the morning air. He wanted to reach over to maybe let his body heat warm her, but all the while she sat there like a timid rabbit.

He turned to Brenda asking, "Are you cold Brenda?"

"A little." She replied.

"The car will warm up in just a few minutes. Is there anything I can do to keep you warm?"

"No. I'll be fine once the heat starts to blow, but thank you for asking."

"It's amazing how time flies when you're surrounded with good people and great conversation." Theo turned to look at her with a smile.

"Yes! I'm glad you feel that way." Brenda turned looking at him smiling. "It seems that my friends think the opposite. Not to say I'm a bad person or anything. It's just that I've been going through some personal problems that I've been trying to work out."

"Don't tell me your boyfriend broke your heart?" Theo looked over at her to see her reaction to the question.

"What makes you think that?" Brenda glanced at him with a how-did-you-know-that look.

"It's in your tone. You sound brokenhearted."

"Wait a minute." Brenda turned her body sideways in the passenger seat with her back to the window. "Somehow or another you have been in my—"

"Your most inner thoughts." Theo turned laughing at her.

"Ah, ha! Who have you been talking to?"

"Let me explain something to you. My mother schooled me on everything about a woman's emotions. I know how to treat her, talk to her, listen to her, and even make love to her."

"Your mother must be very special."

"She is and everything she has taught me tells me that you need someone to love your body and talk to your mind. Am I close?" Theo waited for her response, but her quick move to straighten her body in her seat said it all. "Brenda, your demeanor tells me I'm right."

"You don't have a clue Theo!"

"I do know one thing. In the back of your pretty little head you're still waiting for him to come back to you. My experience tells me once he's gone, he's gone." Theo turned to look at her hoping she would open her heart to him.

"I know he's gone, but my heart doesn't know it yet." Brenda turned looking out of the passenger window.

"That's why you have to let someone else take care of your heart. You need a new start with someone who will take care of it for you."

"It's kind of hard to trust people right now, Theo."

"You mean men. Brenda, I truly understand where you're coming from."

"No you don't Theo! Being a woman is hard enough, but to have someone crush your heart and your spirit leaves a woman like me unsure of what is out there. And I'm not the kind of girl too just throw myself at anyone."

"You don't have too." Brenda's eyes met Theo's as he looked over at her, while they sat at a red light around the corner from Peaton. "Let me throw myself at you. I don't want to sound too forward, but I've wanted to make love to you the first night I saw you. I'm not exactly the kind of guy you fall all over when you first meet me. If what I sense about you is true then you want me as much as I want you."

"What a mouthful. How do I swallow that?"

"You don't. You savor it Brenda James."

Just as he pulled up to the campus Brenda started thinking about what she would have to lose if she gave this man a chance to break the spell. The last few months in school had been lonely. She thought if she gave herself to him on the first date what might he think of her. Then again, who cares! Just as long as he gets her mind off Greg, he would be doing her a favor. Theo pulled into the gate to drop her off.

"Here you go. You have a good night or, I should say, a good morning."

"Theo." Brenda sat in her seat silent and still. She looked over at him with a reserved expression on her face as she gazed into his eyes. "I'm not used to being very forward."

"Yes Brenda."

"I just wonder if you might want to make love to me." Brenda's heart was racing a mile a minute.

"Yes and when?"

"Right now Theo."

"I would be fool to say no, but first let me tell you this. I'm not going to pressure you into anything that you don't want. If we never see each other again, then it was certainly nice that we met."

"Same here Theo."

"Wait Brenda, and if I fall for you please let me down with some dignity and some respect. If you fall for me then I'll have to just catch you in my arms."

"I hope you don't drop me."

"Never Beautiful Brenda."

Theo turned the car around heading back to his place. Brenda was hoping he had what it took to make her put Greg in a small corner of her mind. Theo looked over at her smiling with a glee of wow! She noticed that he was pulling into a subdivision of houses where he parked in front of a quaint brick house.

"I thought you lived on base."

"I did." He parked his car. Then he got out opening the car door for her. "I needed to get a place where I could get away from the everyday hassle of being in the military." Theo led her to the front door where he opened it for her. "Here we go."

"What a nice place." Brenda looked around the living room. "You are very neat. I like that in a person."

"Thank you!" He walked ahead of her down a dimly lit hallway. He stopped in front of an open door. "My bedroom is in here."

"What a big bed for one person." She looked at him smiling. Gazing into her eyes Theo replied, "Yes, but right now it's for two you and me. Come! Trust me to make you feel exactly how a woman should."

"How would that be Theo?" Brenda looked at him with a deep needing desire to let him have his way with her.

"Beautiful." He answered back as he brushed her hair away from her face. He continued to say, "Wanted." Then lifting her hand kissing each of her fingers one by one he slowly replied in soft tone, "and desired Beautiful Brenda. Have you ever had such a feeling?" Theo looked into her gentle brown eyes waiting for a response.

"No!" She replied.

"Then take my hand," He said to her, "and let me introduce you to what I have to offer you."

He grabbed her hand to lead her to the bed to sit down. She followed innocently hanging on to his every word. They sat side by side, and yes they both looked at each other. He began unbuttoning her blouse while she watched him. Slowly sliding off each shoulder of her blouse he began admiring her gorgeous bosom. Theo was very careful not to startle her as he caressed her breasts. Feeling her heart fluttering wildly from within, he knew she was very nervous and unexplored. "Relax, Brenda. I won't hurt you." He looked at her. "I only want to please you."

"I'm trying. It's just that you're the second man I have ever been with, and I just need a few minutes to adjust."

"I'll just take my time helping you adjust then." Theo let his hand lead him to her waist as he began caressing her with long soft kisses to her neck. Then he replied in a thoughtful pitch. "Let me know if you want me to stop. I want to make sure this is really what you want."

"I don't want you too." She closed her eyes as she replied to this patient man.

"I'm no superstar, but I promise to give you something to think about."

"Just do what you do best Theo. I won't stop you."

"Your wish is my command Beautiful Brenda."

Little by little she was letting herself feel his touch. Brenda found herself covered in goose bumps with a slight shiver. Her body began responding to his touch as he caressed her. She felt herself falling into a trance of arousal. Her body began to relax, and all of her emotions about Greg suddenly became secondary to her newest sexual encounter.

Pulling down her pants and then her underwear he lifted her legs placing each one on his shoulders kissing her inner thighs. Almost in slow motion his kisses led him to her temple. She found herself in disbelief that this man was licking her; she realized she had never had this unfamiliar act done to her before. She pushed away from the intense pleasure, and like a nursing baby he followed. She couldn't control her outburst of excitement. Just as she voiced her pleasure she also cried, because she was releasing her needs she kept locked up inside for so long. Theo knew right at that moment he had to give her the best of what he knew in order to make her want him. He was a lover by nature, and his display of affection upon her was made evident in the way he made love to her entire body. Like a gentleman he was very attentive to her every moan and to her every tear that danced down her cheek.

"Brenda sit up."

"Why did you stop?"

"Shh! Just trust me." Theo went to retrieve a scarf from his dresser draw. "Let me cover your eyes with this."

"What is it?" Brenda replied.

"It's a scarf."

Brenda sat in the middle of the bed on her knees naked in the dark. He placed the scarf around her eyes leaving the room in a quiet exit. She sat there wondering what in the world he was up to being she was ready for the final step. She thought to herself that Greg always jumped on never having foreplay when they made love, or so she thought it was making love. Then, Theo came back into the room.

"Open your mouth."

"For what? I'm not sure if—"

"Shh! Trust me Brenda."

Brenda hesitated for a minute. Afraid of what he might do; then again he certainly had a special touch as to knowing how to please her. Slowly, she opened her mouth hoping this guy doesn't do something outrageous. Letting her head lazily layback, she slowly opened her mouth letting her tongue lay relaxed. Feeling the cold metal object ease just beyond her moist lips to glide upward to the roof of her palate she could feel the liquid drip onto her tongue. Closing her mouth to taste the unknown she found it to be cold pineapple juice.

"Umm! Theo that tastes so good."

"Just like you. Wait! Don't move. Open up!" He replied again.

"Again?" She asked.

"Yes again!" He responded.

"Umm peaches."

"Just like your breasts." He whispered. "Don't move."

"Again?" She replied again.

"Yes! Oh yes! One more time my Beautiful Brenda. Open up."

"It's so spicy. Ooooh it's hot!" She moaned.

With a sensual tone he replied as he reached for her. "Like you!"

While she wore her blindfold Theo erotically yanked her waist, and threw her head back grabbing her hair kissing her deeply to taste the hot, spicy twang that flavored her mouth. He laid her back and Brenda thought to herself as she surrendered to him. "Greg had nothing on this magician." She was breathless over the way this wizard opened up her most inner thoughts about sex and bringing to life some of her fantasies that she kept secret in the corner of her mind. No one, not even Brenda herself knew she could enjoy sex as much as she would right at that moment. Holding on tight as he stroked down she could feel her body jolt and twitch as she pulled him deeper and deeper within her. She suddenly realized she was having a crybaby orgasm something she always heard about, but never had the sensation or the experience of coming close too. Somehow she knew this was it! Brenda couldn't hold back her hysterical release of true satisfaction. She blew her top and she was released in a sailing wind of absolute pleasure.

"Ooooh! Theo oh! Theo!"

"Is it good to you Brenda?"

"Ooooh yes!" Brenda replied hugging Theo as tightly as she could.

"Do you want me to stop?"

"No! No! Please don't stop!" she cried out.

"Are you cumming Brenda?"

"Yes I am!"

After their session of passion the two slept tangled in the twisted sheets completely satisfied, and relaxed. The rising sunlight brightened the bedroom where Brenda lay in Theo's arms. Feeling the sunrays warm her skin from the skylight above his bed brought a smile to her face. Everything seemed right with the world as she lay next to her liberator. Her body felt free of all of its pain and sadness from her broken heart. A renewed cycle had begun to spin for her. An outlook on the future seemed easy and less likely of becoming a disaster.

Theo awoke to Brenda's soft hand rubbing his hard chest. He looked down and greeted her with a soft kiss to the forehead. For a few minutes they were completely silent. Brenda was wondering to herself as she lay next to him. "What does one say after having the best sex ever?" Theo lay there hoping she was satisfied with his performance.

"Brenda!" He said.

"Yes." She softly replied.

"I hope I see you again."

"I hope so too Theo." She wrapped her arm around him replying, "You are really a special guy."

"Who me?" He laughed.

"Yes you. I have never had anyone make me feel so open and free."

"You mean the guy, or I should say the man who broke your heart never took the time to make love to you?"

"I guess not. He never did what you did."

"Always remember if you're not dazed and shaken after making love to someone then it's not love making. It's just sex."

"I'm at a loss for words, and I can't describe what you made me feel."

"Just as long as you're happy that's how I want you to feel."

"I'm very happy. I am so glad I let you make love to me. I hope this won't be the last time for us."

"I won't go away until you want me to Brenda."

"Do you really mean that?"

"I do!" Theo tilted his head down to look at Brenda looking up at him. "I've found myself thinking of you each and every day since we met. I must have written your name thousands of times on little pieces of paper in my office. Brenda do you know how many times I've imagined tasting your lips in one day?"

"No! How many?"

"I don't think there is a number. All I can say is that nothing seemed to go right until you called me back."

"Really!" Brenda was hanging on to his every word.

"Really! Do you believe in love at first sight?"

"Right now, I don't know what to believe, but I do know one thing. I finally found someone who made love to me for me."

"Brenda give me a chance to show you what true love can offer."

The alarm clock went off. Theo had to get ready to leave for Columbia to see his mother who was very ill. They dressed quickly to get an early start. Brenda wanted to get back to campus so that she could get some sleep before her first class that morning.

Theo drove her back to school where he parked outside her dorm room. "Call me. I'll be in Columbia for a few hours. I'll be back this evening."

"Definitely! You have a safe trip. Give my best to your family."

"I will. We'll finish our conversation later."

"Sure! Be safe Theo."

Brenda kissed him goodbye. After stepping out of the car she watched him pull off toward the campus exit. She quickly ran up to her room hoping Lee was still asleep. As she pushed open the door there was Rachel asleep on the bed, and Lee was missing in action as usual. Brenda walked over to Rachel who was asleep on Lee's bed tapping her on the back.

"Get up." Brenda leaned down to whisper in her ear. "Rachel this is Samantha. Get out of my husband's bed."

"Huh!" Rachel was startled by Brenda's voice.

"What! What! What! Phillip! Brenda!"

"Having a dream about somebody Rachel?" Brenda stood back laughing at Rachel.

"No! I am not having a dream about anybody Brenda. I hate when people wake me up out of a dead sleep."

"Okay I scared you. What do you want Rachel?"

"What time is it Brenda?"

"It's almost nine o'clock."

"Well, I see you must have been taking care of somebody's business. You slept with him didn't you? And don't lie because it's written all over your face."

"Is it like that? Damn! I must really be happy."

"It shows. You're glowing. Start flapping your lips."

"He was definitely a breath of fresh air. He brought me to my knees girl! I can't wait to see him again." Brenda fell backward onto her bed kicking her legs up and down. She was completely lost in a bowl of happiness.

"So was it a divide and conquer, a sneak attack, or aim and fire?"

"Neither! He put some alien shit on me. He's from outer space because what he put on me was off the hook. This man can't be an earthling. No way!" Brenda sat up in her bed and looked over at Rachel. "Black men don't just do what he did to me."

"What was that?" Rachel replied.

"He romanced me, he talked to me, he teased me, and then he made love to every inch of my body. How could I let myself be cheated out of such a beautiful feeling all these years?"

Brenda slapped herself on the face. "I now know what you guys mean when you talk about having a crybaby orgasm and never looking at sex the same again."

"I am so glad for you Brenda. See, you let yourself enjoy one of nature's pleasures. It takes a special man to bring a woman to her peak, especially a woman who never had a chance to enjoy such a thing."

"You're right! Greg didn't invest the time it took to let me enjoy the moment. Theo took me step by step. He certainly knows the art of making love to a woman."

Brenda and Rachel talked for a little, while she got ready for her class. Rachel was getting somewhat aroused at some of the steamy details of Brenda's night of a rude, but sweet awakening. Brenda was walking on air. She was skipping around like a little girl who found a nickel on her way to school. A new beginning had begun to spin for Beautiful Brenda.

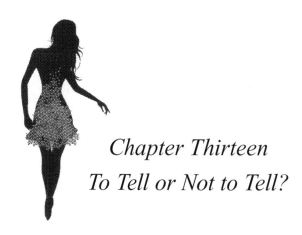

Chapter Thirteen
To Tell or Not to Tell?

Rachel found herself having to run to the light company for her professor who was out of town during the holiday season. She needed to pay a bill for him, because he would not be back in time to pay himself. Rachel decided to go toward the end of the day to bypass any crowds during the early afternoon. The local light company was a block away from the mission where Samantha worked, and having paid the bill with some time to kill downtown Rachel wanted to just pop in to say hello to Samantha as well as invite her, and the kids to the campus for a family event. When Rachel arrived, she didn't see Samantha anywhere.

After taking a few minutes to ask around for her a worker at the mission told her to look in the director's office down the hall. Strolling along the dimly lit hallway looking for the office Rachel noticed the director's door partly open. Knocking lightly to see if anyone would answer she opened the door and walked in. Finding no one there she took a little notepad to leave a note for Samantha. Sitting at a desk to jot down a message for her, Rachel could hear voices coming from down the hall. Standing up at the desk Rachel was ready to greet whoever might pass the door in hopes they could tell her where Samantha was. With her back to Rachel, Samantha was embraced in the arms of another man other than her husband as they kissed backing themselves into the office. Looking on in shock Rachel couldn't fathom what she was seeing. Samantha turned around to see Rachel standing there by the desk in the room with a pad and pen in her hand.

"Rachel! What in the hell are you doing here?"

"I was told you were in here, but I didn't see you, so I wanted to leave you a note. I just wanted to say hello and to let you know Peaton was having a carnival, and I thought you might want to bring the kids." Rachel hung her head down.

Samantha asked the gentleman that she was embraced in a kiss with to excuse her while she spoke to Rachel alone. "Okay. This is not what you think Rachel."

"Samantha— I don't think anything. Actually, it's none of my business. I just work for you Mrs. Daniels." Rachel threw down the pen and pad on the desk pissed and angry thinking to herself that this fuckin bitch would cheat on a good man like Phillip.

Rachel turned to leave. Samantha got nasty with Rachel because she had a holier-than-thou-look on her face. Rachel made Samantha feel she was better than she was. "Rachel, you think you're better than me because you caught me?"

"Like I said I don't think anything Mrs. Daniels. I'm just the help."

"You little stuck-up ass I bet you feel I should explain myself. Well, I am not going to. Do I care if you tell Phillip? All little girls like yourself are tattletales."

"Mrs. Daniels whatever you do is your business. However, a man like Phillip is hard to find. So if I were you I would think twice about the grass being greener on the other side. Most of the time the grass on the other side is browner than shit."

"Rachel you do have a tacky side. Such foul language for a young lady like you, and for heaven's sake stay in your place little girl before you hurt yourself."

"I have to go! I didn't come here for this. I was just trying to be a friend."

"You could never be my friend because you're the help in my house!"

Rachel walked from behind the desk to grab her bag off the chair. Samantha looked at her as she proceeded to leave the office. Rachel about faced then she rushed up into Samantha's face to give her a piece of her mind. "You know what! Women like you mess it up for women like me. I could appreciate a man like Phillip. You don't even know how lucky you are. If I had a chance I would—"

"What Rachel take my husband? Well you can't. See he likes women like me. Classy, well-to-do financially—oh! Don't forget creamy and sweet. See, I made Phillip who he is. I gave him the courage, the status, and two sons. Rachel do you understand? Phillip had nothing when he married me, but I had power, money, and backing. He had a vision, and I helped create what is now one of the biggest companies on the East Coast."

"Samantha, you are so shallow. Do you realize how much Phillip loves you?"

"Yes! I love him too, but he's all business. I need a man at my disposal to give me what my husband won't. I want to feel wanted."

"You're a selfish self-centered bitch!"

"That may be true, but right now I am the most satisfied self-centered bitch I know."

Rachel hurried out of the office leaving Samantha standing in the doorway. Finding her way back home she paced back, and forth debating whether to call Phillip on the phone to tell him what she found out about his wife. Late that night Rachel heard the phone ringing. When she picked up it was Brenda on the other end.

"Hey, girl it's me Brenda. I was hoping you were up."

"Yeah I'm up. I can't sleep."

"What's on your mind?"

"A lot of things."

"Like?"

"Samantha Daniels."

"Isn't that Phillip's wife?" Brenda replied.

"Yes! The one he should leave."

"Back up for a second. Did I miss anything Rachel?"

"She's cheating on Phillip."

"Get out!"

"I don't know exactly when it started, but today I showed up at the mission. I wanted to see if she might want to take the kids to the carnival at the school next week. Just as I was writing her a note the next thing I knew, she was hugging and kissing some guy when they came into the office where I was standing. I didn't feel good about what was happening."

"Then what Rachel?"

"We had a few words, and I left."

"Rachel are you going to tell Phillip?"

"Hell no! That's not my place besides I just work there. I'm not going to put my job on the line. I'm keeping my mouth shut on this one."

"Good idea!"

"Although Phillip and I have become good friends I'm feeling like a calloused heel by not at least trying to say something."

"Friends or not leave it alone. You're the one who will end up paying the price of being the bearer of bad news."

"Brenda, you mean if I were in this situation you wouldn't tell me?"

"I'm not saying that. I'm just saying if you're not emotionally ready to handle a friend telling you the man or whoever is cheating on you, then no. I wouldn't say a word. Somehow or another the friend who tells is the one who ends up getting kicked in the butt."

"You can't be serious Brenda."

"Yes I am!"

"There is no way I would ever go against you if you came to me about someone I love hurting me."

"Rachel are you sure?"

"Yes! I'm sure. Why, you don't think I would hear you out? You're my girl."

Brenda sat on the other side of the phone in silence debating if she should come clean about what she knew about Blake. A moment later Brenda decided to come clean and clear her mind of this once and for all, because Brenda never wanted to ever have anything come between them.

"Rachel remember the night in the library when I tried to tell you about what I heard about Blake?"

"Yes! Why?"

"Remember when you said to me you didn't want to be poisoned with half-truths?"

"Yes! So tell me the half-truths now."

"Okay. Blake used to beat his girlfriend Tisha. They broke up a few weeks before you guys started dating."

"What! And you didn't tell me?"

"I tried, but you were not ready emotionally to hear what I had to say. Rachel! You were hell bent on making sure nothing got in the way of something tarnishing Blake's beautiful exterior."

"What! I just! Forget it Brenda." Rachel retreated without a reaction.

"Rachel—"Brenda paused before she continued say, "I hope you're not mad at me."

Rachel sat on the other end of the phone listening to Brenda speak. She couldn't get angry with her friend who tried to warn her of the possible danger. Rachel thought to herself, "If Brenda did tell me what she knew was I ready to change my mind about Blake? Would I have still gone out with him? Yes! I would have still wanted to make that man my man." Rachel's a leader who must see for herself. Still she thought, "Blake didn't seem the type. How could I have known? I had a chance to know, but I walked away from wanting to hear the truth. Damn! I was stupid."

Rachel pictured Samantha in her mind. The perfect rich girl with a color struck husband was something to leave alone. Who would believe the little black girl working for her as the weekend nanny? That thought frightened Rachel; she figured it would be in everyone's best interest for him to find out on his own. Brenda kept trying to get Rachel to answer her question. "Rachel are you mad at me?"

"What?" Rachel replied.

"I said are you mad at me?"

"Brenda, I can't blame anyone but myself. No, girl I am not mad at you. I'm mad at myself. I should have just listened to what you had to say and looked beyond Blake's perfect shell. To tell or not to tell that is the question. It depends on how the wind blows when that time comes. Right Brenda?"

"Yes Rachel!"

Chapter Fourteen
Breaking Up Is
Hard to Do!

The pressure to perform at home and outside was getting to Ethan. Between Lee and Victoria his motor was about to blow, and he knew that he couldn't last much longer trying to make love to two very sex-thirsty women. It was time for a rest, because the python was not responding to its call to nature. The time spent away from Lee gave him a chance to rekindle the sparks between him and Victoria. The talks, the walks, and the passion that was once there had finally found its way back to his heart for his wife. The feelings he felt were fresh and new.

Ethan knew it was time to end the affair with Lee. Trying to soften the blow of breaking off the relationship Ethan stopped accepting all of Lee's calls at the office. He hoped she would get the hint. Caring and even loving her in his own way only made it harder for him to drop Lee, but his love for his wife was more than what he felt for her.

Lee was becoming tired of waiting for him to find time to make love to her. She knew he couldn't be so busy that he could not return any of her many calls. Waiting by the phone for Ethan to return one of her many texts for thirty-minutes, Lee decided to drive over to his office to see him. Driving up to the building where he worked she found that his car wasn't there. Being so early in the morning, he must be still at home. She quickly turned her car in the direction of his house, and she hit the gas. She always knew where he lived because he told her, but she promised to never come there under any circumstance. Nothing was going to stand in the way of her getting what she wanted—not even a promise to stay away. Slowly driving down the street where he lived she found his car sitting in the driveway. Just as she parked the car he came out of the house to get the morning paper. He shut the door and she got out of her car to go ring the bell. Wondering what she would do if his wife answered, Lee thought she might tell Victoria the truth about having an affair with her husband. Then she thought that just walking away was going to be too easy. Just improvising would have to do. Lee loved adding some excitement to every part of her life, because it made her feel as though she was in total control. Being the dominatrix in her relationships was her ultimate goal. No man was ever going to leave her unless she let him go. After tapping on the door, she stepped back to let him get a full view of her in her birthday suit when he opened the door.

"Who is it?" He yelled.

"It's the police!" Lee replied.

"The police? Just a second."

Lee banged on the door. "Sir you must open the door right now!"

When Ethan pulled the door open, Lee let out a big laugh. Ethan stood in the doorway with a dreadful look on his face wearing his bath robe at eight-forty-five in the morning. Lucky for Ethan, his wife was at work. Lee opened her jacket to reveal her nude body. Ethan snatched her arm, pulling her into his house where she had promised to never come to. He slammed the door behind her.

"Lee! What the fuck are you doing here?"

"Coming to get some of your hot love! See what I got." Lee opened her jacket to flash him again.

"You know you can't be here. Why are you playing games with me?" Ethan shook her arm.

"I wanted to see you, and you didn't return my text. What's a girl to do?"

"Close your jacket. Let me help you to the door." Ethan pulled her by the arm to the front door.

"Where's your wife?"

"She went to work! Thank God!"

"Ethan, I came to give you something. Wait a second."

"This is not the place or the time."

"Ethan, you always wanted to be adventurous!"

"Yeah in a bed that's not in my house Lee!"

"Listen! I came all the way over here to give you something."

Ethan let her arm go. "What Lee!"

"Me!"

Ethan snatched her arm again pulling her to the front door. "Not here you won't!"

"Ethan this is the perfect place. It's so homey. Stop pulling so hard."

"Close your coat and leave."

"Don't be so pushy Ethan. You didn't act like this the last time we saw each other."

"That's then and this is now. Come on let's go."

Just before he could reach to open the door Lee wrapped her arms around him kissing his cheeks. Somehow, she untied his robe and like lighting, she dropped to her knees and began sucking his python. Ethan let his male-driven hormones take over, and he gave in. His sudden quickness of trying to get her out of his house where he and his wife raised two children became another cheap get-off spot. When they were finished Ethan lay on floor in his living room satisfied with an overpowering sense of guilt. He knew he had to get direct with her.

"We have to stop doing this Lee."

"No we don't! I'm willing to keep a low profile."

"No, no, Lee! This is over right here and now. We can't do this anymore. It's not fair to Victoria."

"Don't do this Ethan. You know you love me. We're good for each other."

"No we are not! I'm married and I want to stay that way."

"No you don't! She can't love you like I can."

"Lee listen! It's over. I can't see you anymore. Do you understand?"

"No! I love you Ethan." Lee was frantic with tears in her eyes. Ethan grabbed her jacket pulling her up from the floor to throw her out.

"Get out Lee!"

"No! Don't do this to me. I'm in love with you Ethan."

"Well– I don't love you. It's for the best so leave."

"You can't be serious!" Lee pleaded with him. She pulled away from him as he tried to push her out of the door.

"Lee, I am very serious!" Ethan pushed her out of the open door. "Get out!"

Breaking off their relationship abruptly wasn't how it was supposed to be, and Lee wasn't prepared for such a drastic move without her say so. Ethan stood by the window shaking his head as to how he let things get so out of hand with her. He knew this way would be the best way to let things end for good.

When he slammed the door after he pushed her out Lee banged on the door as hard as she could and repeatedly yelled out his name begging him to answer. Twenty-minutes later she realized he was serious. She kicked the door as hard as she could. "I hate you Ethan! I'm going to tell your wife and I don't give a fuck what happens! You can't just treat me like this! Ethan you think breaking up is hard to do? You wait motherfucker you ain't seen nothing yet!" Lee got in her car and pulled off.

Chapter Fifteen

Unexpected News,
Bad Timing, and
Flashbacks

Brenda and Theo became very dependent one another. For Brenda, he was the man who brought about a sexual awareness that helped her overcome the hold Greg had on her heart. Theo on the other hand was dealing with his mother's illness that was slowly killing her. Emotionally, he was in need of Brenda's touch to help him deal with the everyday toll it took on him. Several weeks just before graduation, his mother took a turn for the worst and she was hospitalized to stabilize her failing health. Knowing the end was evident at any time Theo needed Brenda to be near him more than ever. After he called her early one evening, Brenda rushed over to be with him. Lee dropped her off at his door. After taking off her coat she sat next to him on the couch holding him tightly.

"Thank you for coming over."

"Theo are you okay?"

"I just wanted to talk."

"Okay then." Brenda gave him all of her attention. She didn't even blink an eye. She wanted to make sure she didn't miss anything he might say to her.

"Since my mother took the turn for the worst my sister has been there for me. You can sort of say she stepped into a mother's role of taking care of everybody in the family. I truly respect her for that. Being she had become the backbone of the family leaning on her now wouldn't be fair. Jackie can only handle so much."

"I'm glad there is someone who cares for you just as much as your mother." Brenda wanted to continue, but she knew telling him she loved him now wouldn't be the right time. So, she held back.

"I am glad to have her as my sister, but I'm not used to spilling all of my emotions out in the open. See, I am the only man in the family and I need to be strong for her. I don't want her to see me fall apart, because I want her to know that I'm there for her."

"You're only human, and you have the right to cry just like everyone else."

"Let me finish Brenda."

"Okay."

"I was just thinking about life and how short it can be. No sooner than you're born time just jumps right off. It's like a race you run. Just when you think the race keeps going and going it's over. The finish line pops up out of nowhere, and then I realized that when you see someone you love dying right before your eyes, and there is not a damn thing you can do to help them what do you do? The only thing I came up with was to find a place where I can cry. The only place I thought of was in your arms."

Brenda wiped a small tear from his eyes. "Theo, I am here for you and I want to let you know I love you."

"I love you too Brenda."

Brenda slid over wrapping her arms around Theo, and suddenly he began sobbing like a child in her arms. She found herself sharing his pain and tears. As they sat together they watched the clock ticking away, and she watched him fall asleep in her arms. Just as she placed the blanket over him the telephone rang and she rushed over to pick it up, but she decided to let the answering machine pick up instead. Brenda overheard the message Jackie left to let Theo know their mother had just passed away in her sleep. Wondering if she should wake him from his needed sleep to tell him the news of his mother's death was dreadful. The timing was not good. Brenda wanted to have an issue free relationship, but his mother's death would certainly hinder him emotionally until he has had a chance to heal. She decided letting him sleep for a few hours would be the best, because she didn't want to be the bearer of bad news. However, she would have to let him know that his mother had passed away.

Kneeling down on the floor next to him as he slept on the couch she took a deep breath holding it for just a second or two. As she slowly ran her hand across his soft wavy hair he began to wake up. Brenda made eye contact, and held it steady for the bumpy ride ahead once she told him the tragic news.

Theo looked up with a smile. "Hello Beautiful Brenda."

"Hello handsome." Brenda kissed his warm lips.

"I really needed that sleep. I feel much better. Thank you for being here for me. I hate thinking about you leaving in just a few weeks, but later for that."

"Theo, I need to talk to you."

"Okay let me go and freshen up. I'll be right back." Theo yelled from down the hallway to Brenda. "Come in here for just a second."

"All right!" She just knew he stopped in his bedroom to listen to his messages. Brenda just knew he got the bad news.

Walking down the hallway toward his voice she was startled, because he crept up from behind her from a side room. He grabbed her breasts from behind rubbing his body against hers as he lifted her shirt up from the back pulling it off. Theo guided her against a wall pulling down her pants swiftly. Instantly, they're on the floor going at each other. Brenda didn't want to upset his sudden charge of healthy energy. So, she let him enjoy her as she enjoyed him. When they finished Brenda got up from the floor, and stood over him as he tried to pull her back down for another go around. Reaching for his hand to help him up from the floor Theo noticed her serious stance as she stood looking down at him with her hand out.

"Theo." In a soft patient voice she let him hear the unavoidable news of what had come to rest at his doorway for grief. "I hate to do this to you, but Jackie called a little while ago. It's on your answering machine." Watching her lips part confirming that inevitable moment, made the passion pass through him quickly. He became that of a saddened man who lost his most precious jewel ever sought or found by mankind his mother. Looking down at the floor where he had just made love to Brenda gave him a moment to gather his thoughts.

"Thank you." Theo grabbed her hand to stand up. He looked at her, kissed her, and then hugged her. He walked over to the phone to begin the preparations for his mother's funeral. Brenda stood back looking on at this man—this beautiful man that she knew was truly special.

It had been over a week since Brenda had seen or heard from Theo after getting the news about his mother. She called and called leaving numerous messages to let him know she was concerned about him. After not hearing from him, she decided to give him his space to sort out his emotions. Trying to concentrate on doing some final papers her mind constantly drifted back and forth with the thoughts of Theo making love to her. Still, she wondered how he might be dealing with the death of his mother, and wanted to be close to him in his time of need. Just as she delved into her paperwork Lee walked in.

"Hey Ms. Thing!"

"Hi Lee."

"Got the blues girl?"

"No."

"Then what's up with the long face?"

"Nothing really."

"You lie like a rug. Theo got you thinking dirty thoughts."

"Yes! I feel a little kinky today."

"Good for you. It's about time."

"I wish I could see him right now, but he's still in Columbia."

"That's right. It's been a while since you've seen him."

"He hasn't returned any of my messages. The funeral had to be at least a week ago."

"Brenda maybe he had to tie up some of his mother's loose ends. I know when my father died it took months to just get all of his personal affairs in order. It is very time consuming, and it's an emotional time. It seems time moves very slowly. Just when you think you have finished that box of papers or that dresser drawer of clothes you break down in a stream of tears. Dealing with death is one of the hardest things you'll ever have to go through, especially if it's a parent that you're close too."

"I kind of figured that. It can't be easy saying goodbye to someone you love knowing it will be the last time you'll see them again."

"Especially, if that person is the only one who understood everything about you. On a lighter note when are you leaving for Andrea's wedding?"

"In three days. I was hoping to get to see Theo before I go. At least seeing him would keep me focused on something positive."

"Brenda what's up? That didn't come out right. You sound a little like you're not sure of yourself."

"I didn't tell you Lee?"

"Tell me what?"

"Greg and Lisa got married a few weeks ago. As a matter of fact the weekend before she had the baby."

"What did they have?"

"A little girl."

"I hope you can handle that."

"I hope I can too. After Theo's crash course of bringing the freak out of me, I think Greg better stay clear of me now that I know he's a lying two-timing cheat who happens to be a lame fuck. Please! His looks are the only thing he has going for him and Lisa, well she's a river rat."

"Good choice of words coming from the other woman herself."

"Lee, you know I'm not one to judge people, but I sometimes wonder why you put yourself in the middle of a mess."

"Right now I can't answer that, because it feels right between Ethan and I. I never thought I would be the other woman, but shit happens. You have to be prepared to step over it or in it."

Wiping shit off your shoes is too messy. So, I just step over it and keep on walking because straight ahead there's going to be another pile of it. You can't live your life taking the shit in front of you so seriously. Ninety-nine percent of the time you need to shake the shit off and keep it moving. So, why should Ethan's marriage stop me from wanting to be with him?"

"Still Lee—" The phone rang. "Let me get that. Hi Theo! I am so glad to hear from you!" Brenda turned to notice Lee speaking to her.

"Brenda I'll see you later."

"Just a second Theo. Lee we'll finish our talk. I promise."

"Sure!" Lee left the room and Brenda was able to turn her attention back to her phone call.

"Theo, I was getting a little worried about you. Is everything okay?"

"Yes! As okay as it can be and yes I have been thinking about you Brenda. I just wanted to let you know that I missed you very much. Can I see you tonight?"

"What time Theo?"

"About ten or eleven."

"I'll be there at ten."

"Brenda stay the night?"

"I wouldn't have it any other way. All night in your arms I live for the moment."

"Just don't keep me waiting Beautiful Brenda."

"I won't!"

Theo left Columbia in a rush hurrying to meet Brenda at the door before she arrived. With all that had happened over the last few weeks with his mother's funeral left everything in Augusta backlogged due to his absence. Forgetting to check his messages daily Theo's former lover when he was stationed in Hawaii just happened to leave a message that she would be coming to Augusta to see him. Shauna was eager to see him since he had left the islands for his emergency leave. Shauna and Theo were just bed partners in Hawaii. That was Theo's impression of what they had, but persistence was Shauna's middle name. Nothing was going to stand in her way of trying to win his heart. She figured the timing was just perfect to step in after his mother's funeral. Shauna wanted to make Theo see she was the one for him. The last few months, while he was in Hawaii with Shauna it was a little shaky. Her baby's father was a fellow soldier stationed on the same base in Hawaii.

Being so self-absorbed about her feelings Shauna cheated on her boyfriend with Theo, because she was not being forthcoming with Theo about her relationship with her boyfriend it blew up into a big controversy of lies and crushed feelings. Once confronted with the truth about her relationship with her boyfriend all of Theo's genuine feelings he had for her suddenly became a bad taste in his mouth. After leaving the islands to return to the mainland he left her constant phone calls and letters unanswered. Wanting to forget the mess he left behind Theo spent most of his time right next to his mother. Theo hoped to find someone like Brenda who was free from dealing with a boyfriend, or a ready-made family. When he met Brenda, she was the fresh start he needed to get on with his life.

Shauna had a close relationship with Theo's sister Jackie. She got to know Jackie when she came to visit her brother on the islands for a vacation. It was during that time when Shauna and Theo talked about getting serious with each other. Shauna went out of her way to make sure Jackie had a good time while she vacationed. That led to a friendship between the two women, who eventually began talking to each other every weekend on the phone. Shauna wanted to push herself into Theo's life, so she called his sister to see when he would be returning from Columbia. Innocently enough, Jackie assumed Shauna and Theo were still together. She had no idea that they had a falling out between them. Theo was not the kind of man to discuss his personal life with his family. Shauna finally got Jackie on the phone the night Theo left to meet Brenda.

"Hi Jackie!"

"Hi Shauna."

"I am so sorry Jackie for your loss. Is there anything I can do?"

"No! She is in a better place now."

"Sorry I couldn't make it, but did you get my flowers?"

"Yes! They were beautiful. Thank you for thinking of us."

"I was wondering. Is Theo there?"

"He just took off about twenty-minutes ago back to Augusta."

"Darn it. I just got in about an hour ago off the plane from Hawaii. I was hoping to surprise him by waiting for him at his house. I sort of wanted to prepare a hot meal or something to lift his spirits."

"He never gave you a key?"

"He did, but I lost it and besides he's a little mad at me."

"Shauna, I understand. Every couple has their ups and downs, but I think you being there when he gets in would lift his spirits."

"So he hasn't discussed our relationship with you?"

"No! Theo never tells anyone about his love life. He is very private. I was hoping you guys would hook up and tie the knot."

"I'm working on that right now! Everything takes time when it comes to Theo."

"Oh! I just thought about something. You know what?"

"What?"

"Theo told me he has an emergency key in the backyard under a brick next to the flower bed."

"Thanks! I'll call you in the morning okay Jackie?"

"Good luck Shauna. He's been a little down since the funeral. So be a little patient."

"I love your brother with all my heart. I only want what's best for him and that's me."

Theo pulled up to his house and Brenda was getting out of a cab. Like two magnets they attracted each other. With Brenda's big Kool-Aid smile and Theo's larger-than-life wave hello they both knew it was mutual—that special spark they both had been looking for so long. Being a romantic Theo picked up Chinese to begin his passion filled evening with his lady. Once inside the flicker of soft candles danced on the walls, and the jazz playing in the background released a romantic essence setting the mood. Their hellos were brief and replaced with many kisses and touches of love. No sooner than he put his chopsticks down they began their bedroom tussle.

Hearing the sound of raindrops tap against the windowpane was a sign of a perfect evening ending with pleasures satisfied. Letting their bodies rest on each other they talked themselves to sleep. They slept long and hard after they reunited rhythmically to the music of love. The sky opened up; overwhelmed with liquid and the winds roared like lions in the dusk as the rain poured long hard down on the earth. As Theo and Brenda slept in each other's arms at the front door Shauna was sliding the key in the lock. Wearing only a teddy underneath her black trench coat she stepped through the front door with thoughts of hearing Theo say, "Girl, you are something else!"

Shauna took off her wet coat as she looked for his bedroom down the hall. Before she walked in Brenda got up to use the bathroom. Once Brenda closed the bathroom door Shauna entered the bedroom. She saw a shadow of a body lying in the bed. Standing over him looking down at his face in the hopes he would be elated to see her, Shauna pulled the covers back kicking off her pumps, and slid between the covers. Lying down close to him so he would be able to feel her cold body next his, Shauna whispered to Theo as he slept.

"Theo, Theo, Theo, surprise baby. Guess who?"

"I don't need to guess." Theo took his hands rubbing Shauna's body up down thinking it was Brenda. "Baby you're so cold."

"I am. So heat me up with your body."

"Just a sec. Let me get something to drink from the kitchen."

Theo turned to step out of the bed from his side. He turned on the light that sat on his night table at his bedside. Like clockwork Brenda came out of the bathroom looking over at Theo getting out of bed. Brenda wondered who was lying next to him, and Theo turned to see who was coming out of his bathroom. When he saw Brenda in the doorway of the bathroom he turned to look at who was in the bed next to him. Theo hopped up yelling at Shauna.

"What are you doing here Shauna! How did you get in my bed!" Theo looked over at Brenda and saw she was in disbelief. "Brenda just a minute please!"

"Theo who is that?" Brenda stood in the doorway of the bathroom with his robe on.

"Theo who in the fuck is she?" Shauna got out of the bed with her black teddy on and with her hands on her hips. "I hope she's the plumber."

"Shauna why in the hell are you here?" Theo pointed his finger at her yelling, while Brenda scrambled for her things on the floor.

"Theo, I had no idea you were seeing anyone else." Brenda was looking for her shoes on the floor. "I thought you loved me!"

"No! Theo doesn't love you. He loves me!" Shauna walked over to Theo by the door of his bedroom looking at him.

"Shauna stop it!" Theo stepped around Shauna trying to get Brenda to stop and listen.

"I had no idea you had a girlfriend Theo!" Brenda yelled in Theo's face while he tried to get her to stop from leaving.

"Yeah! I'm his girlfriend right Theo?" Shauna yelled at Brenda from across the bedroom. Brenda stood still waiting for Theo to answer.

"Yes. I mean she was. No! She is not my girlfriend!" Theo yelled at Shauna.

After he replied that she wasn't his girlfriend Shauna responded in a ghetto fabulous attitude as she twisted and rolled her eyes at Brenda and Theo. "That's new to me Theo."

"Shauna cut the fucking games out!" Theo tried to stop Brenda from leaving.

Brenda bolted out of the bedroom door pushing Shauna aside, as she screamed at him while heading down the hall trying to get out of his house. "Theo leave me the hell alone!"

Shauna followed behind them as she commented just loud enough for Brenda to hear. "Theo after a year you're just going to leave me for some other bitch."

Theo turned around yelling at Shauna to stop once again. "Shauna don't call her out of her name." Theo grabbed Shauna's arm trying to shake some sense into her. Shauna pulled away replying, "What! That bitch means something to you? Not too long ago you were in love with me. What about Rebecca? She's been asking for her daddy!"

Brenda heard what Shauna said and shook her head. She couldn't believe Theo was playing the same game Greg had played on her not so long ago. Theo ran to the front door to try to explain this misunderstanding. Brenda didn't want to hear anything he had to say to her nor did she want anything to do with him. She was trying to get around him as she tried to hold back the tears.

"Theo I'm out of here. I can't be caught up in this mess. I refuse to go through this shit again. Get out of my way Greg!" Brenda stopped after she realized what she had just done. Calling Greg's name she put her hand over her mouth realizing she had a flashback of the emotional turmoil she had felt not so long ago.

"Brenda please!" Theo pleaded with her, but Brenda was all shook up.

"Theo what are you going tell me? This woman is just a figment of my imagination with an open invitation to get in your bed. Oh! And she is somebody who got mixed signals about your friendship if that's what you want to call it."

"Brenda she doesn't mean a thing to me. Please don't run out like this. It's not what you think. I swear!"

Brenda looked at him crying like a baby as she replied, "Isn't that something? It's not what you think. Let me tell you what I think. I was thinking a few hours ago I could really love a guy like you forever!" Brenda wiped her eyes and continued on saying, "Not because of the things we do in bed, but because just for one split second in my life I felt like your heart was beating just like mine. Why?"

"Brenda, I swear to you! I need you! I want you to be in my life forever too! Please believe me! Shauna is no threat to you."

Brenda looked at Theo then she rushed forward pulling the front door open and looking back at him while replying loudly, "I know she's no threat to me Theo because I'm gone!"

Brenda ran out into the rain away from Theo's house to call a cab to pick her up. When she hung up the phone to wait for the cab to come, she stood crying in the pouring rain. Theo rushed back into the house to put some clothes on to run after her. As he walked back into the house there was Shauna standing there waiting in his pajama top. She was furious about the situation, because she was only being concerned about her feelings and wants.

"Theo, I can't believe you!" Shauna said.

Theo looked at her as if she were out of her mind. "I can't believe you Shauna. Why in the hell did you think I would still want you after what you put me through? You are so full of it." Shauna kept following Theo around as he scrambled to find something to put on so he could run out into the rain to find Brenda. "From the first day I met you; you lied to me and deceived me. What did you think? Giving me some pussy would change my mind?" Theo grabbed his car keys off the kitchen counter as he put on his jacket. He turned to say to Shauna, "Listen you fuckin witch it's not about pussy. It's about the woman I love running out of my house into the rain assuming something she shouldn't have too."

Shauna got agitated from Theo's confession of love for another woman. "Theo don't try and play me. I will not step to the side. I'm in love with you. Doesn't that mean anything to you?"

Theo was heading for the door to leave when he turned to yell at her, "Hell no!"

Shauna responded by pleading aloud. "Theo what do you mean no! I'm not some little chicken head you can push to the side. I don't give up easily."

"Shauna, I don't want you or your games. I put my trust in your hands, and you hurt me with your lies."

"That was then Theo." With a sweet luring voice Shauna continued, "I want us to start over again. What we had you can't just walk away from it. The way you do the things you do—well, I'm hooked. I'm ready to make a commitment."

"Don't make me laugh with the dramatics. You're hooked all right on the dick. That's all I am to you some pleasure pillow. You're such a shallow bitch."

"A bitch I am, but shallow I'm not."

"Right now Shauna I don't care what you are. I know what you better be when I get back—that is gone. I mean it!" Theo slammed the door behind him.

Theo ran out to find Brenda hoping she would give him a chance to explain. Shauna went back into the bedroom to get her shoes. Unable to let go of what she felt for Theo, she began thinking fast as to what she needed to do in order to get him back in her life. After walking out to the living room to put on her trench coat, she noticed a small purse on the love seat. Shuffling through the contents inside Shauna found Brenda's school identification card from Peaton. Smiling from cheek to cheek Shauna said to herself aloud, "If she thinks she's going to get Theo then let the games begin."

A few days later before Brenda was to leave for Andrea's wedding she received a phone call from the front desk downstairs in the lobby of her dormitory informing her she had a visitor waiting. Knowing the only person it could be was Theo, she knew she had to see him to let him know it was over for the last time. Brenda didn't want anything to do with a two timing dog with a readymade family. Entering the downstairs lobby Brenda looked around for Theo wondering where he could be. Brenda walked over to the reception desk to ask the girl on duty where her visitor was.

"Hi Karen. You called to tell me somebody was here to see me?"

"Yeah Brenda. Some lady. She's in the ladies room." Brenda was wondering who in the world could be there to see her.

"What's her name Karen?"

Karen looked at the sign-in book to get the name. "As a matter of fact she didn't even sign in. Wait here she comes."

"Thanks Karen." Brenda turned around to see who it might be. When Brenda turned around she saw Shauna coming toward her with a smile on her face, as if she was about to say hello to an old friend. Brenda didn't look happy at all. If things could only get worse here comes her boyfriend's girlfriend. She certainly didn't want to have to deal with this on campus, but the mess she ran into two nights ago was right in her face.

"What are you doing here, and how did you find me?"

Shauna smirked slightly. "A little birdie told me I could find you here. Besides, it's about time we set things straight about Theo."

"Shauna is it? I don't want anything else to do with you or him!"

"Make sure you stick to that now okay Brenda, because if you get in my way I'll crush you."

"Is that a threat?"

"No Brenda! It's just an idea. I just want you to know what's been on my mind. A little college girl like yourself should stick to your books."

"Listen Shauna something tells me you're a sick bitch. I'd advise you to leave me alone, or I'll put you where you belong."

"Back up girlfriend! Stay away from Theo, and I won't have to ruin the rest of your life." Shauna reached out and grabbed Brenda yanking her arm to pull her closer to her. "You don't know who you're fucking with!"

"If you don't let me go—"

"You'll what Brenda? Hit me! I don't think you have the guts, but that's not important now." Releasing Brenda's arm she replied, "There you got your arm back, and I have to get back to my man. He needs me. Have a nice life Brenda."

Shauna walked off leaving Brenda standing in the lobby rubbing her arm. Brenda kept her cool until she reached her room. Frustrated with the unexpected news, bad timing, and flashbacks she slammed the door, and then she let her tears flow like a raging river.

Chapter Sixteen
When It Rains–It Pours!

Sitting in the parking lot of the restaurant waiting for Ethan to show up for their last encounter as lovers Lee kept a constant watch on the clock in her car. One hour then two hours had passed, and she realized that Ethan was either late, or he simply wasn't coming. Lee was becoming furious and impatient. Calling her answering machine in her room to check for a possible explanation for his late arrival, on the third ring the phone picked up with Brenda's voice on the other end.

"Hello Lee!" Brenda said.

"Brenda did Ethan call?"

"No! Actually the phone hasn't rung all night. I've been sitting here with Rachel relaxing. Did you check your cell phone to see if he called?"

"Yes I did! Ethan hasn't shown up yet. He's normally on time, especially since tonight is the last night he could see me before graduation."

"Maybe his wife wouldn't let him out."

"I doubt that." Lee paused trying to think of an answer. "He promised nothing would get in the way of us having a good time tonight. That can't be it."

"If his wife didn't stop him then it could be a family emergency."

"He would've called me."

"Lee it might be that he couldn't handle seeing you for the last time. You know how you got the last time he tried to break it off."

Taking a few seconds to find an answer for that Lee thought maybe Brenda might be right. The last time she and Ethan were together was very hurtful. Threatening to tell his wife of the affair they were having blew up into a big argument that kept them apart for weeks. Not until she called him at the office to tell him she was sorry for her childish behavior, and empty threats did Ethan agree to see her one last time. This evening was to be very special for her. She was going to tell Ethan how much she was in love with him. Not until that day had Lee ever truly understand what those words meant. Being without Ethan was making her feel very empty.

Hoping Brenda's understanding of what she knew of the situation was false, Lee suddenly shot down all hopes of him showing up. Realizing she could have pushed Ethan away from her, Lee figured not showing up for their last date might make her understand you can't play with people's emotions the way she did him. Brenda didn't hear Lee on the other end. Brenda kept calling Lee's name into the phone.

"Lee are you still on the line? Lee!"

"Yes! I'm still here." Lee quickly responded. "After waiting for two hours I better get me a table and enjoy my farewell dinner by myself. I'll be back home in an hour or so."

As she hung-up the phone the truth of the matter had left her speechless. Lee went into the dining area, and requested a private table in the corner so that she could dine alone. She ordered a steak, potato, and salad with a glass of red wine. Lee slowly chewed each mouthful as if it were her last meal. Soon after finishing her dinner alone she hurried to her car before the brewing thunderstorm began coming down in torrents.

Taking the highway back to school to save time from stopping at every red light on the local route, Lee ran into a traffic jam that held her up for twenty-minutes. Idling in traffic in the stormy downpour of rain, she turned on some soft music to keep her mind off of Ethan, while she waited for things to get moving. Once traffic got moving she noticed two cars wrecked in the ditch along the highway. Shaking her head at what the other nosey motorists consider their business to watch someone's mishap as something to view as entertainment irritated her.

Once she got to the campus parking lot she pulled in with ease. Turning the ignition off, Lee sat listening to the rainfall against the roof of her car. Wishing she was in Ethan's arms right at that moment feeling his heart beat with the sounds of rain dancing on the earth, Lee burst out into a frantic cry letting all of her feelings sap her strength. Feeling weak and cold from her hard cry, her body needed to feel the warmth of her bed where she went whenever her emotions got the best of her.

Over the next few days all the seniors were preparing for graduation with rehearsal and lots of parties on and off campus. Lee found herself locked in her room with a bottle of Jack Daniel's. She had been drinking heavily since that night at the restaurant. Going to class with a hangover, not keeping herself up, and wearing dark shades with a baseball cap she let the bottle and her self-pity bring her down. Brenda and Rachel kept a close eye on her making sure she didn't take a dive for the worst. They took turns trying to keep her spirits up, but that proved to be very hard.

"Brenda what time does rehearsal start?" Rachel asked.

"At four o'clock." Brenda replied.

"At least we have some time to pull her together." Rachel stood over Lee's booze-scented body on the floor of her dorm room shaking her head. "Do you know if she took her last final Brenda?"

"Yeah she did. I hope she wasn't too wasted to read the questions."

"Lee has a photographic memory." Rachel sucked her teeth. "Looking at her now you wouldn't know that anything she sees she can recall at the drop of a dime."

"She looks so pitiful. I hate to wake her up." Brenda stroked her forehead. "She's been through hell since the other night."

"Brenda just remember we have to make sure she's sober enough to handle the news. Are you ready to get to work?"

"Ready as I'll ever be." Brenda nudged Lee's shoulder. Like a jackrabbit caught eating cabbage in farmer's garden Lee's eyes popped open in a startling glare. Looking around at the blurry images that seemed to dance around, her head began to bounce up and down like a ball. Sounding like a slurring wino on the corner wreaking of hot musty booze, Lee yelled out at Brenda and Rachel to leave her alone so she could finish her nap.

"Leave me alone!" Lee yelled out.

"I said get up!" Brenda yelled back.

"Get the hell away from me Brenda!"

"Nope!"

"Brenda you haven't heard? Nobody loves me."

"That's not true. Rachel and I love you very much. Lee that's the liquor telling you that we don't love you."

"No! No! It's true. I'm a loser. I fuck married men who break up with me. Oh yeah! My mother thinks I'm a self-centered bitch and my father well I was his sweet little princess, but he's dead. Ain't that some shit!"

"Let me help you to the tub Lee." Brenda said. "Rachel grab her feet. You ready on three. One-two-three!" Brenda and Rachel carried Lee's wasted drunken body into the bathroom.

There they stripped her. "Okay easy now. Slow, slow. Rachel get a comb so we can wash her hair. Lee how is the water?"

"It feels great Brenda." Lee looked up at Brenda taking hold of the collar on her shirt. Lee pulled her wiggly wet body up out of the water to tell her what was going through her head. "Ethan and I used to take warm baths together." Lee looked around the room and began shouting, "Where is my man!" She was hoping he would appear. "Ethan come on and get in this tub with me. I want to play." Lee laughed. She let go of Brenda's collar letting her sluggish body fall back in the warm water to swish back and forth.

"Lee!" Brenda looked at her feeling so sorry for her. "Sweetheart we need to talk."

"Shh! Not now Brenda. She's not ready." Rachel abruptly interrupted.

"Don't shh her." Lee sat up in the water to chastise Rachel with her words. "Shit! Shh damn you Rachel."

"Lee relax!" Brenda held Lee down in the tub with both hands on her shoulders to control her misdirected drunken outburst toward Rachel. "Sit back and close your eyes. Feel the warm water. Now doesn't that feel good?"

"Yeah!" Lee said.

"Brenda don't say anything yet. Wait until she sobers up."

Rachel explained why she shouldn't tell Lee the bad news. "If we think this is something, when she finds out about Ethan she's going to really freak out. Let's get her cleaned up for rehearsal. She can't miss another one. If someone finds out she might get herself banned from graduation."

"Lee please settle down!" Brenda said as she tried to wash her hair. "Let me wash your hair."

"Why?" Lee slurred looking at Brenda.

"Because it will make you feel better!" Brenda said.

"No it won't! Only Ethan can make me feel better." Lee hit the water with her hand.

"I know Lee." Rachel ducked down to get away from the flying water in the air.

"Brenda you are so sexy." Lee looked over at Rachel and Brenda. "Rachel, you are so beautiful." She looked down at herself to examine her physical state. "Lee! Hell that's me!" Lee let out an unexpected outcry of sorrow. "I'm cheap!"

"Don't cry Lee!" Rachel warmly said patting her on the back to console her.

"But I am!" Lee mumbled in her hail of tears.

"No you're not!"

"Rachel, you're lying to me."

"I swear Lee. There is nothing cheap about you. You are one of my best friends. Do you think I would hang out with cheap people with no class? You know how much I love the finer things in life."

"For real Rachel." Lee's tears suddenly ceased.

"For real girl. I would put everything on the line for you and Brenda. You guys are the sisters I never had."

"Brenda do you feel the same?" Lee asked.

"Of course I do." Brenda softly replied. "We are family whether you like it or not. Whatever you go through we go through together. Don't ever forget that Lee." Brenda kissed Lee on the forehead.

"I love you, Brenda. I love you, Rachel!" Lee said with a wide crooked smile and red strained eyes.

After two days of binging and feeling sorry for herself, Lee finally came back from her twirl in the bottle. Putting the ceremonial festivities first she had found something to keep her focused. Rachel and Brenda planned to spend a quiet night together with Lee to reinforce her emotionally, so that she knew she had people who loved and cared for her nearby. Lee was waiting for them to come back with some takeout from the local rib shack.

Bored she turned on the television to catch up on some local news. Listening to the news broadcast while she packed some boxes up to keep her mind busy, Lee was looking through her closet to pack the last of her things to ship home. Suddenly, she came across a sweater Ethan had bought her for Christmas. As she brushed her cheek against the fabric a small tear fell. Slowly folding it to place it in the box of clothing her attention was caught by a broadcast on the television. "Police have released the name of the hit-and-run victim of that horrible collision Thursday night. Corporal Ethan Robinson died just hours ago." Lee inched toward the television very slowly to turn up the volume to hear all of the details being broadcasted. "Corporal Robinson leaves behind a wife and two sons. Police are still looking for the unknown driver of the stolen car left at the scene. If anyone can help the police with this unfortunate accident, please call your local police department. In other news . . ."

The newscaster mentioned the accident on the highway the night she drove home from the restaurant. Lee could not believe what she was hearing coming out of the television. Losing all sense of time and feeling in her body she ran to her car like a bat out of hell. She sped off to the hospital where Ethan had died. She was beside herself looking for the nurse's station in a hail of tears. In her search to find help Lee came upon his family standing around Victoria. Lee saw what she needed to confirm her worst nightmare. He's dead! Feeling like she had nowhere to run Lee's heart led her to the one person who she knew she could always talk to.

Driving on the open road trying to figure out why it had to be him, she kept coming back to how this could be. After driving all night she parked alongside the road. The early morning sun rose with its warm rays. Lee was sleeping in her car alongside the Glory Mathews Cemetery.

Wearing jeans and a tank with her sandals undone she got out of her car to walk through the open gates. Before she began her quest she pulled a few yellow and white wildflowers out of the ground from outside the gates of the cemetery. Arranging them to fall into a perfect bouquet she pulled the hair band from around her hair to wrap the freshly picked flowers to make it just little more than perfect, but personal.

Tasting the sweet air of the new day Lee felt at peace as she walked the familiar path she once took not so long ago. Finally, she reached her destination; she knelt down to place the flowers on her father's headstone which read, "A loving father, husband, and friend." Running her hand against the marble surface she let out a small sigh of grief. "I need you so much daddy! Your little girl doesn't know how to deal with what she is going through." Lee was wiping her face dry from the small tears building in her lost brown eyes. "Daddy, I wish you were here. I'm graduating, and I can't wait. I remember when I was a little girl you always said I had what it took to be the best. I'm not sure if I still have it in me to go on." Lee began sobbing. "Your little princess is so lost right now. I keep losing the people I love the most. I know I'm not supposed to question why, but I need an answer to help me understand. Nothing is going right. Oh, Daddy I miss your magic touch that made everything so right."

Crying herself to sleep on her father's grave Lee awoke to the thunder of an airplane flying overhead. Looking around the graveyard she saw no one present. The late afternoon sun was surrendering to the evening dusk. Knowing it was time for her to head back to school she kissed the cold headstone and said, "I will always love you!"

Detouring off her drive back to campus Lee decided to stop by and see her mother. She had hoped the time she spent away from home would bring a happy greeting. Lee opened the door with her key. She walked straight to the kitchen to get something to eat; after all she had not eaten since the night before. Washing up her dishes and cleaning up the kitchen table Lee went to sit on the front porch to gather her thoughts before the long drive back to campus.

Enjoying the still sky as it yielded to the night she started thinking about the times when she enjoyed sitting on the front porch with her family. Lee remembered sitting on her father's lap watching her mother laugh at her brothers as they clowned around on the front lawn playing ball. Back in those days they enjoyed the taste of summer as they drank lemonade, while sharing warm pound cake. Then they were a real family that was close in love, and loyalty. A smile came across her face. The sound of a car pulling up brought a halt to her soft smile. Watching her mother's car drive up Lee put on her best face, and put aside old hurts.

Needing to reach out to her, Lee hurried to the driver's door to help her out. Tina Jordan her mother saw her daughter walking to greet her. Never wanting to save face regardless of any situation Tina kept her smog grim face as always. Lee opened the door with such enthusiasm hoping her mother might invite a warm hug to her cold, weary body.

"Hello Mother!" Lee said with a dollish smile.

"Hello Lee. What do you want? You should have called before you came."

"I'm sorry. I had no idea that I had to call before I came home to visit. Anyway, I just wanted to stop by and say hi!"

"That's unusual." Tina looked uninterested in her daughter's presence. "Funny how you make time for others." Tina turned looking back at Lee as she headed for the front door. "Lee you don't have a giving bone in your body."

"Why can't you just be happy to see me?" Lee closed the door behind her after they entered the house.

"Lee, I'm always glad to see your brothers and yourself. It's just that whenever we have to share time together we always end up at each other's throats. Besides, your father spoiled you. He foolishly taught you to think that you're supposed to have everything go your way. It's not your fault. I wanted you to have good hard discipline like me when I came up—no laughing and sharing conversations with your parents. Children were seen and not heard."

"Let's not bring up the past. I was hoping we could start over, and simply be mother and daughter in every sense of the word." Lee waited anxiously for her mother's answer with hopes of a happy ending.

"It's a little too late for things like that. I don't have the energy to put into a—"

"You mean me." Lee was becoming very upset with her mother's attitude towards her.

"Well yes! Ever since you were a baby you've been difficult. You're a grown woman now. I'm not going to baby you like your father. Besides, you have been changing your colors in the last few months." Tina shook her head with a disappointed look on her face.

"I've had it! At least I tried! Goodbye Mother!" Lee headed for the door in rush to get away from Tina before she said something she would regret.

Heading for the front door Lee was holding back her pain by not looking back at her mother, a mother she so much wanted to love. Suddenly, the front door opened and in walked her Uncle Keith—the man Tina had an affair with as her husband lay dying in a hospital bed and the man Lee hated for causing her father such pain before he died. Before taking another step forward Lee tilted her head with a shocked look planted on her face looking at her uncle as if he were a ghost.

"What in the hell are you doing here Uncle Keith?" Lee put her hands on her hips.

"Lee!" Keith looked surprised to see her.

"Keith you should know coming in my father's house is a slap in his face. What makes you think you could just walk through that door?"

"Lee wait! We have to clear the air before things get out of hand!"

"Out of hand! You broke my father's heart when he found out you were sleeping with his wife. He didn't deserve that from his brother." Lee paused and then she shouted, "Out of hand! It's a little too late for that!" Lee was standing in front of him yelling and preaching.

"Lee stop it! You might as well know the truth. I love your mother more than anything on this earth. I have always loved her. Please hear me out!" Keith was very agitated at Lee because she completely ignored his explanation.

"I will always hate you. You and my mother are a piece of work. You both deserve to go to hell. And I thought I was cold." Lee stepped around Keith and headed for the door.

"What Lee! You can't handle the truth?" Tina yelled out.

"Yes!" Lee turned around to look back at her mother.

"The truth is Lee, I have feelings too!" Tina shouted out.

"Keith and I love each other. When your father began to take a turn for the worst I needed someone to lean on. He was there." Tina was blunt in her response as well as very insensitive.

"I know why you did what you did. You hated the way my father treated me. I was his favorite person in the whole wide world. His little girl replaced his selfish wife. You can't stand that I'm just like you, but younger and better. So, you had to go get you some attention from somewhere else."

"Lee, you don't have a clue about what you're saying. I will not let you try to put a guilt trip on me. Things happen. Keith and I will not apologize for what we feel for each other anymore." Tina lashed out at Lee.

"Mother don't apologize for cheating my father out of love. Couldn't you wait until the breath left his body and he was cold? He died of a broken heart; knowing you turned away from him when he needed you the most. You egotistical bitch how could you!"

"Lee watch what you say to your mother." Trying to take charge of the situation Keith stepped in.

"No disrespect Uncle Keith, but you need to shut the fuck up. I refuse to acknowledge a backstabbing dirty dog like you." Lee replied boldly. "And you, Mother, I realize you don't love me, especially after you saw how my father, your husband, replaced you with his precious little girl."

Tina knew her daughter was right. She did feel pushed aside by the father-and-daughter relationship Lee shared with her father. It made Tina treat her daughter like the other woman.

Out of nowhere Tina reacted by slapping Lee across the face. Lee stood her ground stoned faced; not letting a tear fall from her eyes. Silence fell upon the room for a few seconds. Turning and running to her car Lee turned the music up and drove off leaving a dust cloud behind. Lee knew when it rains it pours when life challenges come down on you all at once.

Chapter Seventeen
Calm Down!

Returning to school in the wee hours of the morning Lee closed the door behind her to hear Brenda's voice in the dark call out to her. "Lee is that you?" Lee let the doorknob go to find the light switch. "Yep it's me." The light came on and Brenda got out of her bed to rush over and give her a hug.

"Where have you been? Rachel and I have been going out of our minds. When we came back with the food and you were gone!" Brenda franticly shouted at Lee.

"I'm sorry. I needed sometime alone." Lee replied.

"What happened Lee? What made you just disappear like that?"

"I heard about Ethan on the television. I still can't believe he's gone."

"I know. We found out the day after the accident happened."

"How! They just released his name yesterday."

"I know. Theo called me to tell me it was Ethan. The military posted it the morning after the accident happened. The only reason he called was, because I had mentioned on a few occasions that you two were seeing each other."

"When did you and Rachel plan on telling me?" Lee looked at Brenda with a blank look on her face waiting for Brenda to answer her.

"When I found out you went on your drinking escapade and you were wasted almost every day since that night Ethan didn't show up at the restaurant what was I supposed to do Lee?"

"Tell me anyway!" Lee replied sounding angry.

"No! You were like a zombie. You didn't take a bath; you didn't comb your hair. You started looking like a crack head. Lee, you were on the edge and I wasn't about to push you over."

"You should have. Everyone I love seems to leave me one way or the other."

"Lee, I'm not planning on going anywhere. Neither is Rachel."

"I don't know how to feel about anything right now! I am so numb."

"You'll be okay. I promise. Please believe me."

"I have no choice but to Brenda."

Long after the day had passed and gone Lee decided to attend Ethan's funeral. She had to pay her last respects to the man she so desperately loved. To make sure she would be able to keep her mind strong, and her heart steady Rachel and Brenda decided to tag along to give some emotional support to their friend. Driving up to the funeral home the ladies noticed how many people were present for Ethan's funeral. Rachel looked around at all the people heading for the church, and she became very nervous.

"Look at all these people. He sure was popular." Rachel commented as they passed the large crowds of service goers.

"Lee are you sure you want go through with this?" Brenda looked over at Lee in the passenger seat fixing her hair.

"With you and Rachel here I'll be just fine. I can't turn around now, and besides Ethan wouldn't if it were me in there."

"I'm pretty sure he wouldn't because his wife and family wouldn't be in there standing over your coffin." Rachel leaned over the passenger seat to state her concerns. "I just don't want you to fall apart in there. I just don't want you to bring any attention to yourself. You know how black folks are at a funeral. If you cry louder than his wife then people are going to wonder who in the hell is she if she ain't family."

"A professional mourner." Lee whispered under her breath.

"Lee!" Brenda interrupted with a stern tone. "Rachel is right. If you need to fall apart please give us a sign. I don't want to get a king-size ass whopping from his entire family. You do know that there could be hundreds of them in there, right?"

"Don't worry Brenda. You and Rachel won't hear a peep from me. I'll be invisible. I can't let everybody in the church know his mistress is present."

"Good just hold in all your tears until we leave. Then it's only right you grieve however you want." Brenda patted Lee on her hand.

"Brenda, I can't control my every emotion; spontaneous things can just happen. All I can do is just do my best. I am under a lot of pressure."

"Whatever pressure you're under put it in check. Got it!" Brenda stressed to Lee in a nervous cry for calmness and peace. "I'm only telling you this for your own good. This is not the place for you to lose your cool."

"Sure!" Lee rolled her eyes looking out of the passenger window.

Rachel and Brenda looked at each other with an unsure look about their faces. Knowing Lee's unpredictable behavior Brenda, and Rachel wondered what's going to happen from minute to minute with her. Walking into the church they found themselves seated in the middle of Ethan's many family, friends, and co-workers who turned out to pay their last respects.

As the funeral service got underway Lee watched Ethan's coffin as it was carried with the American Flag draped over it. She felt her throat beginning to tighten as she watched the military officers carrying him by. The realization of it all was beginning to be a bit too much for her to handle. She knew she couldn't fall apart so soon into the service. So, like always she put on her shield of being strong and unscathed with what was going on around her. Refusing to let herself cry or think negatively Lee decided to celebrate in her own way by smiling, and thinking of the good times they shared. Brenda and Rachel looked over at Lee, and they were amazed at her calmness after putting her emotions in check with a you-can't-touch-me expression planted on her face.

Lee stood and watched Ethan's wife Victoria being escorted in by her two sons. Watching her go past the pew where she was seated Lee didn't feel a thing. Somehow she sympathized with Ethan's two sons, and the loss of their father. Lee remembered she was once where they were, and she allowed her heart to go out to them. In a soft whisper Brenda leaned over just after the family and the coffin were placed in front.

"Are you okay Lee?"

"Yes Brenda."

"Tap me if you can't handle anymore."

"I sure will." Lee smiled.

The choir stood to sing a hymn from the program. Lee took the time to reflect on her love for him. Having never come across such emotions for someone before, she listened to the jolting power of the music as she felt a spirit take rest in her body as the powerful tones and beats played out in the church. Lee knew Ethan was there with her holding her by the hand to help her get through it. A wide smile, a tap of her shoe, and a few pearly white teeth let Rachel and Brenda know she was okay, or so they thought.

The time had come for the last passing of his remains. Lee knew this would be the last time she would ever see him physically on this earth. Just as the pew in front of them was clearing out for her pew to go past the coffin Lee was slow in her exit. They followed the line of grieving family and friends. The time had come for Lee to walk past. Rachel saw she was beginning to fold. Grabbing her hand she looked Lee straight in the eye and gave her a look of support.

"It's going to be okay girl. You don't have to do this if you don't want too."

"I know, but I have to say good-bye!" Lee replied.

"I'll hold your hand."

"Thanks Rachel."

"We're next. Are you ready, Lee?"

"Yes."

Lee allowed Rachel to walk her to the coffin just as the people ahead cleared the way. Her every footstep felt as if she were walking on drying glue, which made every step harder to take. She felt the hot sweat take over her forehead, and the beads began to roll down the side of her face. Finally, reaching the man she loved so much she saw him lifeless in his full military dress. Looking down at his face her tears sat in her eyes filling them to a glossy shine.

Lee took a long look at him. Letting her hands reach inside to touch his hand one last time, something suddenly compelled her to lean down and kiss him on the lips. Rachel's mouth fell like a stack of bricks, and Brenda threw her hand over her mouth in a moment of shock at what Lee did in front of all who could see.

Victoria stood up in a state of disbelief at the bold display of affection by Lee. She looked at Lee bending over in the coffin yelling out. "What's going on?" Lee's lips locked so hard her lipstick left a hard imprint on Ethan's cold lips. With all the confusion going on by the coffin the preacher couldn't help, but look over to observe the show going on. Victoria and a few larger-than-life older women were making their way over to find out about who and what was going on. Rachel noticed the ladies heading for them, and she didn't take the chance on them coming over to give them a pat on the back. Rachel yanked Lee's hand to bring her back to reality then dragged her away from the coffin.

For the family and friends who saw the incident the whispers began to flow throughout the church. Rachel hurried out the door with Lee in hand, and Brenda followed right behind making sure to look back. Running to their car they hopped in and burned the rubber out of the parking lot. With their quick exit the concerned family members made their way out of the door behind them in hopes to have a word or two with the ladies. Instead, the family members had to watch the car with the mysterious trio disappearing in the distance. Driving at high speed toward the highway back to school Brenda and Lee started shouting at each other at the top of their lungs, while Rachel lay in the backseat breathing uncontrollably out of fear.

"What in the hell were you thinking Lee?" Brenda shouted.

"What is the big deal Brenda? I had a right to say good-bye the way I needed too!"

"That may be true Lee, but did you have to kiss the corpse?"

"Yes Brenda! I did! That was Ethan!" Lee screamed hysterically.

"No it wasn't! That was a dead man laid out in there. I will never share another cup with you again not even for communion!"

"Please Brenda it was just a kiss! The last kiss I will be able to give him. Believe me if it were you, you would have done the same thing."

"Maybe but in front of everybody? Your ass is crazy!"

"You just found that out Brenda."

"I guess so! Lee when are you going to remember you must think of others? How do you think his wife must feel after some woman she didn't know kiss her husband in front of the whole world?"

"Please she'll get over it."

"Didn't you learn anything from this tragedy? Ethan wouldn't have appreciated that one bit."

"Whatever! I don't want to hear it right now. Can't you see I'm grieving right now?"

"You're not grieving; you're trying to justify what you did."

"And what did I do so badly Mrs. Perfect Brenda? You finally got worked over and now you are Miss. Know It All. You don't know shit!"

"Whatever Lee. But I do know this you stepped over the line again. Stop being so heartless when it comes to others. I know you loved him very much, but the bitch came out of you just now!"

"You sound just like my damn mother always wanting me to do what is best for others. What about me and my feelings? Don't they count?"

"Of course they do Lee, only if you remember you're not the only one who loved Ethan! Still, Lee it wasn't your place to display your affair out in the open. You were the mistress."

"Damn it Brenda! Don't you think I know that!"

"Yes, but you forgot you come second in line to his wife. You didn't play the game fair Lee."

"Stop the fucking car Brenda!" Lee began pulling on the handle of the door. "Let me out! I refuse to listen to this shit."

"No! I won't!" Brenda grabbed her shoulder from the driver's seat trying to keep Lee in her seat.

"Then I'll jump out!"

"You may be crazy but you're ass ain't stupid. Rachel help me!"

"Brenda, Lee stop it right now! Let's wait till we get back to campus!" Rachel intervened hoping she could stop the tension.

"Then stop the car right know!" Lee shouted.

"Lee are you crazy? Close that door!" Rachel yelled.

"Wait for me to find somewhere to pull over Lee! I'm in the middle of the highway!" Brenda pleaded with Lee.

"Brenda hurry up and get over!" Rachel reached over the passenger seat from the back to keep Lee in her seat. "I can't hold her down much longer!"

"No Brenda! Rachel let me go!" Lee blurted out in anger.

"No way! If you bail out I'm coming with you!" Rachel kept a tight hold on Lee as she tried repeatedly to stop her from jumping out of the car.

"Stop the car!"

Lee screamed while trying to loosen Rachel's grip from around her neck. Rolling down the highway in the middle lane Brenda tried desperately to pull over to the side of the road to let Lee out. Rachel was hanging over the passenger seat trying to keep Lee from jumping out the door while the car was still in motion. Brenda kept looking for an opportunity to get over while Rachel continued to struggle with Lee to keep her from jumping out of the car. Just as traffic opened up Brenda found an opening to get over. She hit the brakes just in time before Lee jumped out. Lee fell out of the car pulling Rachel over the passenger seat. Lee tumbled on the gravel and landed in a grassy area. Her clothing was dusty with grass-stained streaks. Rachel was turned upside down on the passenger side of the car with one shoe on and the other lying on the floor in the back. Brenda helped Rachel get out of the car, and they were yelling for Lee. Her dusty body was off to the side of the road hidden in the tall grass. The ladies ran to see if she was okay.

"Lee where are you?" Brenda yelled out.

"Please answer us! Please Lee!" Rachel followed with a loud call.

Lee sat up brushing her hair from her face. She stood up shaking off the grass and dirt. Lee was crying and frightened at what she had just done. Looking over her shoulder she saw Brenda and Rachel coming toward her calling out to her. She heard Brenda chastising her.

"What in the hell is wrong with you Lee! I'm glad to see you're okay, but you could have been killed Lee!" Brenda roared.

"Why do you care Brenda?" Lee replied.

"Because you're my friend!" Brenda answered.

"Then why can't you understand that I have feelings too! I needed to let him know that I loved him. I didn't get the chance to tell him!" Lee screamed madly up and down on the side of the highway. "He doesn't know how much I love him. Ethan loved me for me no questions asked. He gave me the love my daddy did by always wanting the best for me, and not putting me down about the way I go about things. They always let me be how I wanted to be! They didn't want to change me. They only wanted to love me. Why did they have to leave me?" Lee was out of control screaming upward towards the sky.

"Lee please don't do this to yourself!" Brenda begged her to stop.

"Brenda, you and Rachel have mothers who love you. I don't have anyone."

"Don't say that. You have your mother; she loves you." Brenda warmly mentioned.

"No she doesn't!"

"Every mother loves her child no matter what Lee."

"Not Tina Jordan that cold-hearted bitch. She could go to hell and freeze it over!"

"Lee please you're scaring me!" Rachel said feverously.

"Rachel!" Lee looked at her crying and laughing in the same breath. "I'm sorry, but I can't be strong anymore. I keep losing the people I love the most. What did I do to deserve this?"

Lee yelled at the sky. "Oh God! Why! Why! Why!"

Brenda walked over to Lee as she held her face in her hands crying uncontrollably. Putting her arms around Lee, Brenda realized she was just like her—human and wounded. Rachel wiped the tears from her face after seeing Lee, her friend who she never saw cry; break down like a crumbling wall after being hit by an emotional runaway train. Rachel made her way over to put her arms around Brenda and Lee. Together they stood alongside the highway holding one another with the hazard lights on as eighteen wheelers roared by.

The next morning brought about a new beginning for Lee. She was all cried out and feeling at peace with herself.

"Good morning." Lee purred. "What time is it Brenda?"

"It's–"Brenda looked over at the clock on her night table "eight o'clock."

"Good! Let's go get some breakfast. I'm really hungry." Lee sounded enthusiastic.

"Are you up to it Lee?"

"Yes." Yawning and stretching her arms Lee found herself feeling rather happy and content. "Today is our last day. I want to share it with you and Rachel like we used too. Remember when we all went to breakfast together for the first time? We didn't have enough money to pay the bill. You could tell we had never been away from home."

"I guess we were so used to having our parents pay the bill. We let our greedy butts live it up with our champagne taste and beer pockets. The manager wouldn't let us go until Rachel promised to go out with him." Brenda laughed.

"Oh yeah!" Lee sat up in her bed looking over at Brenda.

"He was so fine. What happened with him?"

"Girl, you don't remember? Come on Lee. Think for a second."

"That's right. He was living on a two-way street." Lee fell back giggling aloud.

"It's a shame a man like him had to be a loss." Brenda replied.

"Preach on girl. He was too fine to be gay." Lee laughed.

"About yesterday." Brenda turned to Lee to apologize. "I am so sorry that I was so insensitive to what you must have been going through."

"I know Brenda. You didn't mean any harm."

"Then you know that I would never do or say anything to hurt you. I was shocked at what you did. I would have never thought you would go that far."

"Neither did I. Something stepped in and took over me."

"Well, whatever it was promise me that you will think before you do, because poor Rachel almost laid an egg. She just knew her ass was going to be kicked in that church."

"She did look scared. It's a shame she got bones like a chicken because she is so beautiful."

"Lee, you are so crazy, but I love you just the way you are."

"Thanks Brenda. I needed that. Let's go and get our grub on."

Sitting at a booth in the back of their favorite restaurant waiting for their order Brenda, Lee, and Rachel were laughing and chatting about the old times they shared while at Peaton. Lee stepped out to the ladies room to freshen up before their food came. Washing her hands in the sink she felt a presence next to her. After turning off the water she looked over to see Victoria washing her hands right next to her. Lee turned her back hoping that Victoria wouldn't see her, but it was too late. Victoria remembered she was the woman who leaned over and kissed her husband.

"Wait a minute! You're that woman from the funeral."

"Leave me alone." Lee turned to walk away. Victoria rushed from behind her to step in front of her.

"Get away from me!" Lee yelled.

"How do you know my husband?" Victoria replied aggressively.

"Does it matter? He's dead. So let well enough alone lady."

"No! Who in the hell are you?" Victoria yelled grabbing Lee's arm.

"Take your hand off my arm." Lee pulled away from Victoria's tight grip.

"No, I won't! I want to know who you are."

"I don't think you want to know, and I don't want to hurt you Victoria."

"How do you know my name? I have never met you before in my life."

"Please! I would ask that you step out of my face if you see the mole on my chin it means you are standing too damn close. Now move!"

"Really, I am shaking in my boots. You're not leaving until something comes out of your mouth."

"Okay if you insist Victoria." Lee crossed her arms with attitude written all over her face. "Your husband and I were in love with each other."

"Really!" Victoria snickered.

"Yes really! What's so funny? Ethan and I were dating since last year."

"No you weren't dating; you were cheating. You look the type, although you're a little thinner than the last one before you. See honey when you have been married to a man like Ethan you have to accept some things like poor judgment, and bad taste in things like you."

"If that's what you think, but I will always believe Ethan truly loved me."

"You really think you were the first little tramp to come across my path. Hell no! But you are the last. He's dead now and yes I loved him, but I won't lose any sleep over this mess."

"I'm not asking you too. Just get out of my way Victoria!"

"Sure. Don't forget he used you like all the rest!" Victoria snickered loud enough for Lee to hear her all the way out of the door.

Lee rushed back to the table with a flushed look on her face. Brenda and Rachel saw that something was terribly wrong with her. Looking down at the table shaking her head back and forth with her eyes closed and mumbling in an angry chant Lee was livid.

"Ain't this some shit!" Rachel tapped her on the shoulder to find out what was wrong with her.

"I just ran into evil Victoria in the bathroom." Rachel and Brenda looked at each other shocked.

"You didn't say anything did you?" Rachel asked.

"We said a lot of things." Lee replied.

"Like what?"

"I told her about Ethan and me."

"Did anything else happen?" Rachel asked.

"No! Yes! She told me I wasn't his first affair. I can't believe that. He always told me he loved me."

"Lee forget what she said." Brenda put her hand on her shoulder to say, "Don't let her get to you."

"Brenda, I loved him. How can I ignore what his wife just told me? I was one of many and that he used me. She even laughed at me. Shit!"

"We should leave." Rachel stood up.

"No Rachel we are staying. I'm not going to leave because of her!" Lee replied.

"Oh hell!" Rachel looked over her shoulder to see Victoria coming toward them. "Here she comes."

"Rachel relax!" Brenda took charge of the oncoming situation.

"Lee please don't say anything. Just sit and pretend we don't see or hear her okay?"

"If that bitch comes over starting some shit I'll break her fuckin skull."

"No you won't! Handle it like a lady not an animal." Brenda ordered Lee to calm down hoping things won't get out of hand.

"Lee put your lips in park."

"Brenda, she better not play me."

"She won't just as long as she doesn't put her hands on you. Let her have her say because she has the right too. Do you understand where I'm coming from?" Brenda looked at Lee hoping she would just calm down.

When the waiter appeared with their food Victoria made a beeline to where Lee was sitting. Taking her time to walk over she wanted to give Lee enough time to let the waiter finish serving the food. Brenda, Rachel, and Lee kept with the plan to ignore her. She stood in front of the table placing one hand down to give her the leverage to get in Lee's face.

"Excuse me ladies. I need to tell your friend something."

"What do you want Widow Victoria?" Lee couldn't resist. She had to respond and Brenda knew things were only going to get worse once Lee opened her mouth.

"I do remember running into you on the military base not so long ago. You needed directions back to some hotel."

Brenda and Rachel kept eating as if nothing was wrong, while Lee and Victoria went at it. The patrons in the restaurant were looking at the spectacle going on at their table. Still, the ladies kept eating as if nothing was wrong.

"Well, if you must know yes and as a matter of fact I had just finished fucking your husband on his couch in his office. Anything else you want to know?" Lee shouted out.

After Lee made her public announcement the ladies' silverware hit their plates in complete disbelief. Rachel wiped her mouth and moved over to the opposite side of the table hoping to get out of the way of what might be coming after a statement like that. Brenda wiped her mouth moving the dishes out of the way.

"Lee stop it!" Brenda said.

"Stay out of this Brenda!" Lee replied.

"No!" Victoria pointed her finger in Lee's face saying, "But you should know you're going to fuck with the wrong wife one day and get yourself hurt little girl."

"Is that a threat?" Lee arrogantly replied.

"No it's a promise. Have a nice life you piece of filth!" Victoria turned to walk away.

"Lady you're lucky I'm trying to be a lady." Lee crudely replied.

"You are–" Victoria turned to say, "not a lady! Ladies don't get on all fours like a dog. You should know better than me." Victoria snickered aloud again aiming her laughter toward Lee "You little bitch! Ha-ha!"

Lee became angry at the fact Victoria was not taking her affair with Ethan seriously. She stood up at the table and began laughing aloud. "Do you know I fucked your husband on your living room floor? And yes every time he stroked me, I looked over at the picture of you and your lovely family on the wall above your wedding picture. Now that's some funny shit! Ha-ha-ha!"

"So the lady is a tramp. So my husband let you in my house."

Victoria stepped forward to stand erect looking Lee up and down standing behind the table. Twisting her lips around Victoria turned midway to leave. Then she balled a fist and abruptly punched Lee in the eye. Lee fell back into her seat and all the patrons seated nearby were brought out of their seats with startling looks on their faces. Victoria yelled at Lee as she lay back in her seat, holding her eye in pain, "I didn't hit you because you cheated with my husband, but because you disrespected me by stepping foot in my house. I told you; you were going to fuck with the wrong wife one day." Victoria walked off back to her table. Brenda jumped between Victoria and Lee to shield Lee from any further physical contact. Lee was furious at Victoria, but she let it go because Ethan would have wanted her too. She didn't want to do anything to further tarnish his memory in public; besides she knew yesterday had to be left alone to live for tomorrow.

The next day Lee had begun to pull herself together by finding some comfort in sitting on the bathroom floor in her dorm alone. Lee began examining her life. Having to deal with a mother who turns a cold shoulder to her whenever she feels the need to reach out to her; a father's passing that left her devastated and unable to find her way past the hurt, and insecurities of losing the one person who supported and believed in her the most. Lee was lost. Stepping in the bathroom Rachel found Lee on the floor staring at a bottle of Jack Daniel's.

"Lee you're not going to drink that are you?" Rachel asked.

"Good question!" Lee looked up at her. "For the last three hours I have been sitting here with a million reasons why I should and only one good reason why I shouldn't. Rachel now that doesn't add up does it?"

"No it doesn't. Lee don't let the bottle be your temporary remedy. If you drink that you know by the time it wears off everything you're running from will come rushing back at you. However, it will be double the blow, and I know you don't want to have to deal with all of that." Rachel sat down with Lee on the bathroom floor crossing her legs to sit and listen.

"You know that was my only reason why I shouldn't. I'm trying so hard to hold on to reality that it is becoming life or death for me. Do you know how many days I wish I could just die? In so many ways, I did already. When my father took his last breath, so did I. His love was my lifeline to this world. Now it's gone."

"No it's not." Rachel said softly. "It's never gone unless you let it go. See, what you have to do is remember all the good things. Once you do that it's yours forever and ever. You are the primary caretaker of your own happiness, and each time you remember whatever it is, it will bring you a smile even a little giggle."

"I don't want to remember. It hurts too much to know I'll never be able to touch or feel that person again Rachel."

"Look at me Lee. Remember that picture of your father that you took just before he died and I said you look just like him?" Rachel asked.

"Yes." Lee replied.

"Do you know you have your father's eyes? You even have his smile."

"So!"

"See my parents always believe when you possess the features of someone dear and close to you, you have a part of them within you. Lee, they live through you."

"I don't want to hear this." Lee stood up with the bottle of liquor in her hand wanting to leave the bathroom.

"You need to girl." Rachel stood up between Lee and the doorway. "Listen! Every time you smile, your dad smiles, and every time you cry, your daddy cries. No matter where he is right now, he's feeling everything you are because he's apart of you whether you like it or not. That's why I thank God every day that I look like my parents, because if I never see them again every time I look in the mirror they will always be right there in my face looking back at me. Lee just think about what I'm saying."

With tired, watery red eyes Lee found herself standing over the toilet pouring out the half bottle of liquor. Watching the last drop hit the water she knew she needed to deal with her issues with a clear mind. Ms. Jordan knew she had to calm down and take life a bit more seriously then she had before.

Chapter Eighteen
Thinking of You

Sharing the last few months with her left Phillip mesmerized and in need of her presence, and the thought of not ever having the opportunity to tell Rachel what he felt in his heart made him uneasy. His every thought of this intelligent, sensitive, and patient woman made him wonder about the love he had for Samantha. Before Rachel came into his life Samantha was the only love Phillip Daniels had needed or wanted. Somehow, her well rounded attitude about life left him wanting to share more of his time with her. Never before did he ever think there might be someone who could share his world in such a full view as Rachel.

It had been a week since Rachel left the job, and Phillip found himself wanting to spend some time alone with her away from his family. Two weeks before graduation Phillip decided to call and speak with her about attending a business meeting in New Orleans with him. Phillip thought this would be a good experience for her to have since business was her major. He picked up the phone, but put it down again. Phillip sat at his office desk for twenty-minutes thinking about what he would say to her without giving away his true feelings. She was very smart and very intuitive about life when it came to her. Wanting to be tactful in his approach so that she wouldn't think he was a dirty old man trying to get in her pants, he realized he had to be careful with her. Phillip picked up the phone and began dialing her number to the dorm. With every push of the numbers on the touch tone phone he began sweating with a slight nervousness in his hands. The phone began ringing as his heart began beating faster and faster with each ring. Rachel's phone picked up and Phillip's eyes grew bigger waiting for her to speak into the phone. He closed his eyes hoping that what he needed to say would flash before him. For a forty-year old man in a five-thousand-dollar business suit he felt more like a little schoolboy waiting to speak to the girl he had a crush on. Rachel's voice sounded at the other end of the phone. "Hello!"

"Hello Rachel." Phillip responded nervously.

"Just kidding! Isn't this answering machine great! I bet you thought it was me. I'm not in right now. Please leave your name, number, and the time you called. I promise I will get back to you as soon as possible."

Phillip felt a sense of relief as the machine played. Letting out a big gasp of absolute nail biting air, he was filled with fear from asking this woman who stirred his desires to a fast spin of wanting to be with her. He needed to think quickly about the message he would leave in hopes she would say yes to accompanying him to New Orleans.

"Hi Rachel. This is Phil. I was hoping to speak with you directly, but I see you're not in now. I know this is short notice, but I hope you would consider my offer of a weekend away in New Orleans–" Phillip cleared his voice and continued, "as a small token of my appreciation for being such a good person and a thank you for the work you've done for my family and I. Please call me here at the office if you decide to accept my offer. Goodbye."

Phillip hung up the phone hoping she would call as soon as possible to ease his craving. Knowing she was getting ready to graduate Phillip felt she might not want to spend the time hanging with a family man and his boring conversation compared to the young carefree fun she would have with her classmates during her last few weeks of college.

Just as he sat in his office way across town that morning thinking of Rachel, she was returning to her dorm room after taking a long jog to clear her mind of Phil. She knew thinking of a married man was something she could not get caught up in. All the while she worked for him spending numerous hours alone together; he never gave her any notion that he even paid any attention to her in a romantic manner or whatsoever. He was always polite to her as he opened her mind to the different angles of life. Upon entering her room Rachel looked over to check for messages on her answering machine. Hitting the play button and turning up the volume to hear it play from the bathroom she stood in the mirror examining her face. She could hear Brenda talking about what happened between her and Theo the night before then Lee screaming about how Ethan pushed her out of his house that morning and needing some advice about what she should do about trying to get him to understand that she loved him. Rachel shook her head at all the goings-on's in her girlfriends' lives while she was out.

She went to sit on the toilet to relieve her ballooned bladder. As she listened for the rest of her messages the final beep on her machine sounded, and silence played; then Phil began his long and slow request. Rachel cut short her rush of relief on the toilet grabbing her shorts, and stumbled out of the bathroom tripping over her feet, and she tried to keep her balance to stand upright with a super surprised look on her face. Hearing Phillip's message play she let out a huge grin of "Yes, he didn't forget me!" Rachel sat on the side of her bed listening to every word while soaking up each one like a sponge.

The answering machine clicked off, and she looked up to the sky and thought, "Why me!" It had been a week since she left the job, and not being able to just spend a few moments with him was killing her. Rachel didn't care if his family might be around. It was just that she had a chance to be near him, and this was what she needed to fill her cup of wantonness. As she picked up the phone dialing the number to his office, she hoped that he might not be in a meeting, his secretary picked up, and Rachel asked to speak to Phil. She was very nervous and overly excited while she waited for him to come to the phone. Just as the phone switched over she could hear the music playing in the background.

Phil was in a meeting with some of the top executives in his company reviewing the upcoming meeting in New Orleans. He had his stern, hard armor in place as he sat in front of his employees. However, on this day Phil was a man of few words, because he was preoccupied with Rachel returning his call. His secretary informed him the call he had been waiting for was on the phone holding for him to pick up. Phil quickly asked to be excused for a moment, and he walked over to a private phone in the corner of the executive boardroom and turned his back. He spoke softly into the phone to greet her.

"Hello Rachel."

"Hello Phil." Rachel smiled.

"It's good to hear from you." Phil turned slightly looking out of the boardroom window overlooking downtown Augusta. The sound of her voice lit up his smile.

"Same here!" Rachel looked over at the open window in her room gleaming with happiness.

"So–"Phil cleared his voice, "I take it you got my message."

"Yes!" Rachel nodded as she answered him. "I did. I'm surprised at the offer."

"Well, I thought maybe taking you to sit in on a major takeover might give you some insight as to what you would be up against in the real world. Besides, just think of this as a small graduation gift from me to you." Phil looked down at the floor hoping she would accept his logic in asking her to go away with him.

"Will your family be coming along? I would love to see the kids."

"Well, no Rachel. Will that be a problem?"

"No!" Rachel got what she wished for. Some time alone with him. "It's just that—"

"What is it Rachel? I'm married?"

"I don't want to offend Samantha," She said sounding sincere and concerned about his wife's feelings. However, deep down inside Rachel felt Samantha could go to hell for all she cared.

"She won't be in town. She took the kids to visit her family out of town for the next couple of days. She wouldn't even notice that I was gone."

"Are you sure about this Phil?"

"Rachel, I never been more sure about anything in my life. Absolutely, I promise you won't offend anyone, but me if you don't accept my invitation."

"Okay! But I don't have much money."

"Don't worry about anything. I will take care of everything including you."

"I already know that Phil." Rachel felt doughy all over.

"So are we all set?"

"When do we leave?" Rachel replied.

Phil let out an enormous smile expressing his happiness in her accepting his invitation. "You leave Friday afternoon. I need to be there early that morning, so I can get the ball rolling for the meeting that afternoon. There will be a driver picking you up at the dorm, and your ticket will be at the gate waiting for you. Okay?"

"Okay!"

"Goodbye Rachel!" Phil hung the phone up.

Rachel jumped up and down like a lottery winner. Her clothes were coming undone as she jiggled and danced around her room. She was sitting on top of the world. Nothing outside of that moment was more important to her. Phil returned to the meeting with a settled boyish daze on his face crossing his legs, leaning back in his chair voiding out everything around him even a question one of his executives asked him. Phil had to hold in his overwhelming happiness to Rachel saying yes to New Orleans. He immediately called an end to the meeting. Leaving the boardroom he walked into his office to get the ball rolling for his weekend away with her.

The day of her departure to New Orleans came quickly. Rachel was still unsure about the outfits she was taking with her. Only the best of her wardrobe was even considered for this once in a lifetime opportunity to be completely alone with the man who steals her breath away, whenever she says his name. Rachel checked and double-checked every outfit, every shoe, even every pair of underwear not wanting to leave any room for error when she needed to make a fashion statement. Brenda sat with Rachel as she ran around the room like a headless chicken. "Rachel relax, relate, and release girl! He's just a man."

"I can't Brenda."

"Why? Because he just happens to have millions; who happens to own one of the biggest design companies on the East Coast, and who just so happens to want you to spend a weekend away with him in New Orleans! This man wants you so bad he would lie to get you alone. I bet he makes a move on you." Brenda preached as she lay back on Rachel's bed, starring at the ceiling.

"And if he does?" Rachel responded.

"Are you prepared to just leave it at a weekend of just sex?" Brenda sat up looking at her.

"I guess I have to think about it." Rachel stood still for a few seconds to think. "He is married, and I know he would never leave his family for me."

"Rachel!" Brenda followed Rachel around the room with her eyes finally asking the question she had wanted ask for so long. "You love him don't you?"

"I do!" Rachel turned facing Brenda with a somber look on her face. "I know that wasn't in my plans."

"You're damn right. Don't be a fool and get in too deep. Just think about graduation, and above all don't get caught up in the same crap Lee got herself into."

"I already know you can't just expect a man to give his whole life away for a roll in the hay. I'm looking at this from a realistic point of view."

"That's my girl, but if you suddenly become compelled to make love just enjoy the time with him. Nothing good can come from getting involved with a married man."

"I know Brenda."

"Rachel what the hell! If I had a dick I would make love to you and you know that's a major statement coming from me. Now does that make you feel better?"

"Yes!" Rachel looked at Brenda wondering where in the world did a statement like that came from. "And by the way you sound more like crazy Lee."

"I decided to go to Andrea's wedding. So I'm getting my crazy side ready for anything. I'm modeling my outbursts according to how Lee might respond."

"Brenda, you got guts."

"Yes! I know Andrea would come to mine regardless of what we may have been through."

"I hope everything goes well for the both of you."

"I hope so too. By the way what's up with Samantha?"

"Nothing! She avoided me every day since that day I caught her in the arms of that man."

"So are you going to tell Phillip?"

"No. I'm leaving well enough alone."

"Good. As a woman I know what she did makes you feel like you have a right to step in and go for it."

"True. It does but it's not right to go at it from that perspective."

"Enough! You got two hours till your ride comes. Let me help you finish getting ready. Just have some fun, and when it's over let go. In the end, you'll be glad you did. Just look at Lee and what she's going through."

"I'll definitely keep her in mind Brenda. That girl is going through some thangs."

Rachel waited in the parking lot for her ride to come. She noticed a black Mercedes stretch limo pulling into the parking lot entrance. She sat there for a moment before a gentleman in a black suit stepped out and stood there looking around for someone he could ask for directions. The gentleman noticed Rachel standing nearby. He began walking toward her. Upon his approach he took off his driver's hat. Rachel was wondering who he could be looking for. For a moment, she thought, "For me! Not!" quickly realizing he must be lost. She smiled at the older gentleman to let him know she was friendly and willing to help him find his destination. "Excuse me! Young lady I wonder if you could help me find someone."

"Sure. Do you have a name or address?"

"Yes." The driver looked at the slip of paper in his hand responding, "I hope I'm saying the name right. Ms. Rachel Tims."

"I'm Ms. Tims." Rachel smiled.

"Mr. Daniels sent me to pick you up for the airport. I'm Jimmy your driver." He extended his hand. "May I take your bag? This way please." The driver stepped to the side allowing Rachel to go ahead of him to the limo.

Rachel was shocked and speechless having never been in a limo before. It was certainly a treat for her. When the driver opened the door to the car she could see the black leather shine just as she stepped in. The inside was everything she imagined it to be: clean, spacious, and filled with lots of goodies to enjoy while she cruised to the airport in style. Popping the bottle of champagne on the bar as the car drove off; she helped herself to some chocolate candies that also adorned the small bar in the limo. She wanted this moment to last forever.

Rachel sipped her champagne very slowly to enjoy her fairy tale to its fullest. The limo pulled up to the airport, and the driver instructed her as to what airline she would be flying. Rachel gave her identification to the ticket agent. The agent gave Rachel her ticket and asked her to board the plane. The stewardess showed Rachel to her seat in the first-class section.

Rachel was impressed with the limo, but a first-class plane ride was not something she expected. Everything was just wonderful. Feeling important as she sat in the first-class section among all the occupants Rachel turned looking around at the cabin with a smirk on her face thinking, "Phil really did take care of everything. I wonder if he left any stone unturned to make me smile. I wonder!"

After a one-hour flight to New Orleans the captain came on announcing the descent to the New Orleans Airport. Rachel was very nervous about seeing Phil. Just before the plane landed Rachel looked at her attire making sure everything was in place just before disembarking. After walking to the ground transportation exit she noticed there was a gentleman standing there with a sign with her name on it. She smiled realizing he did take care of everything even the limo from the airport to the hotel. After checking in at the five-star Hotel Morgan where he had booked her a room, she was given a message from Phil by the desk clerk telling her that she was to call him once she settled into her room. Rachel quickly hurried to her room on the eleventh floor. Flipping the lights on, she noticed that in every corner of the room there were dozens of red and yellow roses. Rachel was stiff from the sight of so many beautiful flowers in her room. She walked through a room that suddenly became a very large suite. On the table in the sitting area was an enormous fruit basket, and on the chair sat a box with a large red ribbon neatly tied around it.

Rachel looked for a phone to call the front desk; she wanted to make sure she was in the right room.

"Hello! Is this the front desk?"

"Yes." The front desk attendant responded.

"My name is Rachel Tims. I was wondering what room was I booked in?"

"Just a moment." After a slight pause the clerk responded, "Your room number is 1108. Is there a problem?"

"No! Thank you."

Just to make sure she went outside to check the number on the door to her hotel suite. She was in the right room, but she could not figure out why all of the wonderful things happening were happening. Without a moment to spare she looked around the suite to find a window view of the many beautiful old buildings in the area. That made her elated. It reminded her of some of the streets in Paris the time she went for a summer vacation a few years back.

The bathroom was bigger than her dorm room at school. It had a separate shower to the side and a bathtub that could hold at least five people all at the same time. The walls in the bathroom had mirrors from the floor to the ceiling. The room was furnished in Chinese Chippendale, and the craftsmanship was meticulous in its detail. Like a little child on Christmas, she ran to open the ribbon tied box that was placed in an arm chair closest to her bed. Inside, Rachel found a long black Gucci negligee with a robe to match. Placed on top of the neatly folded negligee there was a small card that read, *"Thought you might forget something to sleep in. I know I always do. Phil."* She grabbed the negligee and ran to the mirror to place it against her to imagine what it will look like when she puts it on. Swirling around and around to admire the flow of the gown the phone rang. It was Phil.

"Hello."

"Hello Rachel."

"Hello Phil. I just walked in the door."

Phillip smiled. "I see you made it safe and sound. I got a little worried and called the front desk. They said you just checked in moments before I called."

"Yes I did."

"I'm glad you're here." He replied.

"I'm glad I came." She warmly returned the same sentiment.

"I have a little bad news. The meeting went very well. We just wrapped up a few minutes ago. It seems the takeover was rather successful. So, that means we will have to go to dinner right away and jump head first into having some fun. How does that sound?"

"Great!"

"I'll be in the lobby in about ten-minutes waiting for you."

Phil was sitting in the waiting area of the lobby facing the elevators. He wanted to see her from a distance to relish her sway as she walked to meet him. Being very eager to see her, he sat and watched every person get on and off the elevators. Just when he thought it might be her it wasn't. He was beside himself hoping she might be feeling the same as he was.

The moment he sat back in the chair the elevator doors opened, and there she was a vision of what heaven might taste like, completely delicious. Everything about her was perfect from her hips to her fingertips. He was slightly taken aback seeing her all dressed up. Her hair was done up in a French bun, and she wore just the right amount of make-up to let her natural beauty stand out. He stood up to greet her as she came closer. She smiled and Phil did the same. Stepping forward to meet her was hard. He didn't just want to shake her hand to greet her, he wanted to reach out and hold her in his arms giving her a lengthy soft kiss hello.

"Rachel!"

"Hello! Good to see you Phil."

"You look exquisite!"

"Thank you!" She replied.

Unable to keep his eyes off her, he quickly forgot they had a dinner date. The ding of the elevators brought Phil back from a moment of solitude within her beauty. He found himself feeling mushy all over. Right at that moment, he realized he was the happiest he had ever been in years.

"So Rachel what would you like to eat? The sky is the limit."

"I would love to try some New Orleans crawfish."

"Great! I know a little jazz spot in the area that serves a mean crawfish."

The two walked towards the front door of the Hotel Morgan. Rachel could not help but embrace this moment with him. Just to be walking next to him was good enough for her, because she knew he wanted her there with him. She felt special, appreciated, and loved. While walking next to him all she could think about is, "Yes thinking of you is what I could only do before this moment had presented itself." She felt blessed to be given this time with him. She would not take for granted this gift she had prayed so long for.

Chapter Nineteen
Silent Whispers

After arriving at the jazz club they sat and enjoyed a few drinks, while listening to the musicians play as the lady songbirds wrap them in a spirit of enthusiasm with their mean vocal sounds. Phil couldn't help but keep his eyes focused on her as she sat across from him at the table. She was so natural and subdued in the way she carried herself. He was amazed at the way she adapted to the many aspects of his life. To him, she was an impeccable human being that was made the way he had always envisioned his perfect woman and friend to be. They wiped their hands clean of the juices from the crawfish, while they waited for the check. Rachel wanted to leave and walk off the hefty meal they had just indulged in. Phil escorted her to a beautiful riverfront with many different cobblestone streets. She could smell the river in the air as they walked.

"This is so beautiful." Rachel replied as she looked at the view in amazement.

He looked over at her and replied in a very gracious manner. "Just like you Rachel."

"Thank you for the compliment, but this view is absolutely gorgeous more so than me, Phil."

"So what are your plans after graduation Rachel?"

"Well, I'm glad to report that I landed an entry level position in a small, but aggressively growing investment company. The pay is okay for a newcomer like me."

"That's great! So where is this new job?"

"It's located in Malibu, California. I'm so excited. I'll be taking my first few steps to becoming a giant in the business world of movers and shakers."

"I hope you call me if you need some advice or just to talk." Phil looked over at her smiling.

"Of course I will if that's no problem. I know you are a very busy man." Rachel looked over smiling back at him with her arms placed behind her.

They walked for a while talking about dinner and the things to see in New Orleans. The moon was shining, and the sky was midnight blue without a cloud in sight. The soft wind was warm bringing with it a mood of tranquility. They stopped to look at the river watching the stars shimmer in the water as it shifted back and forth.

"Can I ask you a question Rachel?"

"Shoot!"

"Being a black woman did you ever wonder why I married Samantha?"

Rachel turned away from the river view to face him. She was surprised at the question he threw at her. Phil looked at her waiting for her response. She laughed then looked away, then faced him again. She answered him slowly.

"At first I did."

"And now?" Phil asked.

"I still wonder sometimes why black men just push women like me aside for a white woman or just a complete off-the-wall minority group. I think I'm intelligent, understanding, ambitious, patient, and I think I look rather decent. Wouldn't you say?"

"By far you are one of the most beautiful women I have ever seen in my life not just physically, but your mind also."

"Thank you." She took a chance by asking, "So there were no women like me running around Harvard?"

"Actually yes! There were a few, but—"

"But what?"

"But I didn't have a snowball's chance in hell with them and believe me when I say; I tried to date all of them."

"It figures as good-looking as you are." Rachel said.

"I wish. I was fifty pounds overweight, no sense of style, and tongue-tied when it came to women."

"Get out!" Rachel laughed.

"No! I'm dead serious. The only thing I had going for me was my brain and a driving ambition to own my own business. Rachel, you have to remember some of us have to go through a metamorphosis in order to get total acceptance. Now, someone like you must have been a beauty from day one and probably never had a problem getting a date. There was a time what you see now wasn't what you saw then."

"Mmm!" Rachel gestured nodding her head at him.

"I wasn't much of a ladies' man in high school or college. Learning the dating game was not part of my curriculum. I was the guy the girls walked past. They only saw me as the guy who could get them a date with my friend."

"Ooooh !" Rachel chuckled.

"So when I got to Harvard, I just knew there had to be someone doing the same thing I was. Like studying hard and getting ready to conquer the world with the same ambition as myself. True there were some, but I wasn't exactly what they had been looking for. I had no money, two pairs of shoes, four pairs of socks, and three pairs of underwear, four white shirts, and two pairs of jeans. Oh! Let's not forget my wool jacket with no buttons. When you attend Harvard and you don't come from a rich family you pray the clothes on your back will last until graduation."

"Where does a rich girl like Samantha come into the picture?"

"Well, I'm glad you asked Rachel. We shared a class together, and she needed a study partner. She asked me, and then after spending weeks and weeks together we became good friends. The rest is history. She was there when I needed love, affection, and just to feel wanted. A man can get lonely just like a woman when he can't find someone to love him the way he wants to be loved. Samantha gave me that at the time."

"Well, that puts a lot in perspective as to why you married her. It's so sad that sisters couldn't see what I see now." Rachel looked at Phil with a bashful glow to her face.

"Thank you. You know I can't understand why I always feel the stares burning holes in my back, when I walk down the street with Samantha. It hurts sometimes, because when I wanted to be with a black woman very few gave me a chance, or they just didn't hang around long enough because I didn't have much."

"That sounds like some of us, but not all of us think that way. However, in defense of my fellow sisters first, an apology for being pushed aside and not recognizing you for your qualities. Second, there are women like me looking for a good man like you. Samantha is lucky to have you."

"So, Ms. Rachel Tims tell me something about yourself that might surprise me."

"Okay! Let me think. I have a secret passion."

"Don't tell me. Let me guess. You rob banks in between classes?"

"No!" She nudged Phil on the shoulder as she laughed at his silly question. He laughed as she pushed him. "I write poetry. It's something that comforts me when I need to get some emotional baggage off my chest."

"So not only are you trying to be a tough business person, but you're also a poet."

"I wouldn't say that Phil. Maybe a wannabe."

"Well let me be the judge of that. Let me hear something you wrote."

"I'm sort of in the closet about reciting my work. I get really shy about things like this."

"Come on let me hear just a little something. I would love to hear something you wrote Ms. Tims."

"Okay." Rachel stood facing him with look of shyness about her face. "Before I agree please don't laugh, and you have to close your eyes all right?"

"Sure!" Phil responded as he complied with her request.

"Ready!" Rachel remembered a poem she wrote about him not to long after she realized she had feelings for him.

"Whenever you are Ms. Tims." Phil closed his eyes. He waited for her to begin.

"Once in a lifetime, you find true love. Never, ever, give it up. Alone and sorry, it's what you'll feel. So, don't hold back on what is real. Take both arms and hold on tight. Only a few are bitten twice. As I walk along this lonely path, silent whispers remind me of what we could've had. Questioning why it did not last, silent whispers reminds me of what I should have."

Rachel stood silent as she looked at him. She wanted to lean forward to kiss him so badly, but she was not sure if the kiss she wanted to share would be received with an open-heart. She stepped back from him realizing she needed to leave well enough alone.

"Phil, you can open your eyes now. I'm ready to head back to the car." Rachel turned walking in a fast pace back toward the car.

"Wait a minute!" Phil rushed up from behind her to catch up. "What's the rush? Rachel that was very good."

"Really! Thanks!" Rachel looked behind her as she responded to his praise in her rush to return to the car.

"What do you call it?"

"Silent Whispers!" Rachel kept a fast pace towards the car.

"What does it mean to you?"

"It's about this person–" Rachel slowed down to catch her breath as she continued to say, "who could have been or should have been mine. It means that every time I think about him the silent whispers in my head constantly remind me that he was the one for me. Oh! It's just what we women do when we get our hearts broken. We sit down and write little schoolgirl stuff that adds up to gibberish."

"Rachel!" Phil yelled with love in his voice. "I don't think that was gibberish."

Rachel stopped dead in her tacks just ahead of him. She looked down holding her head in her hands. Phil walked from behind her, and he carefully grabbed both of her hands. Moving closer he spread her arms open lifting her chin looking at her with an edgy eye.

"I hope your silent whispers are about me because the next move I make might tell you what my silent whispers say to me about you."

Phil let his warm hands cuff her smooth neck as he looked deep into her eyes under the streetlight just above them. They both knew it was love. He leaned in kissing her intensely. Rachel threw her arms around him tasting his hot wet lips as they caressed hers. The world around them fell still and silent.

Phil released her lips in a confession from his heart. "Rachel do you know how many times I have wanted to touch you? Everything about you drives me crazy. The way you hold your head when you're talking, the way you walk."

"Phil we can't let this happen. What about Samantha?"

"I love Samantha, and I know that I can't have you both."

"Why me– Phil?"

"Do you love me, Rachel? Because if you do, why not you? What man wouldn't want you? You are so beautiful in every way."

"Yes! I do love you! Yes! I do want you and I can't stop what I feel. I want you, but I'm so scared."

"Of what?"

"Of not being able to walk away."

"You don't have to tonight Rachel. I can't make you any promises for tomorrow."

"Shh! Phil, I'm not asking for promises. My silent whispers won't let me hold back on what is real, because I am taking both arms and holding on tight to here now with you." Phil began kissing her as they stood under the streetlight that illuminated their passion.

Chapter Twenty
On Second Thought!

They made their way back to the hotel without leaving each other's embrace. They were both sure about making love with each other as they rode the elevator to Rachel's room. For the moment, it seemed to be the right thing to do. However, after exiting the elevator to walk over to her hotel room Rachel had a sudden of change of heart. Releasing him from their lover's embrace she stepped back looking at him head on. She knew what they were about to get into was not right.

"Here we are." Rachel looked unsure and frightened.

"Rachel are you having second thoughts?" Phil looked at her.

"Actually yes!" Rachel turned her head looking away.

"Phil, I'm not sure if this is the right thing for us to do." She looked down at the floor hoping she wouldn't give away the fact she wanted to just throw herself at him. Rachel didn't want to end up like Lee desperate and feeling used in the end.

"Rachel if this is something you can't handle then I can understand." Phil smiled at her.

"It's not that I can't handle it. It's the consequences that go along with sleeping in the bed of a married man. What kind of woman would I be if I just—"

"Stop! I understand. Besides, for me to just expect you to give yourself to me is a cheap thought. You deserve better than that."

"You're right! If I make love to you; walking away might not be something I would be able to do. It's not often I let my heart lead me, but I did. And here we are standing at temptation's front door."

"Rachel Tims you are so special." Phillip raised her hand kissing it gently. "Do you know how many women would have probably jumped at a chance to sleep with a wealthy man, because of all the perks that go along with having done it?" Phil stood opposite her with a smile that let her know he truly respected her and honored her as woman with values.

"Phil what are you feeling right now?"

"Rachel, Rachel, Rachel! I'm so completely lost in your eyes. However, you turning me down adds to the respect I have for you, and that is the feeling I was referring to; it's called—let's wait till the end and I'll let you know what that feeling is."

"Thank you for understanding. I have to say it has certainly been hard to resist you."

"Same here." Phil winked his eye at her, she blushed innocently.

"Oh Phil, I wish we met under different circumstances. Maybe one day we will be standing in this very same place on the same day, and maybe we both can, well you know the rest."

"I'll dream the rest tonight, but somehow I know this won't be the last time we get a chance like this. Hopefully, our circumstances will be different, and if they are I guarantee, well you know the rest."

"Good night Phil."

"Sweet dreams Rachel."

Phil leaned over and softly kissed her raspberry painted lips. Rachel closed the door behind her easing off her shoes one by one. She looked around the room at the fragrant roses wondering if maybe, she might ever get another chance just like the one she just passed up tonight. Standing and waiting for the elevator to take him to his room on the tenth floor Phil found himself smirking about how strong this woman was. She actually turned away from all the open opportunities to make love to him, and with him. Still, he knew her strength was something to admire leaving him wanting her even more.

Waking up in the Gucci negligee Phil had bought her, she ran her hands up and down the silky material looking up at the ceiling. With a morning after feeling of guilt of not jumping at a chance to be in his arms right at that moment, she hoped he might be feeling the same. Rachel picked up the phone to dial his room number, but in an instant she needed to let go of what was the night before in order to concentrate on the here and now. As she rolled out of bed to shower, a knock at her door interrupted her path to the shower. Grabbing her robe she wondered who in the world could be at her door this early. Suddenly, she hoped it wasn't Phil catching her at her worst. Butterflies began playing pitter-pat in her stomach. Rachel hurried to the door asking who it was.

"I have a message for a Ms. Rachel Tims. Is she available?" The Hotel Manager asked.

"Just a second!" Rachel tied her robe tightly. She opened the door, it wasn't Phil.

"Good morning."

"Morning Ms. Tims?" The Manager asked her.

"That's me."

"Mr. Daniels is requesting you join him for breakfast at nine o'clock."

"Tell him I accept."

"He is in the café downstairs. Good day, Ms. Tims."

Phil knew he had only twenty-four hours left with her. He wanted to make sure they enjoyed every minute they had left alone together. Getting an early start to the day would give them more time to spend with each other. He had the chef in the five-star Hotel Morgan Café standing by waiting to prepare anything her heart desired. Only the freshest flowers, fruits, and pastries could be placed at arm's reach for the woman he so much wanted to please.

Rachel found her way to the café downstairs. The waiter Phil had waiting for her escorted her to a balcony overlooking the lobby of the hotel. She sat waiting for Phil to join her. Relishing the eye-opening setup of pastries, flowers, and the fruits that looked so sweet, she became euphoric over the way this man just laid the world at her feet. Phil appeared from behind her.

"I'm glad you made it."

"Morning Phil."

"Is everything to your liking?"

"Most definitely! This is wonderful. Besides, where am I going to put it all?"

"Please don't say that. I had all of this done just for you to eat."

"Well, I'll do my best, but first can we get a menu?"

"No!"

"Why?"

"Because the chef will make whatever you want. Just ask and you shall receive."

"Really!" Rachel was lost in his world.

"Yes for you Rachel. Anything!" Phil sat waiting for Rachel to respond.

"Okay! How about some home fries, country crude ham, buttermilk pancakes, and some scrambled eggs?" Rachel smiled at Phil.

"That sounds good. I think I'll have the same." Phil smiled back at her.

Phil summoned the chef over to take their order. Rachel loved the way he just took such care of everything from her smiling to her bedtime attire. This man left no stone unturned and no emotion untouched. While they sat and enjoyed breakfast, they found themselves constantly gazing into each other's eyes as they enjoyed their meal.

"I really enjoyed last night Rachel. I just wished this breakfast could have been served in the bed next to you."

"I was just thinking the same thing too." Rachel let her fork twirl in her hand as she imagined what might have been.

"Really! Looking at you just sets me on fire. I remember the day we met. It's very rare you see someone so naturally beautiful. You took my breath away then and even now."

"Phil—"

"Let me finish Rachel. I found myself tossing and turning last night. I was going to call you, but I needed to respect your decision not to put yourself in the middle of my life. Still, in the back of my mind I thought if I crawled to your door and begged you might give in. Being near you just makes me so nervous yet– warm all over. Remember that feeling I was telling you about. Well, I mean—" Confused about how to tell her how he felt he just let it flow from within. "I can't explain this other than I–." He stopped short of telling her that he loved her.

"Phil don't do this. Stop! We both know there is no way we could be together."

"I know this, but I thought you should hear the truth about how I feel."

"I know what you mean. It hurts me to know that in the morning we will have to go back to our separate lives." Rachel reached across the table to hold his hand. "For right now let's just enjoy our time together."

After breakfast they strolled down some of the many streets of New Orleans. Like two elegant swans at play Rachel and Phil looked so beautiful together. The way they laughed and the way they cuddled each other as they slowly walked side by side; anyone and everyone on the street could see the passion and love in their body language. It was something about the two of them that caught the eyes of people around them. Looking in the different shops in the area for little keepsakes to remember their time together, they came across a little restaurant for a quick lunch break. They nuzzled against each other in a back booth sipping on cool lemonade, while sharing a piece of apple pie. Just as they finished their drinks the waitress approached.

"Excuse me sir." The waitress asked, "Would you and your lovely wife like something else to drink or eat?"

"My wife?" Phil turned nodding at Rachel. "She is certainly lovely isn't she?"

"She is very lovely." The waitress replied, "I love to see young people in love with each other."

"Honey!" With a playful childlike look Phil asked Rachel, "Would you like something else?"

"No thank you honey!" Rachel giggled.

"That will be all for us. Thank you." The waitress left. Phil put his arm around Rachel kissing her on the cheek.

"Phil why did you do that?" Rachel asked quietly.

"I was only telling the truth."

"Phil, I'm not your wife."

"It felt good to be treated normal."

"What do you mean normal?"

"Whenever Samantha and I go out people give off the old questioning attitude are those two a couple? Walking down the street with you, hell just sitting here out in the open I have never felt more relaxed. I'm actually being appreciated for just being a patron in someone's business. I know that sounds like I'm ashamed of my wife, but I'm not. I'm just ashamed of how our people treat us. They can be much crueler than a white person. At least white people whisper under their breath and turn away. Black people—they stare you down, rolling their eyes, sucking their teeth loud enough for you to hear."

"I need to confess something to you. I hated you when I first met you. When you walked out my mouth hit the ground. The first thing to run through my mind was he's a sellout.'"

"Do you feel that way now?" Phil asked her.

"No! I'm just so happy that we got to know each other as friends, because that made me see that you were a man with his reasons—some bad, some good. You're no different than my dad."

"Rachel is wanting to be with you something bad?"

"No! That is something good. It's just that the timing is so bad. That's not your fault." Rachel replied.

Once they arrived back at the hotel Phil checked for his messages at the front desk. Rachel went ahead to his room with his key in hand. After getting his messages he rushed to a courtesy phone to call home. Samantha left three messages that he must call home once he gets in. Things were tense between the two of them over the last few weeks. Phil dialed and waited for Samantha to pick up.

"Samantha is everything okay? How are the kids?"

"The kids are fine. Everything is okay here. The kids wanted to talk to you, but they're out playing in the neighbor's backyard with their kids. You should call them before they go to sleep tonight."

"I'll do that. How are you?"

"I'm fine. How are you?"

"Just great, Samantha. I'll be home by noon tomorrow."

"Phillip, why can't you come first thing in the morning?"

"I just need some personal time to myself."

"Are you sure that's all Phillip?"

"Yes Samantha! Sometime to call my own. You should know what I mean."

"Okay, Phillip let's not get into this over the phone."

"All right! One question."

"What!" Sounding frustrated Samantha answered.

"Are you still thinking about the boys' education?"

"Yes!" Samantha bluntly replied.

"So have you made a decision about what route you want to take?"

"No! We still have to waive some options."

"What options?" Phil sternly replied into the phone.

"Not all private schools out there are out of touch from the real world. Besides, we can afford to send our children to the best. So why don't we? My father feels the same."

"Samantha! Once again, I'm their father and I only want what's best for my sons. Turning my back to the reality of getting a good education is something I'm not going to do. Keeping the boys away from the different people in this world would not be a good thing."

"Phil are you still on that color issue again? What does that have to do with getting an education in a private school?"

"Nothing! It's just that where you want them to go they wouldn't have many ethnic influences to keep it real for them."

"Phil let's give this a break."

"No! Samantha our sons are black. There isn't much of their white side standing out to give them true acceptance in your world. You keep forgetting one day ours sons will be in the real world where their brown skin and dark curly hair yells out minority over here."

"Phillip if color is such a big issue, why did you marry me?"

"I thought because I loved you. Lately, I wonder why you married me. It seems everything about me holding on to my heritage has been making you uptight. Whenever I decide to introduce new things about the boys' heritage; you jump in with your wanting to ignore my reality. You never want to address how being a person of color has its draw backs in our society."

"I do not! I just want the best for our sons Phillip."

"So don't let them forget they are made of you and me; with the me part sticking out like a sore thumb. That means they don't just belong in your world; they belong in mine too."

"We'll have to finish this later. I have to get back to the mission."

"You and that mission! I hope you don't let this new venture in your life come between us. It seems the mission comes before me. I don't know how much more I can take of this. Goodbye Samantha."

Phil took a moment to compose himself after hanging up the phone. Needing to put his personal matters in his marriage aside for the next twenty-four hours was a must. He didn't want to take any more time away from Rachel knowing this would be the last time he might ever spend alone with her. He wanted this night to be special. Needing to express his true feelings to her, Phil arranged a romantic dinner on the rooftop of the hotel with live music and champagne. Just before returning to his room where Rachel was waiting for him, Phil had noticed a large mocha teddy bear in the gift shop window. Standing there looking at its innocent little expression he began thinking about her. His romantic side pulled him to the register requesting that the teddy bear be wrapped with their most expensive ribbon. Phil rushed upstairs to his room with his surprise in his hand.

Knocking on the door Phil yelled out, "Rachel it's only me."

"Just a second." Rachel opened the door letting him in.

"You must have had a lot of messages."

"No. I needed to call home."

"Is everything okay?" Rachel sounded concerned.

"Yes! The kids are fine."

"That's good. I was getting a little worried."

"No need for that. Here's a little something I saw downstairs in the gift shop. It reminded me of you."

"Oh Phil this is so sweet of you! I love teddy bears. Look at its cute little nose."

"Isn't it precious? Its' just like you Rachel."

Rachel and Phil embraced sharing a deep passionate kiss. That was the moment if any their bodies longed for. After a few moments of embracing each other, they lay in the bed holding each other and talking about anything and everything that came to mind. Drifting off to sleep; they lay side by side as the warm afternoon waltzed into the twilight to bring forth a soft warm summer night. Just as he turned his body he remembered, "There she is right next to me." Phil looked over at her wishing he could make love to her, but like a real man he let his drive shift back into park. Phillip wanted to make sure he did nothing to injure or insult the love he had for her. Watching her chest move up and down with every breath she took he brushed his hand against her neck feeling her soft skin. Rachel began twisting and turning with every touch he gave. She rolled over and buried her face in his neck. Smelling his cologne and the feel of his five o'clock shadow Rachel's warm lips crept up his neck to his waiting lips.

"Rachel, I thought you didn't want too."

"I'm sorry. Something came over me. I don't want to lead you on to find nothing. It's hard keeping my emotions under control."

"I know. I don't care just as long as I can hold you until the time comes when we have to say goodbye. I'll take you any kind of way I can get you."

"You really care about me don't you Phil?"

"Yes Rachel! I really do! Believe me; I don't have a clue as to how I'm going to handle not being able to be near you. I've been thinking what it would take to keep you in Augusta . I figured a job with a great starting salary, with good benefits, and a free apartment or house would interest you?"

"I wish there was such a job. I'd hop that bus in a second."

"There is."

"Where?"

"With me! In my company."

"Are you serious?" Rachel sat up running her hands through her hair.

"I'm serious. Why not start on the top and learn from me?"

"Wouldn't that look a little funny to Samantha and your staff?"

"Well, Samantha—she doesn't care who works there just as long as the bank card works. My staff, well they'll just have to adjust to the new employee on board."

"I don't know."

"Rachel just think about it before you graduate. When we get back after a few days call me so we can talk further."

"All right."

"Now let's get ready for dinner. I have a little surprise for you."

"Really!"

"I want to show you something special. So go get ready and I'll pick you up in twenty-minutes."

"What shall I wear?"

"Something nice."

"That doesn't tell me anything."

"You'll figure it out once you get to your room. Just don't take too long. I can't stand being away from you."

Rachel went to her room to freshen up for the surprise Phil had planned for their evening out. Throwing her bags on the bed from their shopping spree earlier that day, she went to turn on the radio to listen to some soothing music while she got ready. After stepping out of the shower and drying off she put on the robe Phil had bought her. She walked over to the closet to look for something to wear. Sliding the door back to open it, she found a ruby red dress with rhinestones. As she stepped back in amazement at the wickedly awesome dress that hung in the closet it made her think this was something only a princess would wear to a ball. Looking down at the dress in its full length she noticed a white box. It was sitting on the floor just underneath the dress. She picked the box up, and began laughing at the shocking revelations that were taking place in front of her. Closing her eyes, she pulled the top off. Inside was a pair of matching shoes with a clutch bag to complete the ensemble. Rachel knew Phil had kept his promise to take care of everything even making her feel like the most important person on earth. She smiled letting out a big yes! She stood up shaking her behind off to the beat of music in the background. After she was done dressing and fixing her hair not a moment passed before he knocked.

Knock! Knock! Knock!

"Coming! Who?"

"It's me Phil."

"Come in! It's open." Rachel twirled to let Phil see her in the gown he had bought her. "Well, is this okay?"

"Absolutely stunning!"

"How did you know what I would like?"

"Looking at you only the best will ever do. Don't you know?"

"No. I don't know."

"Rachel make me a promise."

"If I can Phil."

"Remember you are gold, and like gold, you are precious. Like precious things they must be handled with care and lots of love. Never forget us. Let tonight be your guide to show you how you should be treated every single day of your life. Putting the world at your feet is man's responsibility, especially if he cares for you."

"You have made me so happy. Who would ever think a man like you existed? Where have you been?"

"I've been here the whole time, and yes Rachel we do exist. Sometimes we're overlooked to only to be found when you least expect it. "

"I have never been so− "

"'So lucky Rachel!"

"If you call it that."

"It's not luck. It's what you deserve. Come let's go to the top of the world."

Phil held his hand out and Rachel extended hers allowing him to lead the way. Escorting her to the elevator that led to the roof of the hotel, Phil held her hand tightly as they were lifted to the magical wonderland he had planned. The doors of the elevator opened to the steel doors that exited to the roof. He guided her through the door onto a red carpet that covered the once tarred rooftop. Rachel was taken aback with the length this man had gone to exude his love towards her. The live band played a sentimental tone, as they walked around the decorated rooftop that lit up like a soft candle flickering in the distance. Everything was perfect: the weather, the stars, the food, and Phil in his black tuxedo.

Rachel and Phil danced with each other for hours as the band played. This fairy tale Phillip Daniels conjured up in its details, and romance was ending after the music stopped and the dinner dishes were cleaned up. Rachel was wrapped in Phil's warm strong arms as they stood together overlooking the beautiful view of lights that glittered in the downtown area of New Orleans. Watching the clouds drift by in the deep blue midnight skies, they both knew time was running out. Rachel and Phil sat on the roof of the hotel to spend their last night together. They held each other until Sunday morning brought about a sunny still sky that looked down on the world like a songbird prancing in the wind. Everything about that morning felt so right—so wonderful just to be alive to see the new day begin. Just two hours were left for them to pack and board the plane back to Augusta.

Phil escorted Rachel back to her room. He kissed her, and she thought to herself as he kissed her, "I have to leave things the way they are. It's the only smart thing to do." Gently pulling away Phil let her go to pack for her flight back.

After packing her things the bellman came to take her bags to the lobby for checkout. Rachel took a few minutes to look around. The beautiful room of red, and yellow roses allowed her take a good picture for her memory to keep in its own permanent scrapbook of keepsakes in memory of their time together. Rachel walked toward the door to exit the room. She stopped one last time to pick a yellow rose from one of the many vases of flowers allowing herself to smell the fragrant blossom in her hand. Just as she turned to open the door to leave Phil knocked; she opened the door for him.

"I'm glad I caught you before you went downstairs."

"Come in. I already sent my bags down."

"Rachel, I wanted to give you this before you left. I jotted down some of my thoughts about you. Don't open it until you get on the plane."

"All right. I really had a great time. I will never forget this as long as I live."

"You better not. Rachel please think about what I asked you. No strings attached."

"We'll see. I really need to think about this."

"Please call me as soon as you make a decision."

"Okay Phil. I'll be thinking about you. "

"I'll always be thinking of you Rachel, right here in my heart and my mind." With that he kissed her goodbye.

Just as the plane took off from the airport Rachel opened the envelope, and inside was a folded piece of paper. Rachel opened the small letter, and began reading. It read,

"Rachel, you have made me see things I had forgotten about over the last few years, and I found something I thought didn't exist for me: a woman who has the knowledge of a scholar and yet the qualities of a Nubian Nile Queen. Where have you been all my life? I don't know, but I am glad we found each other. When I was in need, you were there.

Every day of your life, know that you're the only one in my world. I'll cross any mountain, swim any sea. Hell, I would even crawl down on my knees. There's nothing in this world to ever keep me from you. Thinking of you brings a ray of sunshine to my heart. Love never seemed so warm, so kind. I'm not afraid of what I feel. Take my heart, take my soul. It's all yours Rachel. I love you!"

Rachel let out a big smile leaning back in her seat looking out of her first-class window. She watched the clouds in the sky go by. She began thinking about his soft brown eyes and his warm touch. On second thought, she felt she might need to change her plans and stay in Augusta with the man she loved. Rachel fell asleep cradled in warm thoughts of love like a baby in a warm blanket.

Chapter Twenty-One
Chitchat

"It's a crime Brenda that you didn't let your foot loose into Theo's ass the other night!" Lee continued to suggest to Brenda. "It sure would have created an extra hole for him."

"Lee what was I supposed to do? Fight over a man who obviously didn't love me? Lowering my standards by fighting over a man, I refuse! Greg wasn't worth the headache so why make Theo one?" Brenda replied.

"Brenda, you can't go on letting people just hurt you and get away with it." With great enthusiasm Lee stood up to preach.

"I did let him know. Sit down Lee."

"How Brenda?"

"I did what any woman with class would. I yelled and walked out and I didn't even breakdown."

"What a statement!" Lee sarcastically waved her hand at Brenda. "When you make a final exit make sure to leave a lasting impression."

"Like what Lee?" Brenda turned with her hand on her hip.

"Break his freaking nose or just slap the shit out him!" Lee stood up on her dorm bed jumping up and down. "Fuck you should have smashed his car's windshield. Hurt that motherfucker's car, you break his heart. How could you forget Blake?"

"I don't need to get ghetto with him or anyone. That's not my style. Walking away is easier. I hate having confrontations. To me nothing gets resolved by losing your cool."

Lee stopped jumping on her bed. "I always lose my foot in somebody's ass if I get into a confrontation. However, when Victoria punched me, you refused to let me get up so I could get to work."

"Lee, you didn't need to get into a confrontation with Ethan's wife. Besides, you were wrong for telling her you screwed her husband on her living room floor." Looking over at Lee, Brenda had a look on her face to let Lee know she had it coming to her.

"Okay!" Lee plopped her bottom onto her bed. "I admit I was wrong, but that still didn't give her the right to hit me; although I would have done the same thing if the roles were reversed."

"Good because I'm glad you see. Well for me, I just need to get myself together and learn to make better choices about the men I give my heart too."

"How do you figure out who's the right one?" Lee asked.

"I don't know yet, but I hope that someone or something up above gives me a sign."

"Brenda, I hope you find what you're looking for. Seeing you hurt over some jerk is not something you deserve. Theo had a lot of nerve to break your heart like that."

"Yeah, he did. Didn't he?"

"Of course! If he couldn't see you're a beautiful intelligent person with a heart of gold then it's his loss."

"I am so tired of hearing about how beautiful and intelligent I am." Brenda sat on her bed looking over at Lee standing in the window from across the room. "That's not working for me. With all my pluses I keep getting a negative reading in the category of male companionship."

"Brenda everything has a place and time for it to come together." Lee strutted from across the room to look in their well packed miniature fridge. "You have to remember Greg and Theo are your stepping stones to the big love mountain ahead." Lee crunched down a piece of celery. "If we didn't get our hearts broken from time to time, then when we find the right one, we wouldn't know how to appreciate what we've found."

"That sounds so nice in a make believe world." Brenda lounged in her bed looking at the ceiling. "I hope things go my way someday, because I don't want to grow old and lonely by myself."

"Brenda just think positive."

"I guess that's all I have left to do." Brenda moaned.

"No you don't. You have to get ready to go get on the plane and show your face at Andrea's wedding."

"I forgot about that Lee." Brenda sat up in the bed. She began rubbing her face as though she just woke up.

"No, no, no! This is your coming-out party. You have some ass to chew on just like I am chewing on this celery. Listen. *Crunch! Crunch! Crunch!* Don't forget what we discussed."

"How could I forget that being nice is hard, but being a bitch is much better. Lee, I hope we stay friends forever because you have so much to teach me." Brenda stood up to go get her suitcase for her weekend trip home.

"Where am I going Brenda! You and Rachel are the only two people who would put up with me."

"You're right Lee, but we love you all the same." Brenda put her suitcase down to give Lee a warm hug.

"I'm glad to have the both of you in my life. You guys are my family." Lee held on to Brenda's hug for dear life. She needed to feel loved.

"Lee are you okay?" Just for a moment Lee drifted off into a deep thought about her mother and their relationship.

"I'm fine." Lee released her grip from around Brenda. "Nothing important! Right now my friend Brenda needs me to be there for her." Lee tapped Brenda's chin and smiled as if nothing was wrong.

"Thank you for listening and making me think girl. You always help me put things into perspective. I love how we chitchat. I learn something new every time." Brenda finished packing her bags and chatted with Lee until it was time to go.

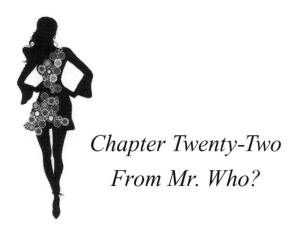

Chapter Twenty-Two
From Mr. Who?

Arriving at LaGuardia Airport Brenda walked through the airport tunnel to the pickup area. Keeping her mind on graduation she hoped to put aside any thoughts she may have had about Theo. Sitting and waiting at the curbside for her was her mother. With a big grin, and wide eyes Brenda picked her spirits up in order not to let her mother see that she was lost and bothered about anything. Getting into the car her mother greeted her.

"Brenda! How's my baby girl?" Janice kissed her daughter hello.

"I'm fine. Where's Daddy?" Brenda sounded curious.

"He had to work late today." Janice hit the gas before heading for home. "So I came instead. Are we getting ready for graduation?" Janice looked over with a big smile.

"Yes Mommy. I'm getting ready for graduation." Brenda looked out the passenger side window to avoid looking at her mother, because she always knew her mother could spot when there was something wrong with her little girl.

"Good! Because I wrote everybody in the family to let them know."

"Mommy it's not a big deal." Brenda looked over at her mother with a disgusted look on her face.

"My baby is getting ready to graduate. Yes it is a big deal!" Janice stopped at a red light, and she looked over at Brenda. "You are the first to graduate from college and you don't have any kids. Shoot! I am going to yell it into every ear that will hear me."

"Please don't make such a big fuss over this. You know how I hate when you make such a big fuss over me." Brenda brushed the side of her face shaking her head and wondering what was so significant about her graduating.

"You are my prize." Janice drove diligently along the highway heading for the off-ramp to get to their house. "I wanted to have a little girl and I got her."

"That may be so, but remember that time when Aunt Jo Ann put Lindsay up against the rest of the kids in the family as the one to make the breakthrough; she ended up having a baby and dropping out of high school." Brenda sighed with a hint of nervousness.

"Brenda, you're graduating from college. That's very different from high school. At this point, you can pull down your pants and run through the streets backwards. I would still be just as proud of you as I am right now." Janice let out an excited high pitched praise to God,

"Hallelujah! You don't have a clue as to what you have truly accomplished." Janice twisted and grinned in her seat as she drove homeward.

"Mommy are you okay?" Brenda looked at her mother wondering what in the world had gotten into her.

"I'm fine baby! I'm just enjoying the fruits of my labor." Janice patted Brenda's thigh as she explained to her. "Forget about being the first female in the family to graduate college, but think about this way you have broken the cycle of non-accomplishment. Baby, you have shown every woman in this family that if you put your mind to it you can do anything."

"I never thought of it like that." Brenda rubbed her chin to think about what her mother had just relayed to her.

"You should. You're a pioneer in higher education when it comes to the women in our circle. I didn't have a chance to go, but I knew if I had a daughter, I'd make sure she had a chance."

"Mommy?" Brenda glanced over to ask her mother a question. "Why didn't you go to college?" "Back when I wanted to go money wasn't available for college like it is now. I came up in a time when getting a job was all I needed to build a secure future. By that time, I was a mother and a wife there was no time to think about going back to school. As time went on technology changed the world around us."

"So why don't you go back now?" Brenda inquired.

"The thought has crossed my mind, and I am looking at the community colleges in the area." Janice looked over at Brenda to give her the thumbs up.

"That's great!" Brenda clapped her hands excitedly for her.

After the long ride home from the airport Brenda jetted up to her room to rest her tired mind after putting on her favorite T-shirt. She fell onto her pillows and let her body just bounce up and down from the springs in her mattress. Sleeping through until the next morning she lay there thinking about the day she bought her favorite T-shirt. It was the first time she and Greg had spent the night together. They rented a hotel room in New Jersey where she lost her virginity. Realizing she didn't bring anything to wear Brenda went to this little shop in the area that sold only T-shirts. It took her a whole hour to pick out the red heart-printed shirt that read, "My heart beats for you." Looking down at the washed-out print Brenda smirked, rose up, and took the shirt off. She balled it in her hands; then tossed it in the garbage can next to her dresser. When the shirt made its swooshing plop in the garbage can Brenda realized, she mentally tossed her emotional baggage remaining from Greg. He seemed to be just an aftertaste in her thoughts right at that moment. Scratching her head, she began thinking about what in the world she was going to do when she runs into him. Letting her thoughts roll down her back, she decided to let whatever happens happen. Brenda's only thought was to fix what hurt she felt about Andrea's part in the affair that broke her heart. Lost in her thoughts Brenda's mother yelled for her from the bottom of the stairs with a loud pitch.

"Brenda! Brenda! Are you up yet?" Janice stood at the bottom of the stairs waiting for Brenda's response while she sipped her coffee.

"Yes!" Brenda rolled over in the covers to answer her mother.

"I'm getting ready to get in the shower. Why?"

"You better come down here when you're finished." Janice replied.

"Okay." Brenda pulled the covers off. Sitting up, she answered her mother, "I will only be a few minutes."

Stepping into the shower she let the warm water run against her face. Brenda let herself forget about her heartbreaks. In her midst of thoughts about all that had gone wrong over the last year, she suddenly felt blissful about life and her future. Nothing was going to stand in her way of being one of the best in the architectural field. Rushing out of the bathroom to get dressed, she then hurried down the stairs to the coffee scented kitchen. Brenda hurried in to see what the big fuss was all about; she stepped into a flood of pastel-colored balloons and dozens of red carnations accompanied by a heart-shaped box of candy with a little gray mesh box on top.

"Mommy who sent you candy and flowers?" Brenda pushed aside the many balloons in her pathway.

"Nobody I know." Janice kept sipping her coffee with a smile on her face.

"What did Daddy do?" Brenda sniffed the fragrance of the carnations on the kitchen counter.

"Nothing." Janice put down her coffee cup. "These are not for me." Janice sniffed the rich red carnations. "They're for you."

"For me!" Brenda looked shocked. "I can't imagine who could have sent this!"

"Here's the card. Read it." Janice handed Brenda the card trying to peek at who it could have been. After taking the envelope with the written message inside Brenda thought this awesome surprise must be from Theo. Preparing to read the card she thought to herself, "If I open it then I have to deal with this crap right now." Sliding her finger under the seam she pulled apart the envelope. Looking at the card, Brenda began to read. The card read,

> *"Brenda if I had everything to do over again hurting you would be the last thing*
> *that I would do. Admitting when you're wrong is hard, but my love for you makes it so*
> *easy to get on my knees and beg you to come back to me. We could do so much*
> *together as one. Please think about us, and about our forever."*

With a soft unsure smile of acceptance she walked over to the flowers to take another sniff. Standing and waiting anxiously to find out whose heart her daughter captured was chipping away at Janice's nerves. Tapping her fingers on the counter top with a rapid beat she leaned over to see the card Brenda left upside down on the counter.

"Brenda who is he?" Janice asked.

"Somebody who needs to do a lot of begging!" Brenda said.

"Poor fellow. At least he's starting out on the right foot. What's his name?"

"Theodore Shell."

"Where did you meet him?"

"I would rather not say." Brenda walked over to the stove to get a cup of coffee.

"Why?" Janice asked stirring her cup.

"Because Mommy you might not like it." Brenda sipped the hot coffee slowly.

"I'm an open-minded person. Come on give me a shot." Janice quickly noted.

"Okay." Brenda put down her coffee cup on the kitchen table. "I met him in a military club."

"You're right I don't like it." Janice stopped stirring her coffee to let the spoon twirl in the cup by itself.

"See! I told you Mommy." Brenda took another sip from her cup.

"Is he married?" Janice inquired.

"No."

"Oh god! How many babies did he have with how many different women?" Janice asked.

"None that I know of." Brenda replied.

"Well how long have you been dating him Brenda?"

"About four months, but right know things are on hold."

"Are you in love with him?" Janice sat down at the kitchen table.

"Good question. If I had to answer that truthfully, right now yes. I guess I am." Brenda confessed to her mother.

"Does he love you?" Janice asked.

"I don't know and I don't care. Right now, all I need to do is to forget about him." Brenda punched one of the balloons in front of her.

"What happened between the two of you?"

"Another woman." Brenda looked at her mother poking her lip out.

"I am so sorry sweetheart. Are you going to be okay?"

"Eventually with time and lots of shopping." Brenda smiled.

"If you want to talk about it we can." Janice warmly mentioned.

"No." Brenda abruptly wanted to change the subject. "He's not worth having a conversation about."

"Good let's open up all the goodies and get our chocolate groove on." Janice suggested with a lighthearted grin on her face to get her daughter to lighten up a little about her mishap with her beau. "Whatever he did, he sure is thinking about it hard to send you such lovely things."

"He should after what happened." Brenda muttered.

Opening the gray jewelry box with less than high hopes of finding something to really catch her attention, Brenda lifted out a tennis bracelet that made her eyes bounce in her head. Taken aback by the peace offering, Brenda held it up to the light to see its sparkling glitter. Sitting back at her kitchen table relaxed in the firm base of the chair, and eating some chocolates Janice's sweet tooth suddenly came to a sudden halt after admiring the dazzling love trinket being placed at her daughter's feet.

"Oh boy!" Janice pulled the chocolate-caramel cluster away from her mouth. "He's got taste."

"Yeah he does! I guess I should call him when I get back. I don't want him to think he didn't get my attention."

"Brenda that thing is so beautiful. You should call him to say thank you. Even if he was a jerk always try and be a lady."

"You're right. I will call, but not today. This would go perfect with my dress for the wedding."

Brenda held the bracelet up to the light as she exited the kitchen to walk up to her room to dress for the wedding. Brenda called Lee and Rachel to update them on what was going on with her. Brenda was unsure if she should be mad at Theo or just be happy that he was trying to win her back. The pulling of her heartstrings were being yanked and stretched as she thought over her decision about her mixed feelings about this. Brenda dialed the phone to call Lee, and the answering machine came on. "Hi Lee. I see you're not in as usual, but I just wanted to say Theo is begging me to come back. Call me later for the full details." Brenda then dialed Rachel's number. The phone picked up.

"Hello Rachel."

"Hello Brenda." Rachel replied.

"I got some good news Rachel."

"What Brenda?"

"Theo sent me a peace offering."

"Get out! What did he send?"

"Candy, balloons, carnations, and a tennis bracelet." Brenda laughed into the phone.

"Let's see how much this is worth. Just a second. Let me get my make-up figures out. My figures come to a phone call to thank him, a new outfit every day of the week for six months, dinner at least three times a week for a year, and he has to write five-hundred thousand times, I will never pull the wool over your eyes again."

"Oh stop Rachel."

"What are you going to do about this relationship Brenda?"

"I haven't decided yet. I really need to think about it. Just this morning I made my mind up to not get involved with anyone else right now, but after this display of admitting he was wrong maybe I should reconsider."

"Brenda, I'm not going to lecture you or try to sound negative. I just think you should leave well enough alone. I was only kidding when I said those things about letting him make it up to you. You don't need to be dealing with a lot of drama just before graduation. Girl take some time to think about what's good for you."

"Maybe you're right. Let me not deal with this mess right now. I have a wedding to go to, and I have a lot on my plate today."

"Yeah you do." Sounding off with a militant tone Rachel reminded Brenda how to attack. "Make sure you get a side of Lisa and a bite of Greg. Yep! Your plate is full. Good luck."

"Thanks! I'll need it. When I get in tonight I will call you with a full report. By the way make sure Lee doesn't forget to pick me up at the airport."

The champagne dress Rachel lent her for the wedding was perfect. The strapless gown was cool and eye-catching. It complemented Brenda's hourglass figure. The tennis bracelet from Mr. Who was the needed touch to give the dress its bubbly essence.

Chapter Twenty-Three

*I'm Glad to Know
You Care*

Brenda and her parents arrived at the church a little early to get a good parking place. On the way over to church Brenda found herself having unsurpassable doubts about events of the evening when she would encounter Greg, Lisa, and Andrea. Brenda got out of the car to go in the church hoping to speak to Andrea before the wedding. Walking up the church steps Brenda felt a warm rush take over her body. The closer she got to the door the more she felt unsure and frightened. Opening the door to walk into the church she felt a cool soothing breeze pass through her. As she stepped in the door letting it close behind her the doubts and fears had melted away. Looking around the church corridor and feeling its stillness eased her worries leaving a calm tranquil feeling within her.

Brenda found the dressing area where the wedding party was getting ready for the festivities. Taking a few quick deep breaths Brenda knocked softly not to disturb the tranquility of the church. She could hear the many voices from the other side of the door, while waiting for the door to open. Thinking about Andrea and wanting to reunite with her good friend, Brenda had an optimistic look on her face. The quick swing of the door opening to the dressing room presented Lisa, the last person she ever planned on running into just before the festive ceremony. "Well, well. Hello Brenda!" Lisa greeted Brenda with an aloof demeanor.

"Is Andrea here?" Brenda asked respectfully.

"Yes!" Lisa paused before going any further. She looked Brenda up and down in her champagne dress with an unwanted look on her face. "But she is too busy to talk to you right now." Lisa began pushing the door closed saying, "So come back later."

"I!" Brenda pushed the door with her hands to keep Lisa from shutting it in her face. "I wanted to let her know I was here!"

"She'll see that you're here when you show up to the reception okay Brenda! We're busy right now. Later!" Lisa pushed the door against Brenda's force.

"I'm sure Andrea would like to see me Lisa." Brenda shoved the door open making her way through. Brenda aggressively stated, "Excuse me! I would hate to make a scene Lisa!"

"Brenda you're right. Making a scene right now would not be the best thing. So why don't you roll away!" Lisa stepped forward to confront Brenda.

"Where would you like me to go Lisa?" Brenda chuckled.

"I'd rather not say due to the holy grounds we stand on." Lisa shook her head. "Why don't you use your imagination?"

"I already did and I can't imagine you wanting to think so ill of me. After all you're the one who stepped out of line." Brenda got savvy bringing forth some of Lee's quick responses she often heard her say. "I forgot you're the kind of bitch who breaks her leash every night to roam the streets. Oops!" Brenda put her hand over her mouth to pretend to watch what she said. "I should watch what I say in a church."

"You better watch what you say to me Brenda!" Brenda's response angered her.

"Or what Lisa! You're going to kick my butt? Better yet, you'll steal my next man. Lisa if I were you, I would get out of my face real quick all right darling?"

The ladies who were getting dressed could hear the confrontation that got louder and louder as Brenda and Lisa got madder and madder. Andrea walked out of her dressing room to find out what was going on. She saw Brenda and Lisa facing each other wrangling. In a quick pace Andrea hurried over to them before things got out of hand.

"Come on ladies!" Andrea pushed them apart stepping in between them. "Lisa back down. This is not the time or place for this. We have to put this behind us." Andrea looked at Lisa as she pleaded with her. "At least for the day ladies, please!"

"Okay! I'll go finish getting ready." Lisa replied as she walked off to finish dressing.

"Brenda!" Andrea smiled.

"Hi Andrea! I bet you thought you wouldn't see me so soon." Brenda replied.

"No, but I'm glad you're here. How are you Brenda?" Andrea asked.

"Amazingly, I'm great! And you Andrea?"

"I'm okay. I am so glad to hear that you're okay. I didn't think you were coming until your mother called to say you were going to be here."

"Under the circumstances I should have stayed away, but my mother had her say as usual, and how could I live with myself if I didn't come to see you say I do."

"I'm so happy to have you here with me." Andrea reached out hugging Brenda.

"I had to come and see you before you made the biggest step in your life." Brenda continued to say, "Remember when we would lay on your bed in your room talking about our wedding day?"

"Yeah. I would marry Michael, and you would marry—"Andrea caught herself before she blurted out Greg's name.

"Greg." Brenda responded.

"I'm sorry that I brought him up." Andrea apologized.

"It's okay. I'm not going to fall apart if I hear his name or if I see him. I have had some time to get him out of my system." Brenda smiled.

"That's good. You look absolutely beautiful Brenda."

"Thank you. However, the bride is picture perfect. I maybe beautiful, but you are so awesome. I knew you would be stunning."

"I sure have missed you, Brenda. So many nights and days would go by, and all I could do is wonder if we could get through this mess Lisa and Greg created. There were so many times I wanted to tell you, but so many things got in the way."

"I know what you mean Andrea. I need to apologize to you. A real friend in a situation like ours would have done the same thing. I had a chance to walk in your shoes, and boy let me tell you it was hard. You were right to stay out of it and let it run its course. I wasn't ready then to hear what you might have said. My ears were clogged, and my heart was weak. Let's just say I was under a love spell, and the only way to break it was dealing with Greg's cheating first hand."

"I'm glad you understand I didn't want to have to choose between my best friend and my sister. I have always hated being in the middle of conflict. You should have known that about me."

"I should have realized that Andrea, but at the same time I didn't see things as clearly as I do now. Regardless of what they did you had nothing to do with it. I'm sorry for being stupid and judgmental. Our friendship is too important to me to just let anyone take it away."

"No. I should apologize too. I could have done something, but I didn't Brenda. I felt so helpless only because there was nothing I could do to soften the hurt you would feel."

"Andrea let's forget all about yesterday's blues and get ready for your big moment. I didn't come all the way from Augusta to dwell on the past. I came here to see my best friend tie the knot."

Once the church was filled; the wedding party was ready to march. The ladies and groomsmen were waiting for the queue to be given. Brenda sat between her mother and father in a pew that was closest to the aisle. Brenda sat quietly in her champagne glittered dress. When the queue was given for the march to begin the guests looked to the back of the church as each individual couple marched down to the altar. Brenda watched on with a smile. When the time came for Greg to march down with his partner Brenda saw him from her seat. She turned her head holding it down in order not to let him see her as he passed by. Seeing him brought back feelings she felt the night he told her about Lisa. Janice noticed her daughter trying to avoid letting Greg see her. Janice tapped Brenda on the shoulder to get her attention.

"Brenda." Janice whispered in Brenda's ear. "Don't let him make you feel ashamed of being in the same room with him. Remember, you have nothing to be ashamed of Brenda. Now hold your head up and let him know what he did to you didn't break you. You have to show him you're stronger than that."

Brenda lifted her head after her mother's strong admonishing demand. Brenda looked on as he passed with his escort. She admitted to herself he was certainly a fine brother, but he was a cold bastard who could pull the carpet from underneath you if you're not looking. Greg and his escort reached the altar to stand alongside the other members of the wedding party. Greg took his place next to the other groomsmen. Looking out into the audience of guests and friends, he looked just past the twelfth row to see Brenda seated between her mother and father. He was locked in on her sexy presence. All the while, he had not noticed that Lisa his wife of two months had begun her Matron-of-Honor March down the aisle. Greg stretched out his neck trying to get a closer look at Brenda.

When Lisa made her way to the altar to take her place, she noticed Greg had not looked over in her direction once. She looked over hoping he would feel her looking at him, but he was lost in another world out in the audience of people in the church. Lisa looked out at the audience, hoping to find what he might be looking at. When she looked out in the audience, she found that his nose was pointed in the direction where Brenda was sitting. Lisa rolled her eyes clearly upset and bothered that he was looking at her.

The bride's march began and all the guests and friends stood to receive Andrea in the holy presence of marriage, commitment, and fidelity. However, Greg and Lisa were not in the receiving mode at the time. The altar Andrea would soon approach was surrounded with jealously and regrets. Greg finally came back from his trip around the world to look over at Lisa and smile at her. Lisa smiled at him, and then suddenly her face faded to an angry hateful scowl. Greg shrugged his shoulders wondering what was wrong, as Andrea was making her way down the aisle. Lisa turned her head looking away from him. Greg was wondering what could be the matter. He looked out in the audience again, looking at Brenda as if it was the first time he had ever seen her face.

Soon after the, I do's the reception got underway at the Manson Hall. The music was pumping, and the dance floor was full. Everyone was having a great time, even Brenda. While, her mother mingled and her father sat and ate she let herself get lost in the moment. She danced with every single guy in the room. Young or old she flowed with the music in her champagne dress that made her glow in the lighting from above.

Just as things were winding down Brenda sat at the table where her father was seated. She looked over at him smiling with an unfolding measure of true happiness that seemed to come over her at that moment. Barry, Brenda's dad had just finished his third plate of red beans and ribs. He wiped his hands so he could pick up his glass of ice water to wash down the hearty meal he had just put away. Barry looked over at Brenda to mention to her how beautiful she was. "Pumpkin you look so pretty tonight." Barry smiled at her then continued to say, "I know how hard it must have been coming tonight and trying to keep your chin up."

"No Daddy it wasn't that hard after all." Brenda smiled leaning over to kiss her father on the cheek.

"You know Brenda you are just like your mother—so strong and positive. I am so glad you are my mighty little girl." Barry relaxed in his chair and began rubbing his full stomach.

"What Daddy?" Brenda looked at her father with a suspicious glare in her eyes wondering what he was up to. "Daddy is there something you want to say?"

"What makes you say that? A father just can't sit and talk and chat like old chums? What only you and your mother can share a heart to heart!"

"Daddy wait! You know I can't talk to you about boy stuff."

"Why not! I have feelings too."

"Okay Daddy what is it?" Brenda sat waiting for her father to come clean.

"I know Greg hurt you, but why didn't you come to me?" Barry squeezed a nearby napkin waiting for her response.

"I!" Brenda was taken aback by his concern over her broken heart. "Daddy– I didn't think you would understand. Better yet I—"

"You don't think men suffer heartbreak like young women. I have some experience in that category. Don't think your mother was the only woman that I have ever loved Brenda."

"I guess at the time I didn't even consider you as someone I could talk too. When a woman gets her heart broken she runs to another woman. Most women don't run to a man unless he might be gay or something like that." Brenda clinched her teeth hoping the explanation she had just given her father would explain her keeping him absent in her emotional turmoil.

"Well, I'm not gay because you're here and your mother keeps me straight." Barry giggled off his little joke. "Brenda, I am your father. I have known you from the moment your mother and I found out about you. You have been my gift from heaven. I have always wanted a little girl. Why? Because your two knucklehead brothers drove me crazy being rough and untamed. Do you have any idea how hard it was to raise two monsters?"

"No Daddy I don't." Brenda sat wondering what in the heck her father was trying to say to her.

"Well, when we found out we were going to have our third child, I prayed every day for a little girl; a sweet little girl and I got her. You!" Barry wiped the corners of his mouth to try to get Brenda to understand what he was trying to say.

"Daddy, I'm waiting. Is there something wrong?" Brenda looked at her father trying to gather his thoughts.

"Brenda what I'm trying to say is that," Barry blurted out what he had on his chest for over a year after finding out what Greg had done to his daughter, "that son-of-butcher Greg, I would have loved to put my foot in his tail for you. I don't mean to use these words I'm using, but a father can only take so much."

"Daddy watch your tone." Brenda let out an excited plea to keep down his voice.

"I hate to bring this up here at Andrea's wedding, but that dirty nasty bastard has been watching you all night. I caught him looking at you in the church, and when you were dancing I caught his doggish tail looking at you from the bar. The only thing that's keeping me from pimp slapping his tail is the crowd in here."

"Daddy don't get bent out of shape over him."

Brenda smiled from ear to ear. She was pleased to hear her father wanting to protect her from her pain. She was honored and touched all in the same breath. "Daddy, I love you!"

Brenda whisked her arms around her father's neck kissing him on the cheek. All the while, Barry kept an eye on Greg over in the corner looking at Brenda. Barry had a bullish red tint in his eyes with the thoughts of charging at Greg, but his daughter's warm hug held him back. Brenda eased up on her gripping hug from around her father. She smelled a hint of an alcoholic aroma on his breath.

"Have you been drinking Daddy?"

"I had one, or five." Barry let out a trembling belch. "Okay! I feel a little mellow. Don't worry darling I'll be cool. I won't do anything to embarrass you or your mother. I know I don't drink much, but a drink here and there won't hurt anybody."

"Daddy, I have never seen you quite like this before." Looking at him amazed that he was tipsy; Brenda was too through as she thought what else could happen tonight.

"I just had to get something to mellow me out. After looking at that toothy loathing fangy, beastie bastard looking at you as if you were prey; I just wanted to jump on his back and eat 'em up. You are my baby girl, and I will do whatever it takes to keep you happy." Barry rubbed both of his hands together looking at the table with a somewhat shameful look on his face.

"I'm glad to know you care about me, Daddy! This moment means more to me than you will ever know. Let me go find Mommy so we can go home, okay?"

"Okay! While you go find your mother, I'll get me another plate of those ribs and red beans." Barry smiled and Brenda walked off to find her mother.

Chapter Twenty-Four
Handling Old Business

From across the room Greg sat staring at Brenda as she walked through the crowd to make her way to the band playing on the stage. She stood still looking around the room looking for her mother in the crowd of people dancing and mingling in the hall. Greg was making his way between the tables to get to her. Lisa was nearby watching his every step in Brenda's direction.

Greg walked over to her very slowly with one hand in one pocket and a drink in the other. It was very hard for him to keep his distance during the wedding, but he had to make his presence known to her. Greg couldn't stay away from her; he needed to be near her. Brenda stood with her back to him unaware of his approach. Inadvertently turning in his direction Brenda was stunned, and shocked at his sudden appearance so close to her person. She was not ready to face him yet, but she had to let things happen as they should—better now than later.

"Hey Brenda." Greg smiled.

"Greg hi." Brenda kept a plain unmoved expression on her face.

"I came over just to say hello, and I just wanted to let you know you look great." Greg nodded.

"Thank you Greg." Brenda looked over his shoulder hoping to see her mother off in the crowd behind him, but she really wanted to keep her emotions bland and unprompted from his person-to-person visit.

"Umm! I hear you're graduating in few days Brenda."

"Yeap! I finally made it despite all of the obstacles in my way. You know what I mean Greg." Brenda refocused her eyes on him.

"Good for you! Brenda you deserve the best!" Greg said sipping his wine as his thoughts flirted with the idea of wanting to kiss her on the lips.

"You're right Greg. I do deserve the best." Brenda was not impressed with his phony appearance of suddenly caring about her well-being. "What do you want Greg?"

"I was hoping that you would give me a chance to say I'm sorry." Greg brushed his hand against her shoulder hoping to spark a smile.

"No need to say sorry. I've moved past all that now. Some of us have grown up Greg."

"Then–" He paused giving his glass to a passing waiter collecting glasses and dishes for the guest in the hall, and he turned to say to her, "dance with me Brenda."

"Please!" Brenda stepped back away from him in total disbelief of his request. "Dance with my enemy."

"I thought you got past all that?" Greg reminded her of what she had stated earlier.

"I did! I'm not going to allow myself to pleasure your need to see if I still have feelings for you. What are you trying to do?" Using an agitated tone with him, Brenda continued to say, "To see if you still got it Greg?"

"No Brenda. I just want to dance with the most beautiful woman in the room."

"Greg!" Brenda waited a few seconds to think about it. She allowed herself to humble him; letting him assume all was fine. "What have I got to lose because I already lost you?"

Greg looked into her eyes as he held his hand out to escort her to the dance floor. Brenda slowly extended her hand to him feeling somewhat shaky; wondering if this might be the right thing to do. Keeping a cautious distance while they danced, Brenda wanted to make sure she kept clear of any possibilities of any reoccurring emotional flashbacks of wanting him or missing him in any way. Brenda reminded herself that this man broke her heart into a million pieces. It was a must that she proves to him he had not blemished her will, or her perseverance to move on without him.

Dancing to the tuneful beat Greg kept his eyes focused on every aspect of her face: watching her every blink; the way her eyes drifted from side to side, and even the way her earrings dangled on her lobe as she swayed to the music. Lisa watched from the distance with an uncertainty if Greg might still be in love with her. Together on the floor they appeared to be the just right couple, as the music played the two danced in step with each other. Brenda's shapely dress that gloved her and Greg's handsome exterior made the two a wonderful delight to see. As they embraced each other it led one to assume a hot passion ran strong through their hearts. Greg felt Brenda's warm skin against his cheek as they danced. He took the liberty to speak openly to her while they danced to the melody being pitched out by the band.

"I'm glad you and Andrea worked things out. I never meant to put the two of you at opposite ends of the table." Greg coolly conveyed to her.

"You did for a while, but we found our way back to each other." Brenda replied.

"That is so good to hear." Greg let his hand cuff her waist to feel her defined curve that reminded him of the beautiful body she had hidden underneath her champagne dress. "What are your plans after graduation Brenda?"

"I'm not sure. Being single and not having any commitments I find myself thinking about many things. Right now, I'm going to enjoy every day like a party." Brenda smiled because she liked what she had just said.

"Will you be moving back home after school?"

"Just for a little while. I have no intentions of hanging around our neighborhood for very long. I have too many bad memories right now. I think a change would be good for me. Don't you think so Greg?"

"I can't answer that Brenda, but I will say it would be nice to see you from time to time if you're going to be home." Greg had a curious yet wondrous look on his face hoping she would give him an open invitation.

"Maybe, but I don't think so. I wouldn't feel comfortable hanging around a married man."

"Brenda, I know I'm married. Still, I can't lie knowing I screwed up the best thing in my life. What was I thinking when I did what I did to you Brenda?"

"What?" Brenda gently and quietly replied wondering where that statement came from.

"I have to be honest. Just a few months ago I realized letting you go was the biggest mistake I ever made." Greg rubbed her shoulder.

"I'm glad you realized what mistakes you've made." Brenda shifted her shoulder away from his affectionate touch and continued to step to the music without missing a beat. "However, Greg when we make mistakes we have to live with them."

"That's what I thought Brenda, but some mistakes you can fix with a little hard work. I know you believe in working hard for what you want." Greg pulled in his lips to moisten them.

"Good luck Greg with whatever you hope to accomplish."

"I don't need luck Brenda."

"Then what do you need?" Brenda looked at Greg and laughed. She continued to say, "You already have a wife you love, a child. Oh! You finally got a job. You have what you have always wanted lots of responsibility. I can't imagine what else you want."

"You can't imagine what I want Brenda?" Greg stopped dancing to look at her.

"No Greg what!" Brenda pulled herself away from his embrace. She shook her head wondering what he was trying to say. "What Greg?"

"I want you Brenda." Greg stood looking at her waiting for her to respond.

The room kept dancing around her as she downloaded Greg's abrupt confession of wanting her back. The music played on and Brenda stood motionless. She backed away bumping into the people dancing around her. Grabbing her chest she ran off into the lobby of the reception hall. Greg rushed behind her hoping she would express some interest of maybe getting together again. He yelled out her name in the crowded room thinking she would stop once she heard her name.

"Brenda wait a minute!" Greg yelled repeatedly.

The people who saw them wondered what was going on as he yelled and pushed through the crowd of people in his way. Greg finally caught up with Brenda in the lobby as she tried to leave the building. He reached out grabbing her hand.

"Brenda please! Hear me out!" Greg pleaded with her.

"Greg, I can't deal with this!" Brenda yelled back at him.

"Why not think about it Brenda! Don't tell me you haven't thought about us just once?"

"Think about what Greg? Wanting to get with you again? Yes, I have over a million times, but each time brings me back to the night you tore my heart out." Brenda's eyes were filled with tears, and like rain the drops began to fall alongside her beautifully painted face.

"Brenda we can get past all the old hurts only if you want too. Just think about us together again, you and me, a couple."

"There is no us! You're a married man with a child. Or did you forget?"

"I know, but I don't have a marriage anymore. What Lisa and I have has been one big nightmare."

"A nightmare you have to live with Greg. I'm not going to get caught up in your life again. I refuse to make the same mistake again."

"I'm not asking you too. Brenda— I just want you back in my life."

"No Greg!" Brenda pulled her hand away from his grip. She began hitting her chest to boldly express to him the pain she felt. "You slapped me in the face with Lisa, and then to find out she's having a baby you both decided to keep. When I was pregnant every word out of your mouth was, I'm not ready for this shit.

You drove me to the abortion clinic to get rid of our mistake." Pointing at him, Brenda continued to say, "Let me tell you something. I am not going to be a fool twice for anyone."

"Then why did you accept my gifts?" Greg asked.

"What!" Brenda's loud angry demeanor came to a halt. Confused by the question she stopped and began to think while looking at Greg to say, "Gifts!"

"The bracelet on your arm!" Greg looked down at her arm.

"You sent this to me? But I thought it was!" Brenda looked at her arm trying to figure out the mistake she made when she thought Theo had sent the bracelet.

"I figured you would be coming to the wedding. So, I wanted to do something romantic, something to show you I was serious about what I was feeling." Greg reached out to hold her hand, while warmly wrapping his long fingers around her forearm. "Believe me Brenda, I know what I want, what I need, but most of all I know what I lost. Looking in your eyes I can see you still love me."

"You're right Greg. I still love you. I can't lie."

Greg leaned over kissing her on her lips. Brenda was stunned by his kiss, and she pulled away without feeling what she once had for him. The love and passion she had once felt erupted into absolute disgust. She thought to herself, "He thinks he could just win me with a few gifts and some wormy words that make me feel like I am easy."

"Get off me." Brenda wiped her mouth with the back of her hand. "Like I said I still love you, but that doesn't mean I want you. You're the last man on earth I would ever give a second chance too." She dangled the bracelet on her arm and then looked at him with a smile on her face. "Thanks for the bracelet you asshole!"

Brenda rushed back into the hall where the guests were still dancing and enjoying themselves. She tried to make her way through the crowd back to her table where her mother and father were sitting and talking with each other. Just before Brenda stepped off the dance floor to get to her table Lisa walked up from behind her with an unpleasant look on her face. Lisa stood nearby at the time Brenda and Greg had their exchange of words in the lobby. She saw Greg kiss her on the mouth, which made Lisa storm off to the ladies room to vent in private. She failed to see Brenda resist Greg's attempt to win her back. When she came out of the bathroom she made it her mission to let Brenda have a piece of her mind. Lisa was beside herself.

Brenda saw her mother just ahead of her sitting at the table and enjoying a drink with her dad. Janice looked up from her conversation with her husband to see Brenda heading toward them. Janice smiled waving at Brenda. From the side, Lisa cut Brenda off just steps away from greeting her mother. Janice saw there was going to be some conflict on the part of Lisa just by looking at her face. Lisa startled Brenda in her quest to join her parents at their table. Brenda stopped in her tracks. She looked at Lisa wondering what she wanted. Brenda had no idea she had seen Greg kiss her just moments ago in the lobby. She just assumed she was bitter that she came to the wedding. Lisa shouted at Brenda to make sure the music playing wouldn't drown out what she had to say to her.

"Brenda!" Lisa yelled.

"What do you want?" Brenda responded in a mildly bewildered tone.

"I want you to stay away from Greg!" Lisa stepped forward to confront Brenda as closely as she could. "He doesn't want you anymore!" Lisa vehemently expressed audibly.

"What!" Brenda let her hair down and attacked back in words and attitude. "You need to tell him to stay away from me!"

"Well, I'm telling you first." Lisa put her finger in Brenda's face. "Stay clear of my husband."

"Lisa, I've given you my leftovers. What else do you want?" Brenda replied.

Janice stood up at her table with a concerned look on her face. She knew things between Lisa and Brenda had come to a head the way the ladies were yelling at each other on the dance floor among the many that were dancing and not noticing the commotion, and those who stood idly watching the ladies go at it. However, Andrea was signing her marriage license in the back of the hall with her groom, the pastor, and her parents. They had no idea of the events that were unveiling on the dance floor. Greg was in the lobby trying to pick his ego up off the floor. Brenda really shattered his hopes in trying to get with her again.

Janice shook Barry to bring his attention to the argument on the floor. Barry attempted to get up from his seat to stop the ladies from arguing. However, Janice felt Brenda needed to handle this on her own. Janice stood watching knowing her daughter needed to finish what was left to fester over the last few months while she was away at college. Lisa became frantic by the comments Brenda kept throwing back at her to counterattack the things she had thrown at her. Lisa knew the things Brenda had said to her were true, and the truth was tearing her up inside. "Brenda, you are such a funky bitch!"

"Bitch Lisa! No!" Brenda was not going to let Lisa get away with calling her a bitch knowing she was the one hurt over what she and Greg had done to her behind her back. Brenda lashed back. "You lay down with a man you know is with someone else, and you dare call me a bitch! Okay, I'll be your bitch, but that makes you a nasty bitch with three baby daddies. So now!"

Lisa lashed out by slapping Brenda across the face, and the music that was playing suddenly stopped. Everyone on the dance floor stopped dancing, and the many guests and friends looked on as the ladies began to go at it. After Lisa slapped Brenda, she reacted with a backhand to her jaw. Lisa fell backward onto the dance floor. Janice saw what her daughter had done to Lisa and began shouting at the top of her lungs, "Brenda, whoop her ass!" Janice stepped on a chair to stand on top of the table to see her daughter let Lisa have it. "Beat the hell out of her. Teach her ass a lesson Brenda." Barry looked at his wife wondering if she had drank more than he did. Lisa tried to get up off the floor before Brenda had a chance to make it over to her. She looked down at Lisa. Brenda shook her head to make fun of her before telling her off.

"I told you that you was a nasty bitch. Lisa the next time I'll kick your ass for fun not over a man. If you ain't heard a real woman wouldn't lower herself to the ground over some dick like you did right here in front of all these people. You have a nice night now." Brenda turned and walked over to her parents' table where Janice stepped down off the table to hug her daughter.

The morning after the wedding Brenda and her mother were sitting having breakfast together at the kitchen table. Brenda was lost in her thoughts over Greg and Theo. Looking sad and furious all in one her mother saw that her daughter had some worries on her mind that had nothing to do with school or the fight she had with Lisa the night before. Janice pulled her coffee cup away from her mouth taking just a few seconds to analyze her daughter.

"Brenda what's on your mind?" Janice asked looking at her with a motherly smile.

"Nothing important Mommy." Brenda replied sadly, twisting her fork in her eggs.

"That's not what your face says. You can always talk to me about anything. I always say if you do not have anything good to say about anybody come sit next to me." Janice waited for Brenda to laugh, but she kept twisting her fork in her eggs. "Things can't be that bad Brenda."

"Really! Nothing's wrong Mommy." Brenda mumbled.

"Okay. I have something on my mind that I've wanted to talk to you about." Janice said.

"Yes." Brenda replied.

"I didn't want to bring this up with the wedding and all, but why didn't you tell me about what Greg and Lisa had done to you?"

"Nothing to tell." Brenda replied with no expression on her face.

"You mean to tell me the man you have been in love with since high school cheated with your best friend's sister, and you don't have anything to say?" Janice looked stunned.

"What was I supposed to do? Beg him to stay with me after what he had done to me?" Brenda looked frustrated and bothered by the subject matter.

"No Brenda. I'm not saying that. It's just that when I told you to be a strong woman, I didn't mean you couldn't mope or cry about getting your heart broken." Janice reached across the table to firmly hold her daughter's hand. "You're only human baby."

"I did mope and cry. The beginning of the school year was very hard for me. I almost didn't get on the plane the day I left. There were days I didn't want to get out of bed, but I had too. I turned down so many dates; it was ridiculous. Lee and Rachel were beginning to think I might have turned gay over what happened between Greg and I." Brenda confessed to her mother with a somber face.

"So did you get him out of your system Brenda?"

"Yes I did. It was rather quick." Brenda let her fork hit her plate and continued to say, "Then I met Theo, but things didn't turn out exactly the way I planned."

"What happened?" Janice asked.

"Well, what didn't happen? Just when you think you have a good catch, the catch had already been caught. His girlfriend showed up on his door when I was there. The rest is history."

"Is this the guy who sent the flowers and bracelet?"

"I wish. Greg did."

"What!" Janice was surprised at Brenda's reply.

"He told me last night at the reception."

"What's with Lisa and the baby if he's sending you flowers and jewelry?"

"He claimed that he doesn't love Lisa anymore."

"I hope you didn't believe that bull." Janice waited for her daughters' answer.

"No I didn't."

"You kept the bracelet right?"

"Yep!" Brenda replied with a smile.

"Good girl. Never give back the jewelry. It's his loss. You'll eventually find somebody who can appreciate how beautiful and smart you are." Janice tapped Brenda's chin winking at her.

"I know. I guess right now I need to concentrate on me. A relationship is not in my future these days, maybe when the time is right."

"That's my baby girl. Brenda things will get better, but you have to give it sometime. He's out there and he's going through some thangs like you, and believe me when you two find each other you'll know it's real. Besides, you'll need a nice bracelet like that to wear when you met him."

"Great Mommy!"

"Brenda don't settle for just any old thing, because you have to understand that you're young. Live a little. Don't tie yourself down too soon or too fast. Life is waiting for you to live, so what's the rush?"

"I don't know. I thought being in a committed relationship would give me wholeness as a woman. I just want what you and Daddy have a happily ever after."

"Honey—you sure have a lot to learn. Your father and I make this relationship look easy, but there is nothing easy about being with the same person for thirty-years. We have our ups and downs like any other couple. We just choose to keep them civil and on the down low. In a nutshell, love has to do with sharing; caring; understanding; but most of all both of you wanting it to work no matter what."

"I didn't think you and Daddy argued."

"We do Brenda, but when the time is right. Nobody's perfect not even me. Marriage is something you have to be ready for and if you haven't lived life to its fullest for yourself to see all you can see, feel and experience how could you bring these things to your marriage or a relationship? Without them you have nothing to guide you or refer to when you take that step. You need to know what's good for you before you know what's good for the other person in your life. Brenda did you catch that?"

"Strangely enough I did. Handling my old business helps me understand how to handle my new business. I got it!" Brenda smiled and finished her eggs.

Chapter Twenty-Five
Decisions–Decisions

With only two days to go before graduation Brenda found herself in a love triangle that had become one big theater production that involved suspense, hate, and a conspiracy to get rid of her indefinitely at any cost. Having to endure late night phone calls with heavy breathing on the other end of the phone, to having her mother's life threatened if she didn't stop seeing Theo was starting to weigh on Brenda's mind. Shauna went as far as slashing Lee's tires simply because she was Brenda's friend. She was going to do whatever it took to make Brenda understand that if she continues to see Theo, she had her to deal with.

Up in Rachel's room where the ladies sat trying to contrive a plan to get Shauna off Brenda's back the ladies were discussing the problem at hand among themselves. Brenda was detectably upset at what she was going through.

"I can't believe this. Why can't she just leave me alone!" Brenda frantically paced around the room with one hand on one hip and the other rubbing her tense neck.

"Because she wants Theo all to herself." Rachel kicked off her shoes to get comfortable on the pillows that decorated her bed. "She seems unbalanced. If I were you, I would leave him alone." Rachel advised with a hint of concern in her voice.

"Why Rachel because she wants me too! I'm not leaving him unless it's my choice to leave. I ran when Lisa and Greg got together, but I won't this time." Brenda stopped pacing to look at herself in the mirror on the wall. "I believe him when he tells me she means nothing to him."

"That's all good, but what is he doing to put a stop to this?" Expressing her true concern Rachel eased to the edge of her bed sitting up looking at Brenda as she looked in the mirror. "This girl is getting a little too close for comfort. She called your mother to tell her she was going to kill her if you don't stop seeing Theo; then she got speeding tickets in your name, and don't forget running up your credit cards."

"I know, but Theo has been trying to get in contact with Shauna. She won't talk to him unless he plans on coming back to her." Brenda said.

"Brenda how did she get your wallet?" Rachel asked.

"I must have left it at Theo's house the night we fell out. At least I reported it to the credit card companies. It was a good thing I was in New York at the time when those charges were made."

"What about the speeding tickets?" Rachel added with an eager tone.

"When I go to the courthouse in the morning to file for a restraining order against her, I'll show them the police report I made about my wallet." Brenda smiled, but inside she was unsure of what might happen.

"Good!" Rachel blurted out.

"I am so glad the tickets she got were issued when I was in New York. I wish I had proof it was Shauna. I would bury her so deep the devil could smell her feet."

"You're going to have to do something quick Brenda. Something tells me she's out to destroy you." Rachel rose up from her bed to get a snack. "I was right! Mr. Dick got a hold on her, and she got it bad." Rachel looked behind her to see Brenda holding her head down trying to think.

"If that's true then that nut got a lot of issues." Brenda started shaking her head with a baffled look on her face.

"You're right. She does have a lot of issues, and you're one of them Brenda." Rachel stood across the room with a serious frown on her face.

"I know." Brenda let her head hang in her hands.

"You better watch your back because I'm pretty sure she has a final ending to all of this."

"I'm sure she does Rachel."

Theo and Brenda agreed to spend a quiet evening dining out together. With Shauna lurking around every corner Brenda kept a full view of her surroundings. Theo could see how uptight Brenda was because of the situation. He wanted to reassure her of his commitment to her, but especially to show her how much he was in love with her. With all that was going on, Theo was hoping their night together would bring about a long lived relationship for years to come. Sitting in the small restaurant on one of Augusta's beautiful colonial-themed streets in the downtown area, Theo and Brenda sat enjoying their dessert after their exquisite dinner. Brenda twirled her fork in her caramel cheesecake lost in her thoughts. Theo looked over at her to see that she was preoccupied. He laid down his fork and cuffed his hands together.

"It's good to be out with you Brenda." He said.

"Same here." Brenda looked up from her plate to respond.

"Are you ready for graduation Brenda?"

"Yes! It's been the only thing to keep my mind off of all the things going on."

"I don't know if that's good or bad." Theo looked fuddled when she finished her statement.

"Neither. It wasn't meant to come off as a bad or good thing Theo." Brenda replied.

"Well, since we're talking about graduation, I was hoping we could talk about what's going to happen to us after that."

"Nothing." Brenda turned to stare out of the restaurant window hoping to avoid the question he asked her. "I graduate and then I leave for New York ."

"What about us?" Theo quickly replied.

"What about us?" Brenda turned to look at Theo. "Why don't you tell me?"

"I was hoping we could maybe be more than just girlfriend and boyfriend." Theo looked very optimistic.

"Go on Theo. Don't stop. I want to hear this." Brenda gave him her undivided attention as he went on to tell her what he had on his mind.

"I know things aren't perfect, but I do love you very much."

"That's good to know. At this point, love hasn't been working in my best interest Theo."

"That's not true Brenda!"

"It is true Theo." Brenda hurtfully let out how she felt about his response to her. "Greg broke my heart and now your ex-girlfriend."

"No Brenda, my ex-lover. She was never my girlfriend."

"Okay. Your ex-lover is trying to make me leave you. I have taken a lot from her in the last few weeks. I don't know how much more I can take."

"I promise I'll get her to stop Brenda." Theo pleaded with her to understand. "You just have to give me some time to get through to her."

"I don't think you can. She's stuck to you like white on rice. As long as I am around things won't get any better."

"Please don't think like that." Theo reached across the table leaning forward in his chair to reach out his hand to touch the tips of her fingers.

"Unless she slips up in her mission to exile me—" With anger in her tone Brenda continued to say, "I can't prove she's stalking me."

"Brenda, relax. Things are going to ease up."

"I can't seem to stop getting angry at what's happing to me."

"Well, I guess my surprise won't be a welcomed keepsake then. Look under the coffee cup next to you."

Brenda lifted the porcelain cup up from the saucer, and underneath was a beautiful ring that sparkled. The pleasant surprise left her flabbergasted. "Oh my goodness!" Brenda's face gleamed with excitement. "Theo it's beautiful. This is —" Brenda tripped over her words trying to speak. "Listen for a second. I want you in my life forever and a day. I was hoping the circumstances could have been different, but they aren't. All that I know is that I am head over heels in love with you Brenda James. Don't let us die. Will you marry me? A perfect fit. I thought so." Theo smiled from cheek to cheek.

"Theo this is so sudden. I need to think about this."

"I understand. Just let me know before you graduate."

Rachel and Lee were sitting on a bench under the old oak tree that stood in the middle of Peaton's campus. The ladies were enjoying the warm air, hot fudge sundaes, and the bright moonlight. They sat talking about Rachel accepting Phillip's offer.

"Rachel, I would take the damn job." Lee replied as she licked some fudge off her spoon. She looked over at Rachel and continued to say, "Ain't nothing like starting on the top girl!" Lee smiled at her.

"I hear you, but I wouldn't be earning it on my own merits. Every businesswoman wants to be taken seriously when she walks in a room." Rachel licked a string of fudge off her top lip.

"Dealing with men in relationships is hard enough. Somehow dealing with them on a business level is even rougher. You're never treated equally, and I have to keep it real. I need to build my own path." Rachel scooped a spoonful of ice cream out of her cup to eat.

"The path has already been paved Rachel. Remember, you're the top guy's pet."

"That's what's wrong with it." Rachel replied.

"What?" Lee turned looking at her with a dumb look on her face. "I don't see anything wrong with it."

"Think about it Lee. The pet could be hauled off to the pound for a new one."

"Looking at it that way, you have a point."

"Check this out. Business and pleasure never mix no matter what. Besides, if my parents found out what has been going on between Phillip and me, they would lock me up until I turned fifty."

Catching her breath, then eating another scoop of ice cream Rachel had a sudden uncomfortable thought. She turned to look at Lee. "Oh! Don't let me forget my father and my brothers. They would hunt Phillip down like an animal and gut him like a wild boar." Rachel folded in her thoughts of Phillip getting beat up by her family.

"If you're worried about what your family thinks then you better stay in your place." Lee chastised Rachel jokingly as if she were a child.

"That's not it Lee."

"Then what Rachel?"

"My parents raised me with morals. They always wanted me to make decisions that I could live with. I wouldn't want to do anything to make them think they didn't do a good job at raising me. I don't want to slap them in the face like that."

"I take it you've made a decision Rachel."

"Yes! Guess I did."

As the ladies finished their fudge sundaes, along came Brenda strolling down the walkway headed for her room. Light headed and dazzled, Brenda kept looking at the marquis-cut three-carat diamond ring with four little diamonds in a single row on each side of the marvelous rock. It was stunning in all its glitter as it sparkled on her finger. She enjoyed the airy feeling that came from being proposed to. Though she was unable to see Rachel and Lee under the oak tree, the ladies noticed her walking toward them.

"Hey Brenda!" Lee shouted.

"Who's that?" Brenda responded wondering where the voice had come from.

"It's me Lee."

"And Rachel!" Rachel shouted. "Over here under the tree."

"What's going on ladies?" Brenda asked.

"Nothing much. We're just enjoying a nice night under the old oak tree." Rachel replied.

"How was dinner with Theo, Brenda?" Lee asked.

"Look." Brenda lifted her hand to show Rachel and Lee. The light in the campus square was just enough to catch the sparkle of the diamond.

"Brenda it's beautiful." Rachel jeered.

"It is everything a girl wishes for." With an unmistakable dejected timber in her voice Brenda continued, "The dinner, the ring, the best sex ever, and the man. Still, I'm not happy."

"Brenda don't let Shauna ruin this for you." Patting her on the back Rachel felt her pain.

"Rachel– she already did. When you have to fight to be with someone the fight will always continue somehow."

"I love the thrill in a challenge" Lee conveyed.

"Love is supposed to bring happiness and the other frills that go along with it. The love Theo and I share brought along Shauna. In other words, it has become a nightmare!" Brenda replied in frustration.

"So why did you take the ring?" Rachel inquired.

"Rachel why do you always ask why?" Brenda threw out a sarcastic question towards Rachel.

"Because I want to know!" Rachel spat her attitude towards Brenda. "Getting funky?"

"I am not getting funky. I'm sorry. It seemed to feel right. Theo completely came out of left field with this. I had not planned to see him anymore after graduation. I told you guys I was going to break it off." Brenda looked at them feeling as if they missed something she said. "Didn't I tell you guys that?"

"No!" Rachel and Lee looked at each other and responded at the same time. "You didn't!"

"It must have slipped my mind with this crazy stuff going on." Brenda scratched her head.

"You're going to have put all that stuff aside for now because this man thinks you're going to marry him." Rachel said.

"I know!" Brenda replied.

"Brenda don't put him off." Rachel advised Brenda of what she had to keep in mind. "After tomorrow we graduate and he's expecting an answer by then. So?"

"Yeah Brenda, so what are you going to do?" Lee chide in.

"What can I do but say yes!" Brenda replied.

"Yes!" Rachel shouted objectively to Brenda's response.

"What's wrong with yes?" Brenda was shocked at Rachel's response. "I do love him."

"Brenda, you haven't been around the block enough to know if this could be the one." Lee added.

"Lee, I'm not basing love on sex like you." Brenda responded with an angry face.

"I'm going to ignore your defensive nonsense. I'm just saying that you need to live a little more." Lee calmly stated.

"I've lived enough, and this is what I want!" Brenda's anger grew.

"Didn't you just say you weren't going to see him after graduation?" Rachel replied.

"Yeah, but that was before I thought our relationship wasn't going anywhere." Sounding simply unsure of her reasons for continuing to see him, Brenda kept coming up with excuses for her wanting to still be with him. "Rachel come on how often does a girl get a marriage proposal?"

"I've had a few guys propose to me." Rachel pleaded with Brenda to see she wasn't ready for such a big step. "Still, I had to realize that I wasn't ready for that step. Don't you want to buy your first car, get your own apartment, and live on your own Brenda?"

"Yes!" Brenda defended her decision to the end. "Theo and I can do all that together."

"No, you can't!" Rachel abruptly expressed.

"Why not?" Brenda took offense to her answer.

"Because we're not talking about him. We're talking about you. Question Brenda!"

"Sure Rachel." Brenda said.

"How well do you know his family?" Rachel asked.

"Not very well. I haven't met anyone yet, but tomorrow his sister will be in town to meet me." Brenda smiled.

"Okay how much did he really tell you about Shauna?" Rachel asked.

"Enough!" Brenda blurted out.

"Just as I thought bits and pieces of the truth!" Rachel got up in a frustrated state shaking her head in total disapproval of the matter at hand to throw away her empty fudge cup in the trash.

"Let's not do this!" Brenda said.

"Let's not!" Lee stepped in with her two-cents.

"Lee– I don't need you jumping in this too!" Brenda replied.

"I know my opinions aren't always taken seriously, but what Greg did to you is still affecting your judgment." Lee whispered.

"You're right." Brenda shrugged her shoulders looking at Lee as if she were a joke. "Your opinions aren't always taken seriously."

"Then I suggest you take this one." Lee looked at Brenda with a hard serious look about her face. "Letting the past dictate your future is a cocktail for disaster, especially if you haven't completely gotten over the past."

Brenda knew Lee was right, but she did not want to deal with the truth. "I need some sleep." Brenda stood up and headed for her dorm room.

"You're right!" Lee shouted at Brenda as she walked off. "Your head is in a fog. Some sleep would clear a path to what you really need to do about this. You think you can rekindle what you and Greg had. It's over! Stop acting like you have one foot in the grave."

"Good night, Lee!" Brenda waved her off as she headed up the path to the dorms.

"Good night Brenda!" Lee yelled at her as she got farther away. "Oh! By the way don't get stuck on dumb because you're going about this all wrong. Decisions, decisions are what you have to make in this life. Just make sure they are one's you can live with!"

Chapter Twenty-Six
How Thangs
Clear Up!

After a long night of tossing and turning in their sleep the ladies had so much to deal with before graduation. Brenda and Lee slept in late after their heart-to-heart talk under the old oak tree in the campus yard the night before. Lee awoke to the sunlight shining in her face from across the room. The window shade was slightly open. She rolled over to look at the clock. Tasting her morning breath; she rose feeling sluggish as she tried to get to the bathroom to brush away the awful taste in her mouth. As she dragged her sleepy, weak body toward the bathroom, a loud knock at the door suspended her focus on getting to the bathroom. Lee answered the door with the sleep still in her eyes and a thick paste in her mouth. When she opened the door; it was campus security with two detectives from the Augusta Police Department.

"What do you want this early in the morning?" Lee asked.

"Is Brenda James in this room?" Detective Thomas asked politely.

"Yes, but she's asleep!" Lee wiped her face and yawned rudely in their faces because of their early visit. "Can I help you? I'm her roommate." Lee said.

"We need to talk to her now!" Detective Thomas was offended at Lee's rude behavior toward him.

"Don't get so uptight officer who?" Lee replied with a stinky attitude.

"It's Detective Thomas miss." He replied.

"Don't get uptight. It's too early for this crap. Besides, when you disturb a woman's pathway to the bathroom, you should show some respect. Just a second. I'll go get her all right. We don't need any of that America's Most Wanted busting through the door crap."

Lee closed the door behind her, feeling nervous about the whole situation as she went to go get Brenda up. Lee hurried over to Brenda to wake her. She pushed and shoved her shoulder to wake her up. Brenda turned over to see Lee squatting beside her bed. She rubbed her eyes trying to rub away the sleep. Lee had a worried look on her face, and Brenda knew something was up.

"Lee what's wrong?"

"There are detectives at the door asking for you Brenda."

"Did they tell you what they wanted Lee?"

"Nope! They just want to see you." Sounding worried Lee went on to say, "For them to come here so early in the morning something really deep must have happened."

"I hope not Lee." Brenda replied as she got out of the bed to put on her robe and house shoes.

Brenda headed for the door, and Lee trailed behind her in a short nightshirt. Before she opened the door she tied her robe tightly, and cleared her voice before turning the knob. Pulling the door open to see two men dressed in casual wear with guns hanging off the side of their waists in their holsters Brenda knew something was really wrong.

"May I help you? I'm Brenda James."

"My name is Detective Thomas from the Augusta Police Department, and this my partner Detective Webber. I hate to disturb you so early in the morning. We would like to speak to you if you don't mind." The detective asked nicely.

"Is this about my wallet and those speeding tickets?" Brenda chuckled about what she thought was a mistake she would take care of that morning. She went on to say, "You guys sure work fast and door-to-door service too. Great!"

"You must be mistaken about why we are here." Detective Thomas replied sternly.

"What mistake? This is not about my wallet and the speeding tickets?" Brenda lost the chuckle in her voice to reveal a grave look on her face.

"Ms. James, we would like for you to accompany us down to the station for questioning about a stolen car involved in an accident." Detective Thomas waited for her response.

"What stolen car?" Brenda's voice rattled as she responded to the detective.

"A car was reported stolen a few weeks back, and your wallet was found in the car that caused the accident." Detective Thomas went on to say, "This accident had a fatality."

"Somebody died?" Brenda was concerned.

"Yes Ms. James." The detective replied.

"I don't have a clue as to what you're talking about, and as for my wallet I was on my way down to check on my police report later this morning."

"That's all good Ms. James, but we still need to have you come down to the station and talk us about what you may know."

"I don't know anything that could help you." Brenda replied to the detective.

"To make sure come downtown and talk to us."

"If I don't are you going to arrest me?"

"If we have to Ms. James. We're trying to avoid that step. We just want you to come with us on your own free will. It will make things easier for everyone involved."

"Since I have nothing to hide, sure, let me put something on first."

The detectives let her close her door to go put on some clothing so she could go with them downtown. When she turned to walk toward her closet, there stood Lee in the doorway behind her. Brenda saw Lee was scared for her.

"What is going on Brenda?"

"I'm not sure Lee. Something about a stolen car that killed somebody and my wallet being found in that car."

"You can't just leave with them like that Brenda!"

"Lee, I have too. I don't have much of a choice. Everything will be okay! Don't worry, and don't call my parents until I tell you too! I'll be fine."

Lee watched her friend being escorted away by the police. She stood in the doorway of their dorm room scared out of her mind for Brenda's well-being. Lee snatched a pair of pants off her chair and headed out of the door straight for Rachel's room. She kicked and banged on Rachel's door, hysterical. Rachel swung open her door answering aloud with a grumpy attitude. "It's eight o'clock in the morning. It better be good!" Rachel replied.

"Rachel help!" Lee frantically replied.

"What's up Lee? Calm down!"

"Brenda was taken down to the police station for questioning about a stolen car that killed somebody."

"Oh hell! Let me think. She's going to need a damn good lawyer. Let me call Phil."

"Are you sure he will help you Rachel?"

"For me! Lee, Phil would do anything. I'm sure of that."

Downtown at the station Brenda was being questioned repeatedly about the car, the accident, and how her wallet found its way under the driver's seat. The detective revealed that the person killed in the accident was Sergeant Ethan Robinson. After finding out who was killed, Brenda put her head on the table in disbelief of who she was being accused of killing.

With the questioning going nowhere and her mind being worn down by the perplexity of the situation, she felt the doors closing in on her. The detectives were not happy with the answers she was giving. In the back of her mind, something was telling her this was a setup by Shauna to get her out of the picture so she could get with Theo. Brenda knew she was in deep trouble. Her commonsense told her the cops needed to find a person to blame for the accident that killed a well decorated military officer. She suddenly felt compelled to start praying for a fast miracle.

After an hour in the police station, a three-hundred-dollar-an- hour suit walked in the door of the interrogation room where they had Brenda seated with a warm can of soda in front of her. When the door opened the detectives and Brenda turned their attention to the man standing in the doorway. He closed the door behind him and walked over to where she was seated.

"Excuse me, gentlemen. My name is Craig Long, and I am Ms. James's lawyer."

He turned to speak to Brenda as she sat there looking like hell. She wondered where he came from and who sent him. Craig spoke to her in a sidebar away from the ear shot of the detectives. "Hi Brenda. Rachel had Phil send me to make sure things are in your favor." He smiled at her and immediately asked the detectives to give them a few moments alone so he could talk to his client in private. The Detectives walked to the other side of the room and waited for them to finish their conversation.

"Hi!" Craig was a flash of relief when he made himself known to her as her lawyer. "Brenda did the detectives read you your rights?"

"No they didn't. They never said I was being arrested for anything."

"Don't be scared." Craig leaned over to whisper in her ear. "We'll find the underlying cause of this in no time." Craig looked over at the detectives in the corner talking among themselves to let them know he was ready to discuss his client's charges.

"Okay Detective Thomas. What is my client being charged with?"

"We haven't charged her with anything as of yet, Mr. Long." Detective Thomas replied.

"Then you do know Detective Thomas anything she may have said can't be used against her because you didn't read Ms. James her rights. Let me remind you that you gentlemen didn't inform her that she could have a lawyer present during questioning. Besides, you didn't charge her with anything." Craig turned to Brenda and said, "We're out of here Brenda. If they can't come up with a charge then we can walk." Craig helped Brenda up from her chair. "Excuse me Detective did you explain this to her. Wait– I'm sure you didn't. Never mind. Don't answer that."

"I'm free to go?" Brenda replied with a sigh of relief.

"After you, Ms. James." Responding to her question with a smile Craig nodded his head.

As Brenda and her lawyer walked toward the door to exit the room Detective Thomas had a very unpleasant look on his face. Before they could open the door to walk out the detective thought he should inform Brenda of her boundaries.

"Before you leave Ms. James, I must inform you that you cannot leave the state until we can clear you as a suspect. You all have a good day now." Detective Thomas smiled bidding her and her lawyer a goodbye.

"What!" Brenda replied loudly. "I graduate in two days, and I'll be flying home to New York the next day. What am I supposed to do?"

"I don't know Ms. James, but we have the right to keep you within the state lines for questioning. Don't think about leaving because if you do it will only make things worse for you in the long run."

"Brenda don't worry this matter will be cleared up by then." Her lawyer relayed counterattacking the Detective's intimidating tone by stepping in. "Good day. My client and I have other more important business to attend too."

Taking what was left of the morning, she shared all she knew with her lawyer to try to explain who might be behind this mess. With all the information he needed Craig called in some favors to get their take on how to clear this up quickly. Rachel was the link in Craig being sent by Phil to help Brenda. He told her that money was not necessary and that the tab was being paid by Phil. Craig gave Brenda a lift back to school. Lee and Rachel were headed out of the building for Lee's car to go find Brenda. Just before they got to the parking lot Brenda was walking toward the dorm. The ladies gathered in a circle to discuss the events at hand.

"Brenda are you okay?" Rachel asked.

"Yes I'm fine." Brenda said.

"Phil is footing the bill for the lawyer. Don't worry about that. I'll keep on top of that girl?" Rachel said.

"I'm leg deep in a lot of shit. Shauna really did it this time. She reported her car stolen and—" Brenda turned to look at Lee with a sad face.

"And what Brenda?" Lee said.

"And–" Brenda held Lee's hand to continue to say, "It was the car that killed Ethan."

"What!" Lee yelled out in shock.

"I am so sorry Lee." Brenda consoled her as she stood in shock with her hand over her mouth and tears in her eyes.

"Brenda, Shauna killed Ethan?" Rachel asked.

"It seems to be the case, but the way she is trying to play it is, she's trying to blame me for the accident. She left my wallet in the car, and now she is saying somebody stole her car. The detectives think I'm somehow involved."

"You mean that bitch killed Ethan?" Lee asked.

"Yes!" Brenda looked at Lee and nodded. "She did. I need you and Rachel to help me figure out how to get out of this mess." Brenda looked at Rachel and Lee. "Are you with me ladies?"

"Just promise me I get first dibs on her." Lee responded with an evil sneer.

"It would be a pleasure Lee." Brenda smiled.

With time running out the ladies kept a close watch on Shauna's whereabouts while she was in Augusta. Lee had a friend in the records division at the police station in Augusta. Getting a copy of the original report where Shauna had her address on it was rather easy. Like spies on the move Rachel and Lee were prepared to follow Shauna from the wee hours of the morning to the end of midnight. Rachel and Lee had nothing to report after a long morning of waiting for something juicy to happen, until they tailed Shauna to Theo's house in the early afternoon.

Parking down the block to distance themselves, they had noticed a heavyset lady greeting her in his driveway. The ladies briefly spoke and Shauna got in her car and left. Lee called Brenda to inform her of what they saw and that they would continue to follow her for the rest of the evening. When Brenda found out that Shauna had been to Theo's house early in the afternoon to greet this heavyset lady, Brenda knew it was his sister Jackie down for a visit with her brother. Theo planned to introduce the two since he popped the question.

It was a little strange that Jackie would meet with Shauna in Theo's driveway made Brenda put two and two together. Suddenly, she remembered something Theo had told her about Jackie. She and Shauna had become good friends despite her fallout with Theo. That evening, Brenda was going to dinner with Theo and Jackie. She knew that she needed to find out if Jackie knew anything about the accident. Dinner at Theo's house would be more than a casual chat.

However, Brenda's female intuition was telling her that Jackie must have told Shauna that she would be over for dinner. Brenda arrived at Theo's house a few minutes early. She walked to the front door with a smile and her guard up. Brenda waited for someone to answer the door after she rung the bell. The door opened, and there was Jackie standing in the doorway with an inviting smile to greet Brenda.

"Hello Brenda. I'm Jackie, Theo's sister. Come in." Jackie stepped to the side to let Brenda pass.

"Thank you." Brenda replied as she entered the doorway.

"Theo is running a little late for dinner." Jackie said as she closed the door behind her.

"That's okay." Brenda went into the living room. "This will give us some time to sit and talk."

"Great!" Jackie followed her into the living room. "So, I hear my brother has finally popped the question."

"Yes!" Brenda sat down on the couch and crossed her legs as she continued to say, "He did."

"I tell you my brother is full of surprises." Jackie forced a smile as she looked toward Brenda where she sat on the couch.

"Really! What makes you say that Jackie?"

"Don't mind me Brenda. It's just that after his last girlfriend, I just knew wedding bells would ring, but like I said, he is so full of surprises."

"Would her name be Shauna or something like that?" Brenda sarcastically replied in a snotty tone.

"So, he told you about her?" Jackie replied.

"Not exactly." Brenda uncrossed her legs and sat up. "We met under some stressed conditions that were less than pleasant."

"I hope you two didn't butt heads, because Shauna could be very difficult."

"To say the least!" Brenda replied.

"You have to understand Brenda, Shauna and Theo were very close in every way. You know what I mean? Besides, he adores her daughter."

"That was a nice trip back in time. You have to remember he asked me to marry him. I'm the one true love of his life— me. You know what I mean Jackie."

"Don't mind me, Brenda. It's just that they had it bad for each other and a love like that doesn't just get replaced." Jackie relaxed her shoulders with a hard smile on her face.

"Okay Jackie." Brenda got up from her seat on the couch to get straight to the point with her. "Enough of the small talk! I know for a fact that Shauna was at this house today. What in the hell is going on?"

"First of all don't use that tone with me and second you don't know what you're talking about."

"A thousand to one you know what's going on. What she's doing to me is not right, and she just might turn on you."

"Please you're clueless Brenda. Shauna is a good friend to me. She only wants what's good for Theo, and so do I."

"What are you getting out of this? Why hurt him by trying to hurt me, Jackie?"

"Listen, all Shauna wants is a fair chance to show her love for him. How can she if you're standing in her way?"

"Why are you running away from my question? What are you getting out of this?"

"Listen, my husband left me with three kids and no support. Shauna stepped in and helped me. So, I'm returning the favor. Besides, what does a rich, stuck up little city girl know about hard times?" Jackie stood up to face Brenda as she stood by the couch.

"She gives you handouts, and you sell your soul to the devil!"

"If that is what you want to call it. Yes!"

"This girl is trying to frame me with vehicular homicide. I could go jail for something I didn't do. Jackie, you have got to know this is wrong!"

"I can't tell her what to do. You wouldn't back down. She felt she had no choice, but to do what she needed to do."

"But you do have a choice Jackie. How can you live with yourself by letting this happen to me? What have I ever done to you? I'm graduating from college tomorrow afternoon, and my whole life is on the line because Shauna wants to play mind games. Help me please."

"Help you! I don't even know you. All I know is that you are trying to dog Shauna." Jackie got on the defensive with Brenda. "Besides, if you hadn't continued to see Theo, then maybe she wouldn't have had to turn all of this mess on you." Jackie was frustrated with her trying to get on her good side. "Shauna didn't mean to hit that man—" Jackie caught herself.

Suddenly stopping midway in her sentence before she let out the whole truth, she turned away from her. The door opened, and Theo walked in from work in his military uniform. He had a smile on his face despite the fact Brenda had not given him an answer yet, but to see her with his sister was a nice sight. A new beginning was something he needed since his mother's death. Kissing the ladies hello with a sincere hug was certainly out of place being they both had anger written all over their faces. Theo felt the room had a hint of hostility floating in the air.

"Okay what's going on?" Theo asked the ladies as they stood in the living room facing one another with him between them.

"Hi sweetheart how was your day?" Brenda warmly asked.

"Fine!" Theo replied kissing her on the lips.

Then he turned to ask his sister how she was doing. "Jackie what's up?"

"Nothing Theo." Jackie replied with a hard tense mutter as she looked at Brenda. She continued to say, "Everything is just fine right Brenda?"

"What!" Brenda replied with a surprisingly loud voice to continue on to say, "I don't think so Jackie."

"Jackie–Brenda." Theo looked at the both of them as they stared the other down. He stepped back from between them and asked, "Did you ladies get off on the wrong foot?"

"Ask Jackie." Brenda said.

"Okay cut it right now." Theo yelled throwing up a time-out sign. "Somebody better tell me what's wrong. I can feel something is wrong around here." He waited for an answer.

"Your sister and Shauna feel that I'm not the right kind of girl for you. Ain't that right Jackie?"

"I don't have a clue as to what this girl is talking about Theo." Jackie went on to say, "She has had a nasty attitude since she walked through the door."

"Are you sure about that Jackie?" Brenda replied coldly.

"Brenda!" Theo turned to her with anger in his voice. "Don't accuse my sister of lying. She is my sister, you know."

"And she's a liar!" Brenda shouted.

"Wait a minute Brenda. You better relax. Don't blow this with me." Theo said.

"Blow what?" Brenda replied.

"Us! I don't want any conflict. Shauna has done enough to try and damage our relationship. Don't make me choose my sister over you." Theo replied.

"I'm not asking you to choose anything. You're assuming I'm coming out of my face for no reason." Brenda continued on to inform him of what had been going on. "Did you know Shauna was over here today while you were at work?"

"No!" He replied. Theo started shifting his eyes back and forth at Jackie, while Brenda continued to talk.

"Ask Jackie if she was here today Theo." Brenda asked.

"Well, was she here Jackie?" Theo asked.

"No!" Jackie replied with an attitude that drove a phony tone from within her.

"Well, ask her if she knows anything about how my wallet ended up in Shauna's car, which killed a man?" Brenda pleaded with Theo to ask her.

"Wait Brenda! What are you talking about?" Theo replied not knowing what had happened to her earlier that day with the police.

"Theo, the police took me down to the police station today to question me about a car that Shauna reported stolen. My wallet, which I told you I had lost, ended up under the driver's seat in Shauna's stolen car." Brenda looked at him waiting for him to respond.

"Brenda, Jackie wouldn't know anything about this." Sure of himself, Theo asked his sister for the truth. "Right Jackie?"

"Right!" Jackie said eagerly with a wide smile.

"Theo please!" Brenda grabbed his hand to try to convince him that she was telling the truth. She could see he was beginning to think she was lying. "Look at me and tell me you believe me!" She shook his hand trying to make him see past his sister's lies.

"I don't know what to believe Brenda. This is my sister you're talking about." Theo pulled his hand away.

"Maybe you should ask Brenda to leave." Jackie said. "I think you made a mistake in asking her to marry you." Jackie added.

"Shut up!" Brenda screamed at her. "Theo, you're going to ask me to leave just like that! After all we shared together?"

"I—" Pausing to think Theo continued to say, "I think you should leave. We'll talk tomorrow. I have to think about this."

"All right Theo! I see that you really don't see past what your sister is trying to do here. Before I leave can I share something with you?" Brenda asked.

"Sure." Theo replied nodding his head.

"Jackie, I think you should pay attention." Brenda smiled as she reached inside of her jacket pocket.

"Make it quick." Jackie replied as she stood with her arms crossed.

"Just a moment." Brenda pulled out her little handheld tape recorder she had in her pocket. It was the same tape recorder Lee used to try to trap Rubin earlier that year.

"What is that?" Jackie asked.

"Theo listen up."

Brenda placed the tape recorder on the table next her and turned up the volume. Hearing her voice on the tape as it played Jackie looked surprised. Theo had always looked up to her as a mother figure since the death of his own mother. Theo was forced to look over at her with disappointment on his face. Jackie could not face him as he looked at her. She left the room with nothing to say once the tape finished. Theo hugged Brenda, apologizing for doubting her.

After talking with Jackie for several hours, Theo had convinced her to do the right thing. That evening, Theo along with Brenda accompanied Jackie to the police station to seek out Detective Thomas. After sitting with him, she informed him that Shauna was the driver of the car that had killed Ethan on that rainy night not too long ago, and how she reported the car stolen hoping it would cover up the fact she had been driving. Jackie explained how Brenda's wallet was found in the car. She told Detective Thomas that at the time when Shauna had ran from the accident, she had forgotten she had Brenda's wallet. Not until one of the officers asked her who Brenda James was did she remember that she had left the wallet, and she used it to her advantage.

All pending charges against Brenda were dropped, and she was no longer a suspect in the murder of Ethan. Brenda returned to the dorm feeling relaxed. She picked up the phone to call Lee on her cell phone. Brenda told Lee to go ahead and do as she pleased with Shauna. After hanging up Lee and Rachel who followed Shauna back to her hotel got out of the car, and headed toward her room. Standing outside of her door Lee had tears in her eyes and Ethan on her mind. Lee knocked on the door and waited for an answer. Rachel stood by the stairway that led to her hotel room to keep watch for anyone who might pass by. Lee heard Shauna yell through door. "Who is it?"

"Its housekeeping!" Lee replied aloud.

"Coming!"

Shauna replied as she headed for the door to open it. As the knob turned and the door eased open slowly, Lee pushed it in abruptly. Shauna was wrapped in a towel when the door slammed against her with no indication that she would be under attack. She fell back onto the floor as Lee stepped in to find her laid out on her back trying to get up. Lee jumped on top of her to keep her down. She straddled Shauna's still wet body from the shower she had just taken before answering the door. Lee entangled her hands in her hair to grab, snatch, and pull as hard as she could. Shauna tried to get her hands out of her shoulder-length hair, but Lee had a good hard grip. Lee banged her head back and forth on the floor of her hotel room. Rachel kept watch so that Lee had enough time to introduce herself to her properly. As she stood out in the stairway, she could hear Shauna screaming as Lee pounded her head against the floor.

Once Lee finished pounding her head, she got up leaving Shauna dazed and laid out. She stood over her seminude body to look at her. Lee stepped away from her to leave, but before she would exit she felt compelled to whisper in her ear in a low decrepitly haunting voice, "That was for my man. By the way his name was Ethan Robinson, and he has a lot of people who really miss him" Lee pushed up off her knee with one hand, and as she rose up she continued to say, "Don't think I forgot my tires." Lee bent over and slapped her face as hard as she could. How thangs clear up made this evening before graduation a time to remember.

Chapter Twenty-Seven
The Bosses' Office

Rachel had not made her decision about taking the job Phil had offered her. Promising to give him an answer before she graduated, she decided to venture out to his office just before the ceremonies at school began to tell him what she had decided. She hopped a cab to his office, keeping in mind that she wanted to build her career based on her own merits. Though she desperately wanted to stay near to him it would only prove to be heartbreaking in the end; no matter if he stayed with Samantha or not. Everyone in the mix would lose just a little something, especially the children. Rachel didn't want to be a factor in why Daddy left Mommy.

She walked through the front door of Phil's empire, and it was making Rachel second-guess herself all the way up to the tenth floor where his office was. She could smell the money in the air. Wondering about all that she could gain from just saying, "Yes!" Finally, she could have the world in the palm of her hand, and she wouldn't have to break a sweat to get it. Rachel caught herself thinking, "Easy come, and easy go."

The elevator doors opened to the lavish waiting area. Extravagant with a luxurious ceiling that domed the large space; the deep money green-colored carpet greeting the business-minded-driven visitor, and the majestic waterfall that magnificently standing alone; suggested passion and depth to a would-be sightseer who sought out money and power. Rachel stepped off the elevator heading to the secretary's desk outside of Phil's office. She politely introduced herself and smiled. The lady behind the desk with her professional manners warmly introduced herself in turn. Phil asked that Rachel wait for him in his private office until he arrived from a meeting that ran over. After a few moments of waiting Rachel was led into his office where Phil's secretary closed the door behind her as she left.

Rachel took a long good look at what being on the top could look like. The leather chair behind his desk could have only been made by the best craftsman due to its curved fit to the frame along with its shiny buttery brown skin. She knew this was a chair made for a man of power and taste. Unable to resist the chance to sit at his desk in his leather swivel chair, she sat down and spun herself around to get the feel of power and where it all begins. As she let the spin of his chair stop on its own, it yielded to face the downtown view of the city. The enormous view of downtown Augusta provided an exhilarating moment. She lost herself in its many splendid sights and scenes.

Forgetting she was a guest Rachel reclined in his chair to enjoy being on top of the world. With her eyes closed, she could hear the door open from behind her, she smiled and put on her soft charming voice to let Phil know she was there waiting for him as he had asked.

"Hello Phil. I'm glad you could see on a minutes' notice. I have truly missed you. New Orleans has been on my mind constantly, especially what you asked me. My eyes are closed. Come around here and kiss me."

Rachel kept her eyes closed waiting for him to kiss her. Feeling the presence she assumed was his in the room with her, Rachel sat waiting for Phil to steal a passionate kiss of hello. However, Phil looked very much like Samantha who just happened to pay a visit to her husband's office unannounced. Samantha eased up behind the chair and placed her purse on the desk behind her where she sat. Taking her hand to turn the chair back to face the desk, Samantha leaned forward saying hello to Rachel.

"Rachel!" Samantha smiled like a sly fox looking at Rachel coldly.

"Samantha!" Rachel stuttered. "What am I supposed to say?"

"Absolutely nothing!" Samantha stood up to gaze down on Rachel's startled face as she looked up at her. "So you're the business he had in New Orleans."

"I should leave." Rachel pulled herself out of the leather chair to try to leave in a hurry.

"Hell no!" Samantha yelled at her to stay. "Let's chat for a few."

"I have nothing to say to you Samantha." Rachel tried to head for the door, but Samantha stepped in her pathway to stop her from passing.

"Then I'll do the talking. You have a lot of nerve. I let you into my home with my husband and my children, and this is what I get in return." Samantha paused hoping Rachel would respond to her comment, but Rachel stood there looking straight at her with nothing to say. Samantha added an extra comment to try to provoke her into responding. "Are you fucking my husband? You dirty bitch!"

"No!" Rachel replied in a reserved tone so not to upset her ladylike demeanor. She continued to reply in her ladylike tone, "Correction Samantha, I never slept with Phil. You should thank me."

"Really Rachel?" Samantha questioned her in a nasty, yet bold reply.

"Yes really!" Smooth, but hinted with a brut gesture. Rachel intended to bruise Samantha's ego with her statement. "I let you keep him."

"You are so typical." Samantha made a face laden with disgust as she replied, "Young and stupid. Phil used you."

"That may be so, but at least I'm not willing to abandon my family for a cheap thrill with some stranger on your desk, especially when my family thinks I'm out trying to make a difference in the world. I may be typical to you Samantha, but you're a typical rich bitch who is never satisfied."

"So you're going to tell Phil what? You saw me in the arms of another man? He would never believe you. See, I have the power of love over my husband. Phil would never turn on me for a little nothing like you."

Before entering his office Phil could hear the women exchanging words as he got closer to his door. The door was slightly ajar when he walked in unannounced. The ladies were caught up in the heat of the moment and had not noticed him entering the room. Phil heard the revealing statement with a harsh tone Samantha aimed at Rachel about her affair. Rachel felt something grab her attention just over Samantha's shoulder; it was Phil standing there with a lost look in his eyes. Rachel could feel his pain where she stood knowing his heart was crushed from hearing Samantha admit to being unfaithful to him. When Samantha saw Rachel's expression, she knew she put her foot in her mouth. Phil interrupted by speaking out as he stood in the background, looking at his wife's head drop.

"I don't think I have to say anything Samantha" Phil replied as he dropped the folder he held in his hand onto a table by his side. "You've said enough."

Rachel walked toward Phil's somber grim expression. Facing him as he stood staring at her, she took a moment to take a good look at him because she knew that she needed to distance herself from this situation. The circumstances that had just occurred between her and his wife would cause conflict. Samantha kept her back turned to them with her head hanging downward. Rachel reached out to caress Phil's cheek. Gently, slowly her finger felt the definition of his masculine jaw line as she gazed long and deep into his warm liquid eyes as she replied with tears in her eyes.

"I am so sorry. I can't stay because if I do things won't be the same now. Goodbye Phillip Daniels. You have truly been an experience I will always remember."

Rachel leaned in giving him a soft kiss on the lips letting her warm hand give way to her exit, as she walked out the door toward the elevators. She left with waves of sadness visible in her eyes not from having to leave him, but having to see Phil get his emotions stepped on.

Phil walked over to Samantha to look at her from behind as she stood looking out at the view of the downtown area. As she turned around with a smile trying to hide her anger from getting caught by her own lips, they both knew they had much to say, but Phil jumped in first not wanting to let her make a fool out of herself. He wanted to let her know he too had someone else. "For a moment I thought it was me, but it wasn't. Don't explain your actions because I'm not going to explain mine. All that you need to know is that I never slept with her. I gave up everything for you, and starting right now it stops."

Phil grabbed his jacket rushing out of his office as Samantha stood looking at him. She was lost in her thoughts trying to figure out what just happened. Phil slammed his office door behind him. Samantha screamed out as the door met the slam when it closed. Running down the stairs from the tenth floor Phil knew he had to catch Rachel before she left. Outside in front there she stood waiting for a cab. Just as the cab pulled alongside her, she reached out to open the door to get in. Phil lunged out to reach from behind her to grab her hand before she grasped the handle of the cab. Rachel was startled by his sudden appearance out of nowhere. Out of breath, he was eager to express his feelings.

"I love you. Don't leave. Rachel, I know now what you mean to me. Everything—you mean everything to me. I may have a kingdom, but I don't have a queen to share it with me. Oh baby please don't go!"

"I love you too, but too much has happened Phil." Rachel replied as she let the tears of love glide down her trembling face. So, overwhelmed by his daring attempt at trying to keep her with him, she truly wanted to risk it all. "Maybe one day we will be standing in the same place, and hopefully, our circumstances will be different, and if they are, I guarantee– well you know the rest."

"If I ever get another chance Rachel, I swear I will not let you go."

"Same here, but now you have to Phil."

Phil tried to kiss her, but in his attempt Rachel turned away. Instead, she gave him a loving hug goodbye. Rachel didn't want to prolong the inevitable of having to leave. She hopped in the cab and closed the door. Phil stood on the curb with his hand against the glass. Rachel put her hand up against the glass from the inside of the cab with tears in her eyes and love in her heart. As the cab rolled away Phil stood on the curb with his hand in the air to bid her farewell for as long as he could see. The farther the cab got, the more he felt her warmth leave. The bosses' office handles all transactions when it comes to the affairs of the heart.

Chapter Twenty-Eight
A Few Thangs
Left to Do!

After returning to campus Rachel had little time to get geared up for the festivities that were to take place in just two hours, and the ladies were dressing for the parade. Lee and Brenda were dressing when the phone rang. It was Craig, Brenda's lawyer calling to tell her that Shauna had been picked up earlier that morning by the police. He added that the district attorney was charging her with credit-card fraud, filing a false police report, leaving the scene of a crime, and vehicular homicide. Brenda was very happy that the nightmare was over.

"Yes! They got her, but most of all; she is going to be charged with Ethan's death Lee."

"For real!" Lee turned as she jumped up and down with happiness.

"For real Lee." Brenda ran over to hug Lee. "Ethan can rest in peace now."

"I feel good knowing that. This day is just a little more special Brenda. Yes, oh yes!"

"You're right."

Again, the phone rang and Brenda picked up to find out that her parents were waiting downstairs for her. "My parents are here. I'm going down to meet them in the lobby before we march. You coming Lee?" Brenda asked.

"No. I'll be down right before we line up. I'll be on time." Lee replied smiling.

"Lee—" Brenda stood between the door and the hall; she replied with enthusiasm in her tone, "She wouldn't miss this for anything in the world."

"She missed everything else in my life Brenda. What makes this one any different?"

"I don't know what to say, but if she doesn't come, you got Rachel and me."

"Thanks girl." Frustration laced Lee's face as she smiled at Brenda.

"I'll be downstairs waiting for you and Rachel." Brenda closed the door behind her.

Brenda left the room leaving Lee in the mirror looking at herself in her black robe. Lee took a few moments to bow her head to think of her father knowing he would be pleased that she had made it. Not forgetting Ethan in her thoughts Lee whispered in an airy voice, "I love you Ethan more than you will ever know. I am so glad

I had a chance to experience loving you. You have left me forever changed." Lifting her head Lee had hoped in her heart that her mother would show, because she was prepared to let her arms hug her; something she had not done since she could remember. After all she had been through those last few months, she wanted to make things right between her and her mother. No more arguing and blaming was to ever come into play. Losing her father and then Ethan was enough. A change had to come. Lee hoped a healing of the mind and soul would occur once she placed her hands on that diploma. Downstairs in the lobby of the dorm, parents and friends were everywhere. Lee was making her way through the crowd to find Rachel by the door waiting for her family to show. She seemed a little distant in her thoughts as Lee called her name.

"Rachel! Rachel! You should have smile on your face." Lee replied.

"I know." Taking a deep breath Rachel continued to say, "I said goodbye to Phil earlier today."

"Did he take it well?" She asked.

"As well as well could be. The question should be how am I taking it?" Rachel replied with sniffles of sadness in her voice.

"Rachel!" Lee noticed the tears building in her eyes. "It's going to be okay."

"Right now my heart feels like its dying. I can honestly say I truly love that married man. But, I had to walk away. He's going to be in my system for a very long time."

"That's what love will do to you Rachel." Lee pulled out a tissue and handed it to her to wipe her moist eyes as she continued to say, "It will sneak up on you, and before you know it, it's got you. All you can do is surrender."

"That's for sure." Rachel smiled. "Let me pull myself together before my parents see me."

"See what? A girl in love!" Lee poked Rachel in the arm in a kidding manner. "It's a beautiful thing and it looks good on you."

"I now understand what you felt for Ethan. I'm sorry I didn't understand. I love you Lee."

"I love you too Rachel. Look here come your folks."

"Stay and hang out until we march." Rachel asked.

"No! I have to go back to the room and get something. You go ahead. I'll be along in just a few. Go!" Lee turned heading through the crowd of people standing in the lobby as she made her way to the stairway. Lee browsed the room hoping she would see her mother in the crowd.

"Hurry back!" Rachel shouted as she watched Lee make her way through the crowd.

Lee hid out until the march started. The graduates were lining up under the old oak tree in the center of the campus yard. The sun was shining, and the sky was a wide-open crystal blue field for as far as one could see. The ladies stood at attention in the sea of caps and gowns. The chapel was where all the major events since 1890 took place. Taking the traditional march like the many thousands before them, the ladies held their heads high. As they stepped across the schoolyard; then crossing the street to the chapel on the hill the past was almost behind them. Standing at the chapel doors waiting for the school song to begin Lee, Rachel, and Brenda crossed their fingers kissing them at the same time to wish for the best. After being seated, Lee found herself looking behind her to see if her mother had come to see her graduate from college. However, her search of locating her mother in the audience had not been successful.

Once the ladies received their diplomas they accepted their right of passage as scholars. Standing to be commenced the ladies threw their hats in the air while dancing in their seats. As the crowd started to clear,

Brenda and her family were heading back to the student lounge for refreshments with the other graduates and their families. As she walked along the schoolyard, Theo stood by the old oak tree hoping to find Brenda after the ceremony, but she just so happened to notice him off in the distance. Excusing herself from her family, she asked them to go ahead of her so she could speak to someone alone. Brenda walked out to the middle of the campus to the old oak tree. Theo saw her off in the distance, and as she approached him twisting the ring he had given her. She approached him as he met her. She stood opposite of him smiling.

"Brenda." He replied.

"Hello Theo. I was going to call you tonight after everything calmed down." Brenda said.

"You're here now. Are you going to marry me?" Theo asked.

"I can't now. I realize I got a whole lot of living to do, and marriage isn't on the list now." Brenda proceeded to pull the ring off her finger. "Here is your ring back."

"No! Keep it Brenda. Think of it as a graduation gift. I guess I should leave now. Hey, if you're ever in town look me up."

"I promise." Brenda replied.

"By the way you're the best thing that ever happened to me Beautiful Brenda."

Theo walked off leaving Brenda standing and watching him walk away. With the ring in her hand, she stood thinking of what it might have felt like being married. She wore a quick smile, and then the reality hit. Brenda knew life was just beginning for her. Turning around to head back to the celebration, she placed the ring on her right hand where a nice piece of jewelry belonged. Somehow it complemented the tennis bracelet Greg gave her. Walking toward Brenda as she headed back to the celebration in the student lounge were Lee and Rachel. When the ladies met up they began giggling and joking as they strolled along side by side. Brenda let out big yell of joy. Lee and Rachel joined in unison.

"We made it gals!" Brenda replied.

"You damn right we did!" Rachel added, "We have all been through so much this year. I am so glad we made it through together."

"Yeah! Me too." Lee replied. She continued to say, "We just didn't go though some things. We've been Going Thru Some Thangs!"

"I like that Lee." Brenda pointed her finger at Lee; then putting her arm around her neck as they headed back up to the celebration together. She continued to say, "Just going thru some thangs. I guess that's how you would describe what we have been through right Rachel?"

"Yes! You can describe it that way." Rachel laughed as Lee and Brenda joined in and off they went to celebrate.

Walking off Lee kept looking back not in hopes of turning into a pillar of salt, but her mother may out of conscience shown up to participate in her daughter's big day. As she turned her head to face forward; she saw caught a glimpse of a shadowy figure looking just like her mother, but hastily looked away to save her heart any more shock and disappointment. The ladies had a few thangs left to do that day, but the last thing was to leave the past behind and head for their futures.

Before You Journey Any Further. . .

By De Ann Lain

Your past helps you understand where it is you must go.
If you do not know where you come from,
how can you know where your journey will take you?
Everyone has a past.
It's important that you understand you are on a journey.
This journey is called life!
Through this life you will meet other's who will love
you, like you, hate you, envy you, hurt you, abandon
you, talk about you, lie to you, fight you. . .
If you've wondered why me, then;
it's important that you reach back and ask questions.
It's important that you reflect on the mistakes
you've made in the past, and in the present.
It's important that you find out why you are the way you are.
It's important to say I'm sorry for every
wrong you've committed.
Before you journey any further fill in the blanks.
The only thing you will find from the answers you seek,
Is a peace of mind knowing you know who you are!

About the Author

DeAnn Lain born November eighth in Queens, New York is a wife, and a mother of a son. She has a Bachelor's Degree in English from Paine College in Augusta, Georgia and a Master's of Science in Secondary Education from Mercy College in Dobbs Ferry, New York. An educator for many years in the classroom, Ms. Lain walked away from it all to pursue her writing career with the support of her family and friends after the crossroads in life presented her with a life altering career change. Being a woman of a certain age who writes for the drama and the passion, which lives in all of us, her philosophy as an educator is to have her readers' wonder, to explore and to enjoy. Her style of writing can be best described as an *"entertaining expedition"* layered with fun, laughing, thinking, and learning from life lessons that are taught through the lives of others. Ms. Lain's only message is that her readers' simply understand that life is a *"university"* if you just stop and watch for the: who; what; when; where; why and how. DeAnn Lain bundles up a cast of characters that are identifiable to the reader as real people; who are real woman; who deal with real life situations; who find real solutions to their issues.